7 June 2003

Enjoy!

Ian & Chris, Liz & Emma.

Saga Short Stories

Saga Short Stories
Volume One

Copyright © 1988 by Saga Magazine

First published in Great Britain in 1988 by
Judy Piatkus (Publishers) Ltd of
5 Windmill Street, London W1

British Library Cataloguing in Publication Data

Saga short stories.
  Vol. 1
  I. Saga magazine
  823′.01′08[FS]

  ISBN 0−86188−769−1
  ISBN 1−86188−771−9 Pbk

Phototypeset in Compugraphic Times by
Action Typesetting, Gloucester
Printed and bound in Great Britain by
Mackays of Chatham PLC, Chatham, Kent

Contents

Preface *by Roger De Haan*   vii
Foreword *by Sarah Shears*   ix

First Prizewinner
The Exorcising of Ruby *by Robert Wood*   1
Second Prizewinner
One of the Boys *by Arthur Thrippleton*   10
Third Prizewinner
Maggie *by Pamela M. Pennock*   15

Highly Commended
A Nice Old Man *by Ted Hayball*   24
An Evening With Friends *by Monica Goddard*   36
Alone? *by Heather Johnson*   43
The Last of the Christmas Puddings *by Kate Greenwood*   49
Like Mother, Like Daughter *by Barbara Roberts*   61
Cherry Ripe *by Pat Earl*   69
Relative Freedom *by Katherine Parry*   77
Ianto Clown *by Ivor Middleton*   88
Lady Luck *by Eva Lomas*   96
Choc Drop Gran *by Iris Taylor*   101
The Traitor *by Glynne Jones*   107
Greenfingers *by Nell Arch*   112
The Year of the Rabbit *by Bruce Cameron Firth*   119
Dancing on the Promenade *by Mallie Aarstad*   125

The Boiler Party *by Robert Sharpe*   134
Auto Suggestion *by Mary Andrew*   142
Heroes *by Paul Griffin*   149
Mrs. Noah's Version *by Meriel Serjeant*   160
The Man Who Was Scared *by Patricia Nielsen*   170
First Day *by Peggie Cannam*   175
Spider's Web *by Peggie R. Kerr*   181
Hot Cockles For Tea *by The Very Reverend Fenton Morley*   191
Neighbourhood Watch *by Susan Ashmore*   197
Grey Dolphin *by Doris M. Hodges*   207
Poor Betsy *by Helena Bovett*   215
Mr. York *by Dorothy Gibson*   223
A Rather Elderly Buttons *by Heather Johnson*   231
Safety First *by E. P. Fisher*   239

About the Authors   250

Saga Addresses   259

Preface
by Roger De Haan
Publisher, Saga Magazine

The stories published in this book are the essence, the rich and remarkable distillation, of the fruits of a unique competition organised by *Saga Magazine*.

Rich, because they contain the ideas, the themes and the concentration of experience that come through long exposure to life itself. Remarkable, because many of the authors, all aged 60 or more, turned to writing only after completing working lives in non-creative roles.

There is great quality here. And originality. And skill. And depth. And technique. You would expect all of that from writers who, in formative years, eagerly accepted their teachers' urgings to respect the English language; to use its great resource to reflect their thoughts and ideals.

For all that, they are written from a collective frame of mind that is clearly in tune with the 'eighties, and with a freshness and openness that some might think, wrongly, is the prerogative of youth.

Saga Magazine, as you would guess if you are first-footing here, is produced and published for a select group of readers who, although they have put behind them that part of their lives which commits them to full-time employment, nonetheless have an enormous amount to contribute to the society of which they are an integral, substantial and important part.

We invited them, our readers, to submit short stories for a competition which offered holiday prizes as an incentive. Although we did not carry fiction in the magazine, we anticipated a good response. At that stage, there was no suggestion of a book.

'Good' turned out to be a black hole of an under-assessment. More than 3,000 entries were received. The vast majority deserved to be published. *Saga Magazine*, even over a number of issues, could accommodate only a few.

Thus the idea of a book emerged. It, too, can contain only a small fraction of that huge entry. But it is intended to be not only a reflection of the skills and evident abilities of the 'top thirty' selected, with great difficulty, by the judges, but a celebration of the creative qualities of all those fine people who were prepared to let us see the sort of stuff they were made of. The right stuff, as it turned out.

Thank you to them, all of them. To those who painstakingly wrote out in fine-ruled WHS notebooks the stories they'd had within them for years. To the late-emerging neo-professionals who'd taken on board the skills and disciplines of creative writing at a time of life when they were having to fend off suggestions that they 'take it easy'.

This is their book. And I hope your book. Do please enjoy it.

Foreword
by Sarah Shears

Some sixty years ago, at the local Writers' Club, we were invited to question the speaker, a best-selling author.

'How does one become an author?' I asked eagerly.

He studied me thoughtfully for a moment and answered, 'When you can make your reader laugh and cry, you can call yourself an author.'

It seemed simple enough but it took me all of forty years to persuade a publisher that I had taken his advice seriously! At the age of sixty, a modest little book, entitled *Tapioca For Tea*, was finally accepted after being rejected by no less than twenty publishers. It was the proudest day of my life! It started the beginning of a writing career, not the end. To celebrate my eightieth birthday, I started on my twenty-seventh book.

It is never too late to cultivate a talent, however small. The reward in the case of finalists in the Saga competition was the pleasure and satisfaction of producing a polished, highly readable short story. In these *Saga Best Short Stories* all the eagerness and enthusiasm of youth is combined with a lifetime's store of tolerance, compassion, humour, and a seasoning of regret. Each one of the stories told in this delightful book could be the basis of a novel.

Maggie, the third prize winner, is a sensitive story told with feeling and compassion. Only the young at heart can recall the simple pleasures of childhood with such clarity. Maggie is a very real person and her cleverness at outwitting a brutal father reveals an intelligence nobody suspected. The art of the short story, we are told, is the twist to the tale, and here we have it — with a subtle difference.

One of the Boys, the second prize winner, combines wisdom with humour, never an easy feat. The school teacher narrator is cast in the mould of Mr Chips but this story ends with a smile instead of tears.

The Exorcising of Ruby is a worthy first prize winner. Elements of the supernatural, and the author's boyhood fear and wonder at the tale of Ruby, the red-headed fen woman, are given form and substance against the lovingly observed East Anglian background, which has a magic all of its own. The story recreated for me all the wonder of a Fenland landscape as the early mists lift from the furrowed fields, and the wet earth, touched by the sun, holds an unsurpassed beauty.

I hope that every reader of *Saga Best Short Stories* will find as much to enjoy in this and all the stories as I did.

First Prizewinner

The Exorcising of Ruby
by Robert Wood

My granddaughter and I were watching a ball of light drift eerily over the darkening fen. 'That's a pocket of methane gas,' said she in the knowing way of a modern fifteen year old.

The light suddenly brightened and its movements became much faster, going round and round in a lessening spiral. A final pirouette, a final flash, and it was gone.

'In olden days,' my granddaughter continued, 'they would have called it a will-o-the-wisp. Or even – ' glancing mischievously at me from the corners of her grey-green eyes – 'a vision of the Virgin Mary.'

I was not shocked but rather sad that this modern world of Moon walks and Mars probes had taken a lovely, fearful wonder from a Fenland childhood.

'When I was a boy we called them Ruby's Lanterns,' I said.

She was not particularly interested. 'Ruby? What's this about Ruby? No one ever told me about her or her lanterns.'

'It's an old tale I know,' I said, for no one had ever told me of Ruby the Witch of the Fenlands; like the rest of the kids growing up in that misty mysterious world, knowledge of her had come with the very air I breathed. Learned gentlemen call this knowing without learning 'folk memory'. Whatever it was, Ruby was clearly defined in our young minds.

She was a beautiful woman, with dark red hair, who dwelt on a secret island in the Fens. She had a taste for strong rather stupid boys, and on warm summer nights would leave her hideaway, and on tall stilts make her way to the higher farmlands: searching for any lad stupid enough to be out after dark. When we saw her lantern flickering over the Fens, it was into bed and head under the clothes for fear she should see us as she passed by on those tall stilts.

The name of Ruby appeared strangely in one of our seasonal games. We had the usual conker season, the whip-top season, the lovely iron hoop season, and then — in late summer — we would all suddenly be walking the Fens on home-made stilts, and the best performers were always called 'Regular Harry's'. We had no idea why.

The game we played on these stilts was a strange reversal, for the girls chased the boys. Many a larruping I've had for going home coated with mud, having fallen when fleeing from the 'Rubies'.

What this red-haired wraith of the Fenlands was supposed to do with us boys if she caught us, we were not at all sure. But during puberty my chasing dreams were always of running from this wild creature who was coming after me on her seven-league stilts. I always awoke before she caught me, for which I was both glad and sorry, having the feeling that capture by Ruby would be at once wonderful and frightening.

My cousins living in Suffolk had their own folk memory of a giant who had held East Anglia in thrall. When the burial ship at Sutton Hoo was excavated, part of the treasure was the armour of a seven foot warrior. This proof that fact mists into legend fascinated me, and Ruby striding through the Fens became very real.

So much so that when, after the War, I had to write a thesis for my M.A. Degree, the wraith of Ruby was constantly before me, demanding to have her existence proved.

The trail began with Daniel Defoe's *Tour Through The Whole of Great Britain*. At the time of his survey, the bonded female farm workers were literally for sale. He told how, once a year, the Fenmen would leave their watery habitat and make their way to the higher farmlands. Here they would purchase a wife. This they did by paying the bond which enslaved the poor soul to the farmer. It was a yearly happening because women from the dry lands rarely lasted twelve months in the mists and miasmas of the Fens. He noted one old man who at the time of writing — 1724 — was purchasing his twenty-fourth wife.

The supply of these pitiful creatures was endless. Born as often as not in a ditch, they were sold as soon as they could hold a hoe. And unless they could pay back that purchase price they were the farmer's chattel, to be sold in their teens to a strange, half-wild creature, striding on stilts into the mists, towing them behind him in frail coracle. To work and fade and die within the year.

Defoe, city born and bred, was uneasy in that damp macabre land. He compressed his report into a single page, and hurried on to more civilised surroundings.

Not so Parson Godman, Vicar of Fensedge at the time. His journal betrays his doubts about the system; indeed about his God.

A sad day. Married old Jacob the Fenman to his twenty-fourth wife. May and December; the poor girl being barely fifteen years old. Mercifully she was not too bright, and sat happily enough in the boat while Jacob strapped on his stilts. Sitting there with a garland of flowers in her hair, she seemed more a sacrifice to one of the old gods than a bride just joined in holy matrimony.

The bondswoman Ruby of the dark red hair was there to wave farewell. She stood at the water's edge, her arm happily entwined with that of her lover. I could not help reflecting how natural was their union compared with the one at which I had just officiated. Ruby, sharp as a toledo blade, was exactly the right mate for the massive but lack-brained Harry. Their owner, Farmer Meade, had told me that since he had allowed the mating Harry had become worth three men, whereas before he had been so useless that he had been in danger of being turned adrift.

I suggested that perhaps I could bless the union, but he would have none of that. If Harry should ever pay off his bond, he could remain and help the girl gain her freedom. The old rogue gave me a twisted grin, and quoted the Holy Writ: Jacob and Rachel.

So there they stood, enjoying the nearness of each other. Living in mortal sin, and damning themselves for all eternity. Whereas old Jacob and little simple Mary were blessed because of the words I had spoken. But it seemed to me that Ruby and Harry were nearer to a state of grace. I was strangely disturbed, and did not feel close to my God.

Old Farmer Meade died soon after that entry. His widow, watching the delight that Ruby and the gigantic Harry found with each other, was reminded just how old her husband had been. And as spring blossomed she was further reminded of just how young she still was. She had been the old man's fourth wife. She was probably only a few months older than Harry.

So when old Jacob came again she had words with him, and Harry was sent on a four-day sheep drive.

A further extract from Parson Godman's Journal:

A black, black day. Married Ruby to old Jacob. The girl

showed signs of beatings, and stood silent during the service. Jacob, not used to such a lovely bride, was impatient to be gone: so impatient that his trembling hands had difficulty in strapping on his stilts. Ruby had refused to wear a garland, but we had filled the boat with flowers and she sat amongst them, crying softly.

When at last Jacob was towing her into the mist, she called back to us: 'Tell him to wait. Tell him I'll be back.' Poor, lovely child. Perhaps in the Hereafter. I am fearful of the aftermath of today. For whereas Good is often sterile, Evil begets Evil. And today was Evil.

The plotting of the widow Meade rebounded to her discomfort. Far from gaining a herculean young lover, she lost a good workman. For, in robbing Harry of his Ruby, she had robbed him of his will, his wits, indeed of his wish to be with his fellow men. He built a simple hut of sedge and reed on the edge of the Fen; and there he lived – just – and waited for the Fenmen to come out of their mysterious world.

If Jacob had come he would have killed him... but no one came, and the year passed through summer – autumn – winter – and then it was spring again, and still no Jacob came through the reeds. But in that following autumn the recruiting trio came to Fensedge: the Fyfe, the Drum – and the Sergeant with his tales of valour and wonder. And Harry was gone for a soldier.

Came spring, came Ruby, seeming to walk on the water, so natural was her mastery of the stilts. She was three years older, and three years lovelier: and at once there was unease in the village. No woman had ever found her way out of the Fenlands. Old Jacob had seemed as permanent as Father Time, and where was he now? Furthermore, no one came from the mists with the glow of health on their cheeks. The grey, wrinkled look of an English walnut was the mark of a fen-dweller; and yet there was Ruby, walking up to the church, looking like a goddess of spring.

Children were hurriedly pulled from the gardens, and doors were shut and bolted.

Parson Godman again:

Her green eyes never left my face as I told her what had happened. 'It's a hard life, Parson. Just when I need the strength of a strong, simple man.' Her voice showed no emotion, but I felt the need to comfort her. 'Perhaps, child, the Lord will provide.' The green eyes did not waver. 'I have found, Parson, that the likes of me have to do their own providing.' And I was left with a strange feeling of unease.

In the morning Daft Donald, who now looked after the Widow Meade's sheep, was gone.

For the rest of the year the tale grew with the telling. Old Jacob had been king of a faery kingdom hidden deep in the Fenland mists, and Ruby had bewitched him. Now she lived in the faery castle with the young men she had likewise bewitched, and who could never return to the mortal world. Only she could come a-hunting for strong young men to serve her in her faery kingdom.

It was a good tale to tell on a winter's night when the East wind blew unhindered across the Fens. It took root with the telling; and when Ruby came alone next spring, the women hissed and threw stones, and everywhere was shuttered against her.

It made no difference. Well-built simpletons abounded in those inbred communities, and what simple lad would fight enslavement to a faery queen? In the morning another one was missing.

She came no more to Fensedge, but when those strange lights drifted over the marshes they said it was Ruby seeking young men to enslave. Be that as it may, every summer a lad — slow of wit, but large in muscle —

seemed to go missing. Whether Ruby lured them all is open to doubt, but the tales were told as they would be through the centuries.

And then, what was left of Harry returned from the wars.

A fearsome figure he seemed: riding an ancient horse, the tattered uniform flapping against his gaunt frame; and those pale blue eyes looking with hurt bewilderment at an unfriendly world. A fearsome figure indeed – until they noticed that both legs ended at the knee, and what they had taken for swords were two wooden legs hanging from the saddle.

If the village had thought he had come back for pity and Poor Relief, they were mistaken. He rode straight through to where the Fens began, and strapping on his legs began to gather the reeds. The villagers, following at a distance, saw that far from making him a cripple the gods of war had shaped Harry for the Fens. He strode the shallow waters freed from the tyranny of the stilts.

Within a week he had built a hut, and was fending easily for himself. He spoke to no one and no one spoke to him – but everyone knew he was waiting for Ruby.

Harry had arrived in June, and the village said that she had sensed he was around from the very first day. They said her lanterns had never burnt as brightly as they did throughout that sultry summer. Some claimed to have seen her peering from the reeds.

She actually arrived one breezy September morning. Arrived with the swirling early mist. So when Harry looked up from his reed-cutting she was suddenly there, the mist glittering like diamonds in the red-gold of her hair.

He had no words for he had almost forgotten how to talk, but the defensive look began to fade from his eyes.

'Harry,' she said softly, 'you always were my man. And' – looking down at the wooden legs standing so firmly in the Fen – 'you're made to my measure now.'

Final quote from Parson Godman:

Married Ruby to Harry. Married them standing in the Fen. It seemed to me that God had given them the Fens as their own particular Eden. No one attended from the village. Witches' weddings are not for my simple folk. Afterwards I hurried to my church and rang the bell for a full hour; so that my blessing was following them across the waters.

And there the misty curtain of time comes down on Ruby and Harry. Parson Godman died, and there is no further mention of them in any of the Parish histories of the time.

So, did Harry last only the year? And then did Ruby return to that macabre yearly hunt? Those childhood folk memories would seem to say just that.

I could not believe this. There was a strange conviction in my mind that there was a happy ending to this tale. I felt personally involved.

While awaiting the result of my finals I took a wildfowling trip to a remote part of the Fens. My guide, waiting with the punt, was so wrapped and balaclava'd against the cold that only his eyes showed. When we reached the reeds, he strapped on his stilts and towed the punt easily into the hide.

'You do that well,' I said.

'Born to it,' he answered, his voice muffled by the woollen wrappings.

The day turned warmer, and at about ten o'clock we started to remove the layers. When his balaclava came off I was surprised to see hair which Titian would have loved to paint.

'That's a most unusual colour,' I said. 'I don't think I've ever seen − certainly not in this part of world.'

He was not pleased with the remark. 'No, I suppose not. It's a sort of trade mark. If you ever see anyone with this coloured hair, you can bet you're looking at a member of the Fenwitch brood.' He gave a twisted grin. 'It's a bit of a bind for a fellow. Looks smashing on my sister, though . . .'

The happy ending was suddenly there. In my mind's eye I saw Ruby and Harry striding through the waters, each with a bonny red-haired child astride their shoulders. At that moment, if Fensedge Church had still been standing, I too would have rung the bell for a full hour. Like Churchill, I felt I was walking with destiny.

'I'd like to meet your sister,' I said.

'Ruby?' said my granddaughter again 'What's this about Ruby?'

I looked at the red-gold of her hair, and thought of the bloodline that had given it to her.

'I'll tell you one day,' I said.

And so I have; but I doubt if she will understand.

Second Prizewinner

One of the Boys
by Arthur Thrippleton

'It's Mr. Chambers, isn't it, sir?'

'It is! Should I know you?'

This was not the first time that I had been stopped by a former pupil, hurt that I should have failed to recognise him now that he had grown into manhood. They seemed to think that because I had changed only a little, they too had remained the same. Of course they had not. The National Health glasses had been replaced by trendy modern frames or even contact lenses; where there had been a 'short-back-and-sides' costing six old pennies was now a careful coif costing six or seven pounds, basic, from the Unisex Salon – tinting extra; frequently they were hidden behind a moustache or, even worse, a beard.

Invariably they wanted to reminisce and it was a constant source of amazement to me how none of the lads whose backsides I had slippered ever bore any resentment. On the contrary, they would chuckle with pleasure as they recalled what they had done to deserve it. They would probably go into their 'locals' that same night to recount how they had bumped into 'Old Jerry' Chambers, and then proceed to argue about corporal punishment in schools.

Not that I ever used it a great deal, but it was there. I never used a cane at all – nasty things canes, thin and vindictive. No, I always used a large gym-slipper, size thirteen, which would wrap itself around their buttocks with a resounding thwack but cause very little real hurt. It sort of spread it around, not like a thin cane which concentrated the pain sadistically into long narrow weals.

The lads never felt demeaned by a gym-slipper. They would rub themselves ruefully and grin sheepishly as they returned to their seats. When the changeover came and the girls joined us, I threw my size thirteen away. No boy should ever by physically punished like that in front of girls.

Ah, yes! I was telling you ...

'Should I know you?' I asked.

'Breem!' he replied. 'Bobby Breem!'

Then, of course, I knew him straight away but you would not believe the change in him.

At sixteen, Bobby Breem had been puny, the smallest lad in the form. 5C it was – not the brightest form in the school. Now he was a strapping chap with a strong face and well-cared for hands. I noticed them as they rested on the door, because, of course, I had lowered the window to speak to him. It was the heavy moustache which had prevented me from recognising him. Once I had removed that – mentally – I could see his face as it used to be, his cheeky, infectious grin and his lively eyes. I had always though of him as 'Puckish', and he still was. He had not belonged in a 'C' Stream, he was 'A' Stream material, but Palmer couldn't handle him and to have put him in 5B with Bennet would have been worse. No, all the so-called awkward ones were passed over to me.

He had not been with me a week when my treasured fountain-pen vanished. There were several boys in that lot who were known to be light-fingered, but there was also an unwritten law that they did not steal within their own form-room. I took Bobby to one side and explained this tactfully without mention of my missing pen. Within the hour it had reappeared. Apparently it had rolled beneath some papers!

Another time I remember catching him as he emerged from the boiler room where some of them were in the habit of retiring, fairly harmlessly, to smoke, to play cards or, perhaps, simply to enjoy the prestige which such an act gave them in the eyes of their peers. Usually I would sing aloud as I patrolled that particular corridor. I know some of the boys thought me careless, probably even stupid, but not Bobby. He knew.

This day my thoughts must have been elsewhere for I quite forgot to sing and he bumped headlong into me. I could have punished him on several counts, I suppose. Instead I used a fairly common ploy which usually proved effective. I merely said, 'It's a good job that it's not tobacco I can smell on your breath, Bobby.' He stood still, saying nothing, knowing very well that I knew. I sent him on his way.

Naturally I knew something of his background. A shiftless, drunken father; a pathetic, over-strained and ever-loving Mum whom, incidentally, he worshipped; there was never any money coming in; he was badly clothed, badly shod and badly fed but he was always clean and he had a cheerful resilience. He led a gang of some half a dozen young feller-me-lads who were suspected of 'demanding with menaces', but that was never proved.

I remember, at fourteen, he put his name down to go on the ski-ing trip abroad with me. I ran one every year. He brought the deposit and a few shillings every week for about half a term. Then his mother came to see me. Fortunately I had a 'Contingency Fund' for just such occasions and I arranged some pocket money for him from the School Fund. I still had to buy him some warm clothing myself. So far as I know, he firmly believed that his mother had scraped it all together for him. It was better that way. Wherever it came from it was worth every single penny.

In all my years I have never seen any boy mature so quickly as Bobby did on that holiday. He took to ski-ing as a duck takes to water and he helped us enormously with the more timid members of the party. Even the instructors passed comment, and they were a pretty disinterested lot.

Then he had to go and spoil it all.

He was caught shop-lifting.

Everybody else was taking presents home for the various members of their families. Bobby had spotted exactly what he wanted for his Mum, a pair of beautiful, hand-knitted gloves with a matching scarf. They cost a great many more francs than he could afford. The shop-keepers in these ski resorts, especially the ones which cater for school parties – well, by and large, they are a grasping lot and no mistake, eager to make enough in the Season to support them throughout the year. Their prices reflected this, together with an additional percentage to cover theft. Of course, none of this makes what he did right. There can be no justification for theft.

He was caught. The shopkeeper called in the police who, in turn, sent for me. It does not matter how, but I was able to straighten the matter out and he took his present home to a proud and highly delighted Mum.

On his final day at school, after the afternoon break, I went to my form-room to distribute Reports. As I walked through the door I was met by absolute silence, something which I frequently demanded but only rarely achieved. Every single one or them, boys and girls, was sitting straight and still in his or her place. All save Bobby! He was standing beside my desk with a neatly wrapped parcel before him. He gave a tidy little speech, very flattering as I remember it, and handed me the package in a strangely formal manner. The Form clapped. I thanked them. He called for three cheers. All this in spite of the fact that it was school policy for Staff not to accept presents from pupils. Mind you, I don't entirely agree with that for there is a pleasure and a satisfaction to be gained from giving. But that is by the by.

As often happens, Bobby was glad to put his school days behind him and, apart from posting some surprisingly good examination results on to him, that was the last we ever saw of him.

It was not, however, the last we ever heard of him. At the start of the new School Year there was a letter awaiting our return. It came from a group of parents who complained bitterly that their daughters had, at the end of the previous term, been forced to contribute some of their bus-fares towards a present for Mr. Chambers!

There was nothing we could do about it at that stage, and that French-English, English-French Dictionary was on my desk throughout the rest of my teaching days. I still have it at home, well thumbed and a little out of date, but I would never dream of replacing it for all the *coqs-au-vin* in France.

That was over twenty years ago and now here was Police-Sergeant Breem stopping me as I drove away from the White Hart, and me with several large whiskies taken.

'Nice to see you again, sir! You are looking well! It's a good job that's not whisky I can smell on your breath, though!'

I sat still, saying nothing, knowing very well that he knew.

Third Prizewinner

Maggie
by Pamela M. Pennock

Maggie entered my life unobtrusively in the spring of 1942 and before that year had ended, she left it, just as quietly.

I came out of my parents' neat new semi-detached house and there she was, walking slowly by and up the hill towards the farm. I did then what I had always been told not to do – I stared. For in my short, well-ordered life I had never seen another living creature quite like Maggie.

Her face, beneath an old-fashioned felt cloche hat that almost covered lank black hair, was that of neither child nor woman. I could put no age to it then, and the eyes that returned my stare were blank with indifference. I glimpsed a thin cotton dress beneath her ankle-length coat, which was of uncertain style and colour and so heavy that it appeared to drag her shoulders into a permanent stoop. She trudged, in men's farm boots, failing to stop or acknowledge my startled greeting.

We had not lived long on the small estate, moving in with other families when the houses were completed, and it had been exciting to change schools and make new friends. We children played, during those long spring evenings, in each other's gardens or in the relative safety of the road, obedient to parents' insistence that we run home immediately should an alert be sounded.

The war had put a stop to further private building and we made use of abandoned materials. A plank of wood made a perfect see-saw when fitted between the crenellations of a garden wall and I was enjoying this sensation when Maggie made her second appearance.

'Who is she?' I whispered to John Cummings, one of the bigger boys, who at that moment was standing in the centre of the see-saw, working it to and fro with his feet.

'Ah, it's Maggie, the loony from the farm,' he cried, running down the plank and yelling ferociously: 'Get off, loony, we don't want yer here!'

Maggie, after one petrified glance, was moving as fast as her heavily shod feet would let her as John picked up a stone and some of the others made to copy him. Then, suddenly, she stopped and turned.

I had let out a piercing scream. The child on the opposite side of the see-saw had jumped off to enjoy the fun and, as I came crashing down, my hands slid up the wood and a sliver embedded itself deeply between thumb and forefinger.

Instantly, Maggie was beside me and, as the others clustered round, took my hand and put it into her mouth, sucking deeply. Then, after one deep intake of breath, she stopped and returned my hand. Between her teeth was a splinter at least half an inch long.

'There 't is,' she said, displaying it to a now captive audience. 'Tha' must be careful wi' planks, lass. That one's full o' lime – could'a gone badly if we 'adn't got it out.'

'Thank you,' I gasped, trying to hold back tears as blood now spurted from the wound.

'Ah should go 'ome to thee mam,' she said, 'get 'er to put sommat on it.'

And she was gone, moving at her usual pace up the hill and out of sight.

'She's not loony,' I accused John Cummings. 'Don't you ever dare say that again!'

I took to walking home through the farmyard. It was a short cut and many of the children came that way. Dick Ward, the farmer's son, was a friendly lad and often invited us to see newborn animals and collect windfalls from the orchard. But it was Maggie I wanted. The hind's cottage in which she lived was some way from the main building, tucked away in a corner of a field. Dick said her father and four brothers were good workers but had little to say for themselves. The mother had died many years ago and Maggie, who I now gathered was nineteen, kept house for them as best she could.

'Bit simple, poor girl,' said Dick, 'but then, so are the lads or they wouldn't put up with that brute of a father.'

I wanted to know more, but Dick had said all that he was going to and I daren't push him further. Nor, after his revelations, dare I call at the cottage.

I did see Maggie, however, and after school seemed to be a good time. Her father and brothers were hard at work in the fields and my mother busy with her Red Cross work. None of the others teased Maggie any more and if they considered my growing friendship with her strange, they were careful not to say so. She would listen patiently to my fantasies, not trying to out-do as the other children did, but smiling to herself or answering 'That's grand', or 'Th'all do lass', in the quiet, grumbly way she had of speaking.

Once, as we walked through the copse at the edge of the meadow, we heard the scream of an animal.

'Rabbit,' she said, and we stumbled through tangled weeds until we reached a small clearing. A young buck was caught by the leg in a trap, which had so cruelly torn the limb that it had been almost severed. I turned away, unable to bear the sight, but Maggie immediately took control.

'Grab 'is ears,' she said, 'an' 'old 'im tight. Ah'll 'ave ter get this trap off 'im.'

I hesitated but her eyes flashed and I did as she said, gripping the struggling animal while she pulled with all her might at the iron jaw of the trap.

When it finally sprung I would have lost him, but she made a grab, soothing and stroking, regardless of the blood now streaming from its leg and over her dress. Then, just as quickly, she took hold of the good leg, swung the rabbit downwards and with one hand delivered a sharp chop to the back of its head.

Laying the dead rabbit at her feet, she sat down on a tree stump, while I stared at her, disbelieving.

'What did you do that for?' I cried, kneeling beside the prone body, my tears soaking the soft fur. 'Poor little thing – how could you, Maggie?'

'Rather it died slowly and in agony would tha'? 'Cos it would, yer know – it 'adn't a chance wi' that leg. This way it went quick.'

'Yes, I see. But I hope they catch whoever put the trap there. We had better tell Mr. Ward.'

She laughed. 'Wouldn't do much good. He knows. Me father set trap and he'll expect this little fella for 'is dinner termorra, so I'd better get off home wi' it.'

We never spoke of the incident again but I wondered about Maggie's father. Her arms, when it grew warm enough for her to leave off the heavy coat, were often covered with bruises.

It was a glorious summer. I'd play with the others until I knew Maggie was free and then wait by the cottage until she came out, smiling at me. We'd run hand in hand to the buttercup meadow and roll, laughing, in the long grass. Although she was bigger and older than I, it was as if she wanted to capture the essence of my carefree childhood and hug it to herself for the brief time we could be together. We watched the slippery birth of a calf, played with baby chickens, and ran screaming from the orchard when Bessie, the old sow, broke loose and chased us.

Then came the day when I knew I had passed the scholarship examination. In the autumn I would be going to the High School. I could hardly wait to tell Maggie.

'If tha's 'appy, then I am,' she said as we swung from the farm gate. 'Ah couldn't wait ter leave school meself, but if that's what tha' wants...'

'Oh, it is, Maggie, it is! I'll learn all kinds of new things, and wear a super uniform and a blazer with a green and gold badge on the pocket.'

'Won't tha' be t'posh one,' she grinned, and putting her hand on her hip, she attempted to mince towards me until she tripped over her too large boots and we tumbled, laughing, into the grass.

I was the first to stop. I drew up my legs and looked at her, seeing for the first time that summer the shabbiness of her cotton frock. I shivered in the cool wind.

'Maggie,' I said, 'haven't you got a cardigan?'

'Naw,' she replied, contentedly munching on a stalk of grass.

'But what will you do when it gets cold?'

'Ah've got me coat 'an 'at,' she said logically. 'C'mon, lass, it's time tha' went 'ome.'

A few day's later, Mum called me into her bedroom. She was folding clothes into a brown paper carrier.

'Take these down to Mrs. Green, will you, pet? They're for the jumble sale for Comforts for the Forces.'

I fingered a pale pink angora jumper.

'You're not sending the bunny wool one, are you?' I cried, holding it to my face. 'You look lovely in it.'

She was pleased and it was true. The jumper had given a warm glow to her still pretty features and when she wore it I loved to snuggle up close and feel its softness on my cheek.

'It's gone a bit slack, pet, and the colour is fading. Besides, we must give all we can to help our lads over there, mustn't we?'

She pushed the jumper into the bag and gave me a brief hug before I set out on my errand. Already I knew what I must do. I would hide the jumper somewhere safe and next day give it to Maggie. She would remember the silky fur of the rabbit she had had to kill and know that I had understood. I could see the pretty pink wool against her angular body, warming her and reflecting its colour in her pasty face. It wouldn't matter if she were seen wearing it. Everyone would think Mrs. Ward had bought it for her at the jumble sale.

I stuffed it under my blazer. It tickled my skin through my thin cotton dress and I thought of the pleasure it would give Maggie.

She was sitting on a stile waiting for me. One eye was bruised and swollen and she did not smile.

'Maggie, what's happened?' I cried.

'Nowt,' she answered. 'Nowt fer thee ter fret ower, anyways. Let's walk down ter t'meadow.'

We walked in silence until we reached our favourite place, then as we sat down I could wait no longer.

'I've brought you a present, Maggie,' I blurted. 'Go on, take it. I'm sure it will cheer you up.'

She stared as I drew the parcel from my blazer and pushed it into her limp hands. 'It's nothing special, but I *do* want you to have it — open it, Maggie, please.'

All at once she smiled.

'Ee lass, th'art a funny one. I've niver 'ad a present afore. What is it?'

We tore off the paper and the dainty garment, spread across her great knees, looked incongruous. The swollen eye seemed blacker than ever in her putty-coloured face and she made no attempt to touch the jumper.

'Oh, Maggie, don't you like it!' I cried, close to tears.

'Aye, ah like it. I like it fine, but 'ee'd niver let me keep it. The missus gives us stuff sometimes, but 'ee takes it to second 'and shop for beer money. Take it back to tha' mam, lass,' she concluded, with rare insight.

'But your dad need never know,' I persisted, crying openly now. 'Besides, you can't refuse a gift, Maggie. Mum says even if you don't like a gift, you must never offend by not accepting it.'

'Did she? Well I niver 'eard the like. Right then, if that's the case ah'll tek it and me dad'll niver see it. Stop bawling, lass, it's all right. I do like it — it's lovely and ah've niver 'ad anything like it afore.'

She picked it up and held it close to her face, giving one of her great laughs. 'It's like thee, lass — prickly at first, but soft and pretty.'

I pushed her over in the grass and she laughed again, kicking at the air with her ungainly legs. I made a grab for the jumper and we rolled together, giggling and shrieking as the rabbit's wool tickled our nostrils. Poor, strange Maggie. How I loved her then. It was an enchanting moment that stayed locked in my memory to be taken out afterwards to soothe the guilt of my neglect.

For neglect her I did, in the next few months when the days became shorter and cooler and a new dimension entered my life — the High School.

There was so much to absorb: travelling back and forth by train, new friends, school rules, teachers, and coping with homework.

She'd be waiting for me at first, outside the railway station, and I'd slip away from the others and promise to meet her at weekends, but then, when the time came, there seemed to be so many other things I wanted to do. She never approached me, but would stand waiting in the shadows, expressionless, in her old brown coat and that terrible hat. Sometimes, when the others nudged one another and sniggered, I would pretend I hadn't seen her, but her dark eyes reproached my back and when she finally gave up, guilt was tempered by an enormous sense of relief.

Winter approached and night raids became more frequent. One night, bombs fell uncomfortably close and there wasn't much point in going to school next day. The railway line had been blown up and Mum was busy at the hospital. Dad, as an air-raid warden, had been up all night and I had been ordered to wait in the kitchen for his return.

I couldn't sit still. There was no break in the neat line of houses, but beyond, I could see smoke rising from the railway and yet more from the direction of the farm. I ran towards it, inhaling the acrid fumes, warm dust in my hair, eyes and mouth. The farm still stood, windowless sockets agape from the blast of the bomb that had razed the field where Maggie's home had been.

Figures were digging at the rubble. Covered stretchers lay on the ground.

'Maggie ...!' I screamed and ran towards them, as my father, hearing my voice, tried to head me off. I had pulled away the first blanket when he reached me. He held me close.

'She's dead, Jennifer love, but there's not a mark on her. She must have been blown clear out of bed. Come away now.'

I continued to stare down at my friend. Her face had become young; she was smiling and hugging herself tight. Beneath her thin, cotton nightie, she was wearing a pink rabbit's wool jumper.

Highly Commended

The judges also Highly Commended the following seven stories, which appear in no particular order of merit:

A Nice Old Man *by Ted Hayball*
An Evening With Friends *by Monica Goddard*
Alone? *by Heather Johnson*
The Last of the Christmas Puddings *by Kate Greenwood*
Like Mother Like Daughter *by Barbara Roberts*
Cherry Ripe *by Pat Earl*
Relative Freedom *by Katherine Parry*

Highly Commended

A Nice Old Man
by Ted Hayball

The old man sat in his chair outside the almshouses and sourly surveyed Capability Brown's landscape on the other side of the road. Beyond the park wall it was possible to see the Palladian construction of Oakhead Hall, its ornamental lake and the Gothic and Classical temples arranged to present a pleasing aspect.

It was then he noticed the small party approaching and knew where they were bound. Lady Millicent and her house guests were coming to see her ancient Crimean veteran. He cursed silently. Flamin' museum piece, that's me, to be pulled out, dusted and put back again!

He moved his leg against the dozing bulldog by his side. 'Now you mind you behave yourself, Bull's-Eye. Don't go tekkin' lumps out of the gentry's legs.'

'He was our coachman for many years,' explained Her Ladyship. 'Very good with horses.'

I was good with horses once, loved 'em. But not after Balaclava. After that they were just machines for riding and pulling. Haven't loved a horse since old Hiddy...

He remembered sitting on Hiddy, loosening his sword in its scabbard, looking at the thin erect figure in front of the Brigade in the magnificent blue and cherry uniform with its dolman of gold-trimmed fur. He hadn't sharpened his sabre for six weeks for nothing. Come the fog of war and he'd kill Lord Cardigan. He'd slice through his scrawny neck like cutting through a turnip on a bean pole...

Lady Millicent chattered on. 'Very mild, reserved man. He never said anything but I don't think he was ever entirely at home down here. Came from somewhere in the Midlands. I can't recall where.'

I can't remember much about Hinckley except the Horse Fair and the starving stockiners. My mum wer' one, I can still hear her old frame rattlin' away. My dad wer' a villain. I were only a bab then, nobody knowed what he did. They say he ran away to London, lived on the earnings of some drab.

There were a Mr. Hansom lived in Hinckley then. Built some funny kind of carriage. Folk said as it would never catch on. He were an architect too. Designed Hinckley Workhouse in 1838 just in time for Mum and me to enter its crowded rooms.

Mum helped to relieve the pressure on the accommodation by dying in 1840, the year Prince Albert arrived to wed the Queen of this bright and shining land. Lord Cardigan took the IIth Light Dragoons to Dover to escort the Prince to London. Got made hussars for this: blue and gold jackets, furred dolmans, sealskin busbies wi' plumes and cherry-coloured trousers. His Lordship spent a small fortune on them...

'What regiment was this old fellow in?' asked one of Lady Millicent's guests, an officer on leave from the Western Front.

'The IIth Hussars.'

'Ah, the Old Cherry Bums.'

After three years of workhouse skilly, I wer' apprenticed to a stone mason in Stoney Stanton where I soon tired of stone-cutting. The other apprentices reckoned that, after five years of stone-sawing, you might get on to inscribing '*Sacred to the Memory of Ebenezer Smallbeer*' or carving out angels. Angels didn't seem to be much in my line so

I ran off and took up wi' Sammy Lee, a gypsy horse dealer. The Parish came lookin' for me, but by then Sammy and me were halfway up the Watling in search of Welsh ponies for Hinckley Horse Fair.

Pennington in the IIth said Hinckley Horse Fair wer' mentioned in Shakespeare. Perhaps that's why they built Hinckley Workhouse in the Tudor style. Right then I didn't know Shakespeare from a bull's foot, but he did. Became an actor after the Crimea. He wore his old uniform and medals, and milked the gallant charge for all it wer' worth.

Now where was I? Ah, Hinckley Horse Fair. I reckon Shakespeare took one look at it and tore off down the Fosse.

All I learnt from Sammy wer' how to ride and how to doctor some old crock so it could manage to stand. The Welsh ponies wer' as wild as Bashi Bazouks. They weren't so wild after hauling coal tubs in Midland pits. There's only one fate worse than being a man, and that's being a horse.

Sammy would grab a pony by the mane and nostrils and run it up and down a street full of gypsies, yelling, shouting, waving sticks and flags. It was like hell on hooves.

Weedon in Northants was where I parted company with Sammy. For once he'd managed to get hold of some decent horseflesh to sell to the Army.

We hadn't gone far back home when Samy pulled me by the arm. 'See that house?' nodding towards a house a little way off. It wer' a dark gloomy building wi' a kind of tower at the end. 'Looks empty. We might pick up something.'

Sammy was no shining example to set before a simple lad like me, but by then I weren't so simple.

We crept down the drive. Not a soul about. '*Roland House*' said the sign over the door. Round the back we went, like two stoats stalking a rabbit. Half the rear was taken up by this great conservatory that looked like a jungle under glass.

Sammy sniffed. All was silent. To cut it short, we got into the house. The ground floor was full of large carved furniture, seemingly made for giants.

'Nothin' 'ere,' whispered Sammy. 'Let's look upstairs.'

Lady Millicent's party had by this time reached the lodge gates.

'For many years he was responsible for the provision of the horses' fodder and feed. A most reliable man, the soul of honesty.'

The soul of honesty remembered climbing the dark stairs. Sammy eased the first door on the left and the hinges made a noise like a pig in pain.

A quavery voice cried: 'Who's there?'

Sammy shoved me and said 'Get movin', a female voice shouted 'Benskin! Benskin!' and a bell rang. There was bustle from below, feet pounded on the stairs, and mine pounded towards a door at the end of the corridor.

I looked back. Sammy had vanished. I plunged into the dark, winding steps of the tower. Bouncing off one wall on to the other, four steps to each stride, I reached the door at the bottom. It was locked.

I shook with fright until I remembered a small window halfway up the tower. Racing up, I kicked the panes out and dived headlong. Above me a gun went off and there was an almighty crash.

Landing in a bush, I struggled clear and ran to the rear of the house. My feet crunched on broken glass and there was Sammy, threshing about in the conservatory amidst a wild mixture of fallen vines, broken pots and exotic plants. My late comrade must have picked the wrong window.

I always had one principle when a mate was in trouble:

run like the clappers. Flying down the vegetable garden, I scrambled over the rear wall. A fleeing fox couldn't have beaten me for speed across the fields.

Back through Weedon, I ran down the Watling, hiding behind the hedges by turns in case I was followed and caught. At last I sat down to rest by a milestone. Can't remember how many miles it said, only the word *London* stuck in my head. That's the place, I thought, London, the place where the money flowed and a sharp lad could help himself to a piece of it.

I near starved getting there. Ate spuds and turnips out of fields, and leavings left out for pigs at the back of an inn.

At last I got to the City of Gold where for five years I went hungry, begged, stole, ate fruit filched from costers' barrows, slept in thieves' kitchens and led a hand to mouth existence — except that sometimes my hand didn't reach my mouth.

It was while I was there that I had word of my old man. Before he passed on he achieved a kind of fame ... at least I think that was what they called it.

Came the year of the Great Exhibition in 1851 when it seemed that every foreigner in Europe and every crook in England descended on the capital. Darkie Jones and I had rich pickings until disaster struck us at Paddington. This hayseed up from Turnip Land wasn't quite as drunk as we supposed. He grabbed Darkie with a mutton-sized fist and hollered 'Thief! Thief!' with all the force of his leather lungs.

I was tearing down a turning off Praed Street when I was heaved by the back collar and thrown behind a door. 'Stay there!' growled a steely grey voice. Outside the hue and cry went howling by whilst someone on the other side of the door unconcernedly whistled 'Brighton Camp'.

The door pressed back on me so I could hardly move.

I felt like the filling in a wood and brick sandwich. Then, thankfully, the pressure eased, the door folded back, and I beheld the huge figure of a Scots Fusilier Guardsman. The ribbons in his cap told me that he was a recruiting sergeant.

'Ah, mah wee mannie,' he said jovially, 'wha' ha'e we here?' He hummed lightly. 'Ah'm lonesome since Ah crossed the hill, And o'er the muir and valley.'

We were in the entrance to an inn and from the side door, wiping the froth from his moustache, came a Heavy Dragoon Sergeant with a face resembling the butt end of a barrel.

'Eh, Jock, ye've a fine strapping Guardsman there. His bearskin would be bigger nor'im.'

The Guardsman's grip nearly choked me whilst the other hand went diving through my pockets.

'Here, Bob,' he snorted, tossing across the purse. 'Hae a luik inside.'

'Well, well,' said the dragoon. 'Four shinin' jimmy o'goblins!' He shook his head in mock sadness. 'Ah, the villainy of the young. Tut-tut, so small and yet so greatly depraved. Still, that makes two apiece for us.'

'We'll no leave the laddie wi'out a penny, eh, Bob? Shall we gi' him the Queen's Shilling?' And they both laughed like demented ogres.

'But – but – ' I spluttered.

'Of course,' offered the Dragoon Sergeant, 'we could always call the Law back.'

I gulped and shut my mouth.

'He'll no mak the Foot,' remarked the Scot. 'Full marching order would kill him.'

The dragoon ran a professional eye over my bandy legs. 'He's either a horseman or he's had rickets. We'll see if the Light Cavalry will have him. Hussars, not Lancers. Give him a lance and he'd look like Jack the Giant Killer.'

So away I was led, bound for the welcoming bosom of the British Army, and after the first few weeks I began to think that I'd have been more fortunate if I had been bound for Botany Bay.

The IIth Hussars celebrated my entry by kicking me across the barrack square. I can't say that I ever cut much of a martial figure at the start of my military career. When I first tried on my busby, my troop sergeant exclaimed, 'Hivens, a hedgehog peeping beneath a hedge!'

Indeed, I was never much of a parade ground soldier and the regiment would have shown me the door except that they discovered that I was a natural horseman. Even Lord Cardigan, on one of his rare appearances, admitted that. 'He's good,' says he, 'but hide him in the rear rank.'

Mostly I was kept on stable duties, bringing up remounts and breaking them in. I was just becoming seasoned to Army life when the Russkies and the Turks began arguing over the Holy Places, about who should have access to the stable door. To me, they were only the entrances to work.

Then we was off to Varna in Bulgaria. Charming weren't the word for it. Plunging, maddened horses in storm-tossed transports . . . you were lucky if you didn't get your head kicked in.

Devna near Varna wer' a pretty little place, or so we thought at the time. We didn't know the Turks called it the Valley of Death until the cholera hit us.

It was there that I got a new horse, and a flogging. Usually, Cardigan weren't too bad with the lower orders; it was the officers he couldn't stand. But it must be admitted that of late he hadn't been in the best of humours. He'd led some futile patrol towards Silistria where milord had looked across the Danube at the Russkies and they had looked back at him. Then they struggled back, sick troopers in bullock carts and horses dying on their feet.

Back in Devna, it wer' drill and disease, thieving and violence. Someone in the IIth beat up a Turkish coffee shop-owner. Cardigan tried to discover the culprit but he never found out. Then one of the 13th Light Dragoons made off with a turkey which Cardigan was keeping for his dinner. So that when I wer' wheeled up before him he was looking on the world, as they say, with a jaundiced eye.

Lately, I'd been doing a little thieving myself. Nothing much: a few shillings off a corpse or some extra fodder for my horse.

The rum jar wer' unfortunate as they found me dead drunk with it still in my hand. I was tied up to a forage cart and given fifty lashes.

Then my mare caught a fetlock disease and had to be put down. Spare mounts were few when horses were dying of cold, hunger and neglect every day. And then up turns me boyo Captain Nolan with three hundred remounts, all undersized Arabs, so wild they fought one another.

'Look at them!' said a sergeant of the 13th. 'Not one of them big enough to carry a boy trumpeter!' I was turning away in disgust when I saw a larger horse in the rear of this milling mob.

I'd never seen a horse like him, he was the ugliest beast I'd ever met. He'd a head like a hammer, bones that stuck out all over the place, and he was the colour of trodden mud.

After a struggle I got a bridle on him. There was only one word for him — vile. He did his level best to kill me and very near did. We went plunging through the lines, kicking over cooking pots, pulling up guy ropes, and followed by a ripe collection of bad language.

Still, once I'd mastered him, he wer' as quiet as a

lamb, even became fond of me. It wer' strange, affection was something I'd never had much of. Somehow we survived that cruel country, a pair of mongrels together.

His Lordship saw my new charger and we was once more hid away in the rear rank. That's how he got his name, Hiddy. By now, we'd crossed to the Crimea, stood by at the Alma and set up our camp between Sebastopol and Balaclava...

'So he was in the famous charge, was he?' asked the officer.

'Yes,' replied Lady Millicent, 'though I believe he does not like to talk about it much.'

The twenty-fifth of October. Gawd, that's a day I'd like to forget! Sometimes I wakes up in the night, the sweat breaking out on me, and I remember the shells bursting and men and horses being blown into bloody fragments.

It began with Cardigan's shrill high voice giving the order to advance. After that it wer' plain murder. And to cap it all, that Hiddy gave me a real rough ride. He would swerve to the right, jink to the left, pull back and plunge forward, his ears flicking to and fro. I cursed him until I realised what he wer' doing was dodging the shells. The old warrior had been under fire before. After that I just gave him his head. Owing to Hiddy's unusual movements I'd sort of got separated from the rest of the regiment. They'd swerved off to the left flank whilst Hiddy and I went charging into the smoke around the guns. These were silent now, the 17th Lancers had speared the gunners.

I was heaving back on Hiddy when out of the smoke rides milord Cardigan on his way back. He sat on his charger, Ronald, as if he were passing in review on Hounslow Heath. Right, me beauty, I thought, drew my sword and jerked Hiddy round towards him...

Lady Millicent and her party were now entering the

lane that led to the almshouses.

'Yes,' she said, 'he saved Grandfather's life. Very brave of him. The family have always held him in high esteem.'

I didn't mean to, it was pushed upon me. Halfway towards his Lordship, another figure on a staggering, dying horse came between us.

It was the Honourable. He was my troop officer, thick as two short planks but not a bad bloke. Blood streamed from a cut across his forehead and at any moment he was due to go overboard. Cardigan didn't even give him the flicker of a glance but rode on. With so many dead and dying around him, he probably reckoned that one more didn't make much difference.

I swung my horse alongside the Honourable and held him round the waist. His blood dripped on to me. Even there the odd thought came to me that the Army would probably make me pay for a new tunic. I didn't have long to consider this for out of the smoke came a huge great Cossack. I parried, the lance went wide and my sabre sliced into his bushy black beard. He gave a choking cry and fell out of the saddle. My sabre was stuck so fast that the falling body tore it out of my grip — and right behind was one of his mates!

'My pistols!' gasped the Honourable. I pulled one out of the saddle holster. Never fired one before but I knew you had to cock it. Then I closed one eye and aimed. I was within an ace of being a spitted kebab when the pistol exploded and the Czar was short of another Cossack.

Any minute now and the Honourable's horse would collapse so I lugged him out of his saddle and across mine. I knew where I was going — out of this mess. Perhaps I'd get the Cross for saving a wounded officer. So back we went, picking our way through the wreckage of the Light Brigade.

The guns on our flanks were still banging away. We were almost there when Hiddy went down and we both went flying. I staggered up and looked down at Hiddy. You've seen those war pictures where the dying horse takes a fond farewell, looking up with faithful brown eyes at its sorrowing master? Not Hiddy. The shell splinter had torn into his head. He'd gone out like a light.

I heaved the unconscious Honourable over my shoulder, calling him all the dishonourable names I could think of. We wobbled back through the carnage. All those years of good living had made the Honourable no easy burden. Then I passed out and came round to hear a familiar voice saying it was no fault of his.

'Never mind, my lord,' was one hero's remark. 'We're quite willing to go again.'

You speak for yourself, mate, I thought weakly. Then someone was pushing rum between my lips. . . .

'Was he decorated?' enquired the officer of Lady Millicent.

'Indeed he was, the Distinguished Conduct Medal.'

So I was. Didn't get the Cross. There was rather a glut of heroes that day, those that got back.

'Yes,' went on Lady Millicent, 'after the war, Grandfather resigned his commission and came home.'

Yes, the Honourable reckoned he'd seen enough fighting for one lifetime. Still, he took me with him . . .

Here they are . . . better get my medals on and tie old Bull's-Eye up.

'Please don't get up,' says Lady Millicent.

Don't worry, I won't. Behind me the old dog's growling away. He can smell when I don't like someone. We talk the usual fiddle-faddle and I can see she's running out of questions.

'By the way,' she asks, just as they are leaving. 'You were always so good with horses, what was your father?'

'He wer' a house surveyor, my lady.'

Surveyed it to see by which window he could get in!

'Yes,' I go on. 'Fell off a roof and killed 'isself. A sad loss.'

It was. It did the hangman out of a job.

As they are leaving, this officer puts a coin in my hand. Blurry half a crown! The gentry ain't what they used to be.

On the way back the officer remarked on what a horrible beast that bulldog was, but he liked the old man.

'Yes,' replied Lady Millicent, 'he's a nice old man is Troop Sergeant Sikes.'

An Evening with Friends
by Monica Goddard

Being a slow thinker and a poor liar I am often at a disadvantage, but experience is teaching me some neat footwork and evasive tactics.

I was poised with my hand on the dark room door, preparing for a morning session with a roll of film taken at a Salvation Army Hostel off the Old Kent Road last Saturday night, when I heard my wife Helen on the phone in the hall below. There was a pause.

'The Sefton-Smiths have asked us to dinner,' she shouted up the stairs, 'next Friday.'

I cringed. My immediate impulse was to slip badger-like into the dark room and feign deafness, paralysis or amnesia. I pulled myself together, my knuckles white on the door knob.

'It's the South London Polytechnic's yearly show,' I said promptly, 'I'm helping to select the winners.'

There was a moment's silence whilst Helen murmured something about thinking that was next week. I prayed that her hand was over the mouthpiece and with a vast sigh of relief heard her saying in the warmest and friendliest of tones, and with just the right touch of regret, that we were unable to accept their invitation. I moved into the dark room; the prospect of an uninterrupted morning with the drop-outs of South East London delighted me.

Funnily enough, less than twelve months ago the same

invitation from Sarah and Tony Sefton-Smith had filled me with joyful anticipation. Tony had just completed a highly successful series of portraits of leading politicians at their (printable) favourite pastimes, for one of the Sunday heavies. His work was elegant but had great strength and originality. We'd met at college six years ago. Since then I'd watched Tony progress steadily and had attended his happy and suitable marriage to blonde and beautiful Sarah, and two years later the christening party for their first-born, Edward.

Then, last year, we had gone to dinner with Tony and Sarah on a cold evening in early April. The white stuccoed houses looked like wedding cake against the pewter sky as we walked across the heath.

Tony answered the door. I noticed that his face was thinner and his eyes had a slightly haunted look. His soft pink Viyella shirt was shielded by a vast plastic apron across which marched several ducks in bright chrome yellow. He greeted us warmly and clasped our hands; I noticed that his fingers were rather sticky.

I looked along the hessian walls of the hall for the familiar studies of Che Guevara, Tony and Sarah's beautiful Siamese cat: Che resting, pouncing, sunbathing, birding, sleeping. Two years ago Che had graced the long hallway at every point, immaculately mounted and framed. But now his sleek, aristocratic grace had gone and a dozen sharp-focussed records of a day in the life of Edward met the eye. Walking, crawling, crying, sitting, smiling, cooing, sleeping – ending up with a life size close-up of Edward at the breast, squint-eyed and comatose, like a chap with a well-deserved pint at the end of a hard day.

We made suitable and genuine sounds of admiration. Tony smiled and then cocked his head like a nervous animal.

'I think we'd better creep in here – *sotto*, if you don't mind. Sarah's just getting Neddy off and it's a devil of a job. He seems to know when we're having people. Terribly perceptive, even at fifteen months.'

We tiptoed in Tony's wake into the sitting room. The off-white presence of high Art Deco was still there but partly submerged, like a dying civilisation. Superimposed upon it were the brilliant primary colours of play-pen, frame, walking aids, rocking-horse, tricycle, building blocks, and between everything bobbed a sea of small toys, woolly, plastic, wooden, playful or constructive. I felt Helen clutch my arm. To anyone in high-heeled sandals this must have looked like a mine-field.

Tony was gathering things up and throwing them into the play-pen. 'Sorry you missed Neddy but we thought it better if he went up before you arrived; he gets frightfully excited and overtired when we have visitors.' He picked up a wooden board punctured with variously shaped holes into which, by trial and error, a child could hammer suitable matching pegs. 'Supposed to be for eighteen months upwards,' Tony said, somewhat scathingly. 'Neddy cracked it in the first day. Threw it out of the window in disgust this afternoon.'

We murmured our admiring approval and reached the haven of two empty chairs. There, in the furthermost corner of one of them, curled tight as a winkle, was Che Guevara, his cream coat merging like camouflage into the pale leather. He had the switched-off look of a cat admitting defeat; the quiet dignity of a deposed king. Helen exclaimed his name in pleasure and touched his head gently. Uttering a low cry he gazed up at her with all the soulfulness of a Russian emigré at the sound of balalaikas.

During drinks Sarah appeared, cool and unruffled and with only the slightest flush of colour to betray that she was managing both kitchen and nursery. Tony seemed disturbed at the speed with which Sarah had put his son to bed but she assured him with calm sweetness that all was well. When we were bidden to the dining room I observed Tony moving with the stealth of a deer stalker.

The meal was delightful and we were well into the *navarin* of lamb when a strangely muffled sound, as of a far-off muezzin, stole upon the warm air of the room. Tony looked like a startled animal raising his head from grazing. 'Neddy! Neddy calling!' he said, gazing ceilingwards, a forkful of lamb held aloft.

Sarah shook back her hair fringe and smiled soothingly. 'Leave him, darling, till we've finished. He's all right. More wine, Peter?'

As she refilled my glass I noticed a small loud-speaker set into the corner of a nearby book-case. The muezzin clamoured more urgently. Tony rose and left the room. Sarah glanced after him with a slightly rueful smile. 'A little more lamb, Helen?' We heard the rapturous reunion of Neddy and Tony relayed across the room.

A few minutes later father and son arrived. Neddy snuffled a little as he surveyed the scene; he rubbed his fists in both eyes, all the better to see us with.

'There you are,' Tony murmured encouragingly. 'Nice Peter — beautiful Helen.'

Neddy gave a non-committal gurgle and sneezed wetly over us. During Tony's agonising over whether or not the window had been too wide open in the sitting room or the bath water too cold, Sarah drew up a high chair between Helen and Tony, and Neddy was established like a precious fledgling in an eyrie.

Here he had an elevated view of the proceedings and was ready to accept small offerings: carefully mashed carrot, tiny shreds of succulent lamb in gravy, and *petit pois*. The latter are a challenge to anyone's dexterity and should be well up on the list of educational toys. Peas can be flirted, flipped, rolled or just plain chewed and spat out. Neddy proved himself an adventurous and creative eater.

At one point Che walked silently through the room with a proud dignity which touched the heart. He looked neither to right nor left, disappearing into the kitchen and presumably out of the cat flap into the night. Many a cat of lesser breeding would have let the flap slam shut resentfully but Che departed quietly like a sad ghost. I hope he had friends out there.

All talk of the photographic world, of Tony's experiences on his last assignment or his coming visit to the States, was now disjointed and finally abandoned. But not before Tony had amazed me by expressing dismay at the prospect of two months in the USA, photographing retired movie stars.

'Don't want to be away from home, to be honest,' he said. 'Eight weeks is a long time to be away from Neddy.' He fielded a *petit pois* and popped it back on to his son's platter.

'As a matter of fact, that's something I wanted to talk about to you, Pete.' He mashed the peas into some carrot. Neddy lobbed a spoonful neatly into Helen's lap. 'Steady, Ned, old chap. Here, try a bit of lambikins.'

Neddy tried. He raised his face ceilingwards and let the rich, raw umber mixture run from the corner of his mouth where it came to rest below his ears.

Sarah came round and mopped deftly with a napkin. Tony made sympathetic noises at this high-handed treatment and was temporarily distracted whilst the Angel Cake was brought on and distributed. The fresh strawberries inspired Neddy to make several badly aimed grabs at Helen's dish. To be fair, he was hampered by the confines of his high chair and it would have taken a heart of stone to resist those beseeching little hands. I managed all right, being grateful for the table's width and a screen of wine glasses between us.

Halfway through the dessert, and Neddy happy with his father's and Helen's strawberries, Tony came back to the subject of his visit to America. He leant towards me, mashed carrot nestling in the creases of the pink Viyella shirt. 'Pete, you wouldn't fancy a trip to the States, would you?' he asked. His expression was anxious.

I swallowed a whole strawberry without tasting it. 'Me? You want an assistant?'

'No, no! I want you to take over the whole trip! It's an awful lot to ask, I know, you must be pretty busy . . . but I'd be terribly grateful if you could do it.'

I didn't know what to say and watched Helen eat the last and only strawberry she'd salvaged. She was gazing into the distance with a stony look. Tony continued urgently: 'You're the only one I can ask. I can't think of anyone's work I like so much.' The sincerity of his tone shook me.

I thought of Tony's work: the flattering light he often used and the sometimes heroic appearance of his subject. Then I thought of last Saturday night and my own work. I had high hopes of the darkly bleak roll of film taken at a Salvation Army Hostel. Hard to explain, really, but I would like to be to photography what Maxim Gorky is to literature; the lower depths is where I focus my attention and camera. I had a feeling that American movie stars might not like my style.

It was about now that Neddy demanded to get down and go walk-about, and so he stumped off in the direction of the kitchen and there was a general getting up and gathering of dishes which gave me a breathing space. Tony was anxious at the disappearance of his son and so I had time to compose a suitable answer to his request.

I opened my mouth to start on a polite refusal when a half-empty bottle of wine was tipped over; we exclaimed and dabbed ineffectually. Helen, seeing Sarah's hands full of dishes, went off to the kitchen to fetch a cloth. It was all over in seconds – a quick rush, a shriek, a clatter, a crash.

'My God, Neddy!' Tony flew towards the kitchen. But Neddy was unscathed, intent upon the business of draining the last golden drop from the salad oil bottle on to the tiled floor. Helen lay half conscious by the sink, her leg doubled up under her. Tony swept up Neddy, who resisted loudly. He held the child in his arms, his face aglow with pride. 'He'd got the top off that salad oil bottle – no trouble at all. Such dexterity at his age! Amazing, isn't it?'

It was left to Sarah and me to lift Helen up and carry her into the sitting room. I must say the ambulance came very quickly, and the hospital made a lovely job of setting the bone. She was out of plaster within a month.

Alone?
by Heather Johnson

Jim, who had been gardening most of the afternoon, had come in and had his bath and was now sleeping peacefully in front of the television set. They'd had a bigger than usual lunch and decided to have scones and strawberries on a tray that evening, so there was nothing for Lorna to do.

She heard the bubbling cry of a curlew and watched out of the kitchen window as it sailed overhead.

On an impulse, she scribbled a note for him: '*Gone for a walk, back in half-an-hour.*' Adding the time, she changed her shoes and put on an anorak and then let herself out quietly.

There was a stiff breeze and the lark above her was being blown about, but sang lustily nevertheless. Swallows swooped down in swift curved flight, almost as if they were mobbing her.

She turned on to the narrow single-track road that joined their lane, and started walking up the hill, keeping well to the right. When a car came up behind her she turned and smiled at the driver and he smiled back and waved cheerily, passing by her carefully, for his car was large and opulent. She didn't know him but guessed he must live close by – one always beamed at walkers, to show approval and mutual appreciation of the countryside.

She would just walk to the top of the hill, she thought, and see if she could get a close-up of the curlews.

The lark, which had seemed to be following her, fell suddenly and rapidly, levelling off smoothly just before reaching the ground. Then a curlew came over the wall, only a few feet away from her; he was calling fiercely and continuously and she watched his long open curved bill and saw the bright speckled body and graceful wingspan. He settled on the wall and stayed for quite a long time before lifting off and circling round, still calling.

Dark rain clouds hung over the low ridge and the silhouettes of sheep showed clearly in the brighter strip of light along the tops. The further higher hills to her right were black too, with just a sunlit patch of pale green here and there.

She felt a surge of contentment at the beauty of it all and turning, walked back slowly, her eyes caressing the rough moorland, scarred by rocky outcrops and divided and sub-divided by endless dry stone walls built long ago when labour was skilled and plentiful. She listened to the complaining wails of sheep and their lambs; only a short while ago the young ones had nosed timidly behind their mothers, stumbling on thin unsteady legs; now they looked rounded and sturdy in thickening curling coats.

Usually, the broader verges were bright with the now dormant gorse. Once, she remembered, when they were much younger, they had tried to dig up a clump for the garden; but the spiky plant had clung to the bank with roots of steel and, defeated but full of admiration, they had given up.

The blue haze of harebells and delicate pink of lady's smock had gone, leaving the humbler cow parsley, red clover and buttercups.

She knew Jim would say she shouldn't have gone out alone. Gone were the days when lone walks were thought safe – and she resented it. She recalled the time, forty years ago, when she was carrying their first-born, then two weeks overdue, and old Dr. Miller had told her to go for a good long walk round the reservoir to 'shake him down'. Even then Jim had been appalled.

'I don't suppose you gave a thought to what you'd have done out there alone, if anything had started?'

In the end it had taken castor oil and a hot bath and many hours of lonely travail in a bleak labour ward to achieve the joyful deliverance, and Jim only then forgave the doctor for what he had considered sheer thoughtlessness.

Occasionally, throughout their life together, his over-concern and caution irritated her, but mostly she loved him for it. She knew now that if he'd wakened and seen her note he would greet her reproachfully and there would be that ridge of anxiety between his eyes. If he were still asleep she wouldn't tell him she'd been out.

Later that night however, when they lay side by side, she couldn't resist the temptation. She felt for his hand.

'I went for a walk while you were asleep this afternoon.'

He was drowsy, but he still asked, 'Alone?'

'Of course ... you always say you've got too much to do in the garden.'

He grunted.

'It's such a lovely time of the year, there was a lark, and the swallows were bombing around, and I saw a curlew – really close-up, and it stayed near me, on the wall for quite a long time. On the way back I looked for the little owl we saw from the car on Sunday, but I didn't see him. The lambs all look fat and woolly now.'

He grunted again to show he was still awake.

'I felt so happy and fortunate to have so much beauty around me, darling,' she whispered, squeezing his hand. 'Thank you for our lovely home, and garden and ... everything.'

He turned towards her and his arm came round her strongly. She felt the vital warmth of him.

'You've earned it all.' He spoke softly, his lips touching her ear. 'On Sunday we'll walk to the Dragon and have lunch.'

She gave a satisfied sigh and they hugged each other for a long moment.

There were two long hills between them and their nearest pub. The sun was strong but they took their time, enjoying the clear views, identifying the different birds which took flight at their passing, and noticing the growing affluence of the two hill farms along the way. When they had first come to the district, land was cheap and the farms had looked forlorn and neglected; now, since Britain had joined the EEC, more fields were ploughed and around the farmsteads the barns were no longer the rough wooden and corrugated-roofed sheds they once were. In the sunshine there was an air of prosperity all around.

Enjoying their usual 'Dragon Special', they nodded to a couple of acquaintances and grimaced at them as some young barbarian approached the juke box in the corner and a raucous modern ballad blared forth.

'It's not that bad, darling,' laughed Lorna as Jim got up suddenly, excused himself, and hurried out to the cloakroom.

She noticed casually that he was walking with one shoulder hunched, but thought little of it until the landlord came to the lounge door and looked around, glanced at her and then at their friend.

'Henry', he called, 'could you come a moment?'

She felt uneasy and then alarmed; she got up. 'What is it? Is it Jim?'

They carried him in and laid him on the long seat under the window; his eyes were closed and his face drained of colour. She took his hands in hers. Usually so warm and strong, they were limp and cool. She put them between her own and held them to her face. She heard the landlord telephoning urgently. Henry got a blanket from somewhere and covered Jim with it, putting a cushion under his feet. Moving Lorna gently aside, he leaned over the prostrate form and, after feeling for a pulse, started with resuscitation.

When the ambulance men came in with their stretcher he helped them get Jim into the vehicle and, with Lorna, watched them expertly administer oxygen. She went with the ambulance to the hospital and Henry and Jean Maddox followed in their car.

When they joined her, an hour later, they knew at once it was all over.

With their arms around her she allowed herself to be led to the car, and sat huddle in a corner of the back seat, Jean beside her, holding her hands. She felt only that she had lost all feeling, and when they put her to bed in their home with a sedative the hospital doctor had prescribed, she prayed that she would not wake up again.

When she did, in that pretty, sun-filled bedroom, for a moment she had to search for the reason for the black cloud that seemed to hover above her. When she remembered, she gave a shudder of despair, and wept.

Jean came in and sat beside her with a cup of tea, waiting patiently until she could control her tears and sit up and drink, gratefully.

'I'm sorry, Jean,' she said, 'this must be awful for you. Will you take me home now, please? I must telephone the children, I should really have done it last night.' The thought of 'the children', now all adult and settled into their own different lives away from Jim and her, brought on another uncontrollable burst of weeping.

She leaned back against the pillow, closed her eyes and sagged with exhaustion. Then she made a tremendous effort and smiled ruefully at her friend.

Jean said gently, 'It's good for you to cry. Please don't worry about it, I understand.'

Lorna washed and dressed, each movement slow and mechanical. Jean had agreed to take her home if she would promise to 'phone that afternoon and let them know her plans, and to join them for dinner in the evening, unless other closer friends were available and Lorna wished to go to them.

Left alone at home, she looked around the silent rooms with the eyes of a stranger, and then — drawn by the sunshine — went into the garden. Jim's garden. Already it looked somehow empty and forlorn. The annuals he had planted, and which he would now never see, were going to give just that splash of colour he had said he had wanted around the edge of the patio. One of the starlings, which had always exasperated him because they hustled all the other birds from the bird table he had erected, perched on the fence, twitching its tail, the sun glinting on its glossy blue-green feathers; 'urchins' he used to call them.

She thought of the ordeals ahead of her. The funeral, the children coming home, the kindness of friends ... and then the long emptiness. She knew just how it would be: she had watched with sympathy as other friends had suffered.

A curlew called and soared overhead. She shaded her eyes and watched as it came lower and lower, head and bill stretching forward. It was all so beautiful. She was glad she'd told him about her walk. ... Glad she'd said thank you.

The Last of the Christmas Puddings
by Kate Greenwood

When I was six years old my tonsils were removed in a manner which today would be regarded as barbaric, but in those distant times was the norm.

My mother delivered me, quaking and breakfastless, to the Childrens' Hospital at 8.30 a.m. one morning, and collected me at 5 p.m. the same day.

I was trundled home in the family pram with my feet sticking out at the end, a limp, semi-comatose doll, unable to swallow food or drink, and nauseous from chloroform.

After a few days, my Grandma Chadwick came and whisked me off to the depths of rural Oxfordshire. It was late-October, and when we alighted from the train the air was soft, balmy and full of delicious autumnal scents.

Woodbridge Halt was a small farming village through which, en route for the West Country, the Great Central Railway had forged its way, transforming it into a goods and passenger junction, giving permanent, uniformed employment to farmers' sons and casual farm labourers.

My Grandfather was engaged on line maintenance, my Uncle Tom on the foot plate as trainee driver, my Uncle Alfred was in the signal box and my Uncle Jack a clerk in the ticket office.

My Grandmother became the proud possessor of a

railway privilege ticket with which she entrained to surrounding villages for Fur and Feather whist drives, returning in triumph with rabbits, pheasant or fowl, which she baked into delicious pies and casseroles, meanwhile imparting all the local news and gossip she had gleaned whilst counting trumps and totting up tricks.

Grandma told me she was about to start her Christmas preparations and needed my help with the puddings. So saying, next day she gave me a large bowl of washed raisins with instructions on how to remove the stones from them. This I struggled to do, whilst she grated suet, apples, carrots, made breadcrumbs, blanched and chopped almonds and candied peel.

When all the fruit and nuts were prepared, we weighed out sufficient for the cake, added spices, sugar, flour, eggs and butter, with golden syrup and grated rind and juice of orange and lemon.

Next we set aside fruit and suet for the mincemeat. The rest was tipped into her best bedroom wash-hand basin (well scalded out first), and the mixing and stirring of the puddings began.

It was hard work as more and more ingredients were added. Many pairs of hands, under the promise of a wish fulfilled for every good stir, came to help.

John Kingston, the farmer's son, delivering fresh milk from an enormous churn in the back of a pony and trap, came in and stirred mightily, wishing out loud for a lovely gel to come a-courting him.

Isobel Wringham, the blacksmith's daughter, took the spoon in both hands and said: 'I wish I may, I wish I might, get the wish I wish tonight − I mean this afternoon,' then went very red and fled.

Freda and Sally Foot, the daughters of the village baker, came in after school to gossip and stir and wish, dipping their fingers into the mixture to take a sweet tooth of fruits.

Stirring vigorously, they asked if it was true my Uncle Jack was courting the Stationmaster's daughter, Lily Clare? And was it true my Grandmother's youngest, Auntie Flo, had jilted Raymond Fairbrother and was now courting Stephen Smith, the lay preacher's son?

They were told tartly to get on with their stirring and wishing, and then be off and do their homework.

My Grandfather, that evening, stirred long and seriously, sniffed and tasted, and said it needed a good marinade in stout with a nice drop of brandy.

At every opportunity I stirred and wished we might all come to spend Christmas and eat these lovely things.

When the time came for me to go home, revived by fresh, country air and home-produced food, I took a last look at the three cockerels which were being fattened for Christmas, and a final glance round the larder. This was a small room off the kitchen which extended under the stairs. It was a veritable Aladdin's cave.

I breathed in the delicious smells of spices, newly made bread, strings of onions, and counted again the row of six Christmas puddings we had made, as well as the jars of mincemeat.

In a high rack near the ceiling, wrapped in cheese cloth, was a side of home-produced bacon and two picnic hams.

There were jars of pickles, chutneys, jams and preserves, and in the corner a drum of Stilton cheese for Grandad.

On the pantry floor were sacks of home-grown potatoes, flour, corn for the chickens, meal and bran for Grandad's pigs, and a large glazed jar of eggs preserved in isinglass, ready for when the chickens went off lay.

Saying it was time to catch our train, Grandma took my hand and said if I promised to eat up all my dinner every day from now until Christmas, we could all come and spend it with her for she planned to gather her family together to celebrate the passing of the long dark shadow of the Great War, from which all her own had emerged unscathed (except for my Aunt Effie, who was still in mourning for her fallen young husband, and our second cousin George, torpedoed and lost at sea).

Marvelling at the speed with which my pudding stirring wish had come true, I vowed to eat every crumb. Grandma was not only a superb cook, she was also a wise and wily strategist.

We arrived, my Mother, Aunt Effie and Cousin Louise, on the day before Christmas Eve, in order to help with the preparations.

Grandma was already baking in the kitchen, pouring stock down a funnel in the centre of a pork pie to make the delicious jelly round the meat. Trays of mince pies were cooling on the copper, and in a place of honour was a large caraway seed cake for Grandad whose taste did not run to iced Christmas cake.

A glazed earthenware bowl stood in the hearth, dough rising nicely. The smell of baking was like nectar.

Louise and I found Grandad in the outhouse at the bottom of the kitchen garden, plucking the three cockerels. A large bin was full of feathers, and bits of chicken fluff were sticking to his eyebrows and bristly cheeks. Seated on a broken-backed kitchen chair, he was wearing a yellowing old straw boater (the one he used for gardening in the summer) and a striped apron. After we had planted a hasty peck on his rough cheeks and ducked smartly to avoid being brushed by his stubbly chin in return, foiled in his intent, he picked up one of the bird's claws and, pulling a tendon, made it clench open and shut. We shrieked and fled.

He was short and rotund, red-faced, white-haired, and relentlessly jolly. He could never, over the years, remember the names of the growing band of grandchildren who invaded his privacy during the school holidays, but he overcame this difficulty by using the collective pronoun.

Thinking himself a strict disciplinarian, when the going got rough, he would open the parlour door a few inches and shout, 'Now then you little gels/lads, GIVE OVER.' If mayhem broke out after bedtime, and the giggling and pillow fighting got out of hand, he would repeat the formula, first banging on the stairs to suggest he was on his way up, adding: 'If I have to come up there – I'll *WARM* the lot of you.' It never failed to restore law and order.

At Christmas, in his best navy serge suit, with his gold watch chain and sovereign medallion across his amplitude, he moved among us in a benign aura of palm olive shaving soap and cigars, overlaid with a faint whiff of brandy.

He came along presently, with a bucket of potatoes from his allotment, and another one of carrots, onions and sprouts, which my Mother and Aunt Effie peeled and prepared ready for the next two days.

Louise and I spent our time in the parlour, adding candles and trimmings to the Christmas tree.

On Christmas Eve, there was succulent cold rabbit pie, several kinds of pickles and chutneys, and mince pies for supper. After which, my youngest Auntie Flo (eventually we had three aunts of that name) bound our hair into corkscrew curls with rags, and helped us write notes to Santa asking for baby dolls. These we floated up the chimney, hoping he would receive them in time.

Two pillow cases were pegged to the fireguard ready for his visit, and we went early to the spare feather mattress made up into a bed for us in Grandma's front room, with the oven shelf wrapped in several layers of brown paper to warm it. We were warned that Santa would not come while we were awake.

Sleep was not easy. A constant stream of callers came

and departed, talking and laughing went on until quite late, then the village band played carols all along the lane, calling out 'Merry Christmas' to everyone by name on the way.

Louise and I woke at first light and cautiously explored Santa's offerings. There was an apple, an orange, some chocolate coins wrapped in silver paper, a sugar mouse (which we ate straight away), and also something soft and furry, which did not feel at all like a baby doll.

Grandad was up early. He collected all the shoes and honed and boned them ready for the day, then he brought up cups of tea with a dash of whisky for the ladies.

After this, he and my Uncle Alfred went off carrying roasting tins containing the cockerels and a hand and spring of pork to Mr. Foot, the baker, down the lane, whose custom it was to keep his ovens going to cook the Christmas meats for his neighbours. His twin daughters, aged eight, were feared and detested by Louise and me. They were older than us, they swanked because they went on the train to Brackley High School for Girls, and they made fun of us.

We had found not baby dolls but squirrel fur muffs in our pillow cases. After breakfast Grandad said we should take the old sheep dog Fluff for a nice run down to Fisher's field, and wear our new muffs to keep our hands warm.

We set off in our brightly polished shoes, hair in tight corkscrew curls with big bows on top, our new muffs in place, down the lane past Mr. Foot's bakery.

There, to our horror, we met the Foot twins, carrying new baby dolls! How could Santa have mixed up our notes so disastrously?

'What did you have for Christmas?' they wished to know.

'Santa brought us these,' said Louise, displaying her muff. The twins shrieked with mirth. 'Santa brought you? It's not Santa, you donkeys, it's your father dressed up!' They ran off, laughing. Presently, they came back. 'When the doctor brings babies in his black bag, where do you think he gets them from?' they enquired.

Wide-eyed and stricken dumb, we listened as they whispered a second heresy.

In Fisher's field, while Fluff sniffed happily round in search of rabbits, we considered.

Louise was emphatic. 'It can't be your father, because mine died on Flanders field, and yours is still away.'

Comforted by this conclusion, we decided to test the other story we had been told.

When the Christmas cake was cut, we both asked for a slice of Grandad's caraway seed cake instead. As it was growing dark, we postponed our plan until Boxing Day, when we went to the allotment behind the hen house and kitchen garden and carefully sprinkled the caraway seeds round the gooseberry bushes.

We retired behind the pig sty to discuss it. 'If it's true,' said Louise, 'will they grow on the bushes or in the ground?'

'Wouldn't you think they would get dirt in their ears or catch cold?' I ventured.

Throwing a few small apple fallings to Sukie and her piglets, we went back to the house.

There was hand and spring of pork with crackling, roast potatoes, and warmed mince pies with cream for dinner. For tea we had gammon ham, pickles, red cabbage and the remains of the sherry trifle and Christmas cake, of which we made up for what we had missed the previous day.

As was the custom on Boxing Day, the fiancées came to tea. My Uncle Tom brought Florrie Campbell, whom he was to marry in the New Year, and my Uncle Alfred brought Florrie Marriott, the young cook at the Manse, a pretty lady with violet blue eyes and a porcelain-like complexion which she dabbed frequently with Phul-Nana face powder, much to Grandad's disgust.

My Uncle Jack, Grandma's favourite, had come down from London whence he had been recently transferred to the ticket office at Marylebone Station, by the machinations of Peter Clare who feared his Lily had eyes for Jack. Mr. Clare had other plans for her. The Rector's son perhaps – or the Doctor's eldest, currently at medical school.

My Uncle Jack was dark, pale, with Ivor Novello good looks and a rather sad expression. After tea, he came downstairs in his best navy Melton cloth overcoat, carrying a black ebony cane with a silver knob – an unexplained Christmas gift.

Louise flung herself upon him for she was experiencing, at six years of age, the pangs of first love. She begged him to stay but he said he had to see a man about a dog, at which Grandma stared at him accusingly over the silver-rimmed spectacles she wore on the end of her nose when playing whist, but said nothing.

My youngest Auntie Flo brought Stephen Smith, a young man of such dazzling beauty I, too, was stricken to the heart. He had corn-coloured curly hair and the flushed, tanned complexion of a farm worker, for he was stockman at Kingston's. He wore beneath his navy suit a canary-coloured waistcoat which his Auntie Emm had knitted him for Christmas, and had on also Saxe blue hand-knitted socks.

In the evening, while the cards were being shuffled for whist, my mother played songs, carols and 'The Maiden's Prayer' on the piano in the parlour, then Louise and I played duets with two fingers on the black notes until bedtime. We managed to postpone this so that I could count up Stephen's tricks and mark them on the peg board. When we left play for a time, he cracked nuts for us with the flat iron, until we had to say goodnight.

In bed, we discussed the excitement of the last two days until sleep came. Louise said she hoped Uncle Jack had got a nice puppy, and decided to marry him when she grew up.

I resolved privately that if Auntie Flo did not choose Stephen Smith, I would ask him to wait for me so we could have a double wedding with Louise and Uncle Jack.

Next day, we returned home with a pudding stuffed with silver threepenny pieces to eat on New Year's Day. These we licked clean and put away to bring us luck in the coming year.

'Well, girls,' said my mother, 'that's the last of the Christmas puddings. Who knows where we will all be next Christmas?'

Due to those wretched caraway seeds we had sprinkled under the gooseberry bushes, and the rash of babies they caused in the family, our next Christmas was spent at home.

In the New Year my father came home, and in the autumn I had a new baby sister, Dorothy Eileen. My Uncle Tom and his Flo were married and they had a baby girl, Gladys Mary Jane. (Gladys for the famous actress, Miss Gladys Cooper, and Mary and Jane for her two grandmothers.)

My Aunt Effie was swept to the altar by Mr. Roach, our family butcher, who was a widower with grown-up children, and Louise had a baby half-brother, Ernest Edwin (named for Louise's fallen hero father and Grandad).

Out of the blue, my Uncle Jack eloped with Lily Clare. Peter Clare was furious and swore that if, after all the money he had spent sending his Lily to Brackley High School for Girls, she couldn't do better than go off with a railway clerk (even if it was one of Teddy Chadwick's lads), they need never darken his doors again. Nor did they.

My Grandma, on hearing the news, had a terrible 'turn' and had to be put to bed by my youngest Auntie Flo, who rubbed her forehead with a camphor stick, applied the smelling salts, and sent off, post haste, to the Turk's Head for a quartern of brandy.

It was not the time to acquaint her with the latest of Cupid's depredations.

My youngest Auntie Flo was said to be the biggest flirt in Woodbridge Halt. She had two admirers. One Friday evening, Stephen Smith, on his way home from band practice, called for my Aunt, resolved to reach an understanding.

When he learned that she had gone to a dance at Byefield with Raymond Fairbrother on the pillion of his motor bike, Stephen leapt on to his push bike and tore off in pursuit.

Storming into St. Matthews' Church Hall, still wearing his bike clips, he confronted my Aunt in the middle of the Military Two-step.

Leading her by force from the hall, he pedalled off into the summer night with her on his crossbar. Thus, in intimate *tête-à-tête*, he demanded that she choose between her life of reckless pleasure and his true love.

My Aunt was not Grandma's daughter for nothing. Before they plighted their troth in the woodshed, she made her own terms.

Raymond Fairbrother was already on the footplate, firing the Derby Flyer with my Uncle Tom. She could never marry a man who was not on the railway like the rest of her family, and the proud possessor of a privilege rail ticket.

So Stephen gave up the land and took to the rails for his love's sweet sake.

Her last chick fled, leaving my Grandma bereft, she lost interest in Fur and Feather whist drives and making delicious pies from her winnings. There was only Grandad to eat them all.

My Uncle Tom tried to interest her in a little innocent gambling, encouraging her to put 6p each way on an outsider, any to come for a win on the favourite in the next race.

But it was no use. She packed her wickerwork basket suitcase and went off to Derby to visit her sister Sally, arranging for old lady Wood next door to put up my Grandad's snap and cook him a hot meal when he came off shift.

Some weeks later, she returned with two small boys in tow, orphans whom she had undertaken to foster.

One was a quiet, ginger-haired little lad, Joey Bosworth, who had a weak chest and a disarming grin; the other, Johnnie Handley, a dark-eyed charmer who turned out to be a wilful young varmint.

Grandma rolled up her sleeves and took them in hand. She rubbed Joey's back and chest with goose grease, and stitched him into a brown paper vest, in which he creaked (and ponged) until the spring, when she let him out and plied them both with brimstone and treacle, 'to cleanse their blood'.

As for Johnnie, always in trouble for breaking her gas mantles with blown up balloons, and putting monkey nut shells into the dough left to rise on the hearth, she dealt with him summarily.

As a youth, Great-great-grandad Chadwick had been whipper-in to Captain Reeves' pack at Friars Marston. His dog whip hung strategically by his portrait near the kitchen door. She would chase Johnnie round the kitchen table and out into the garden, cracking the whip in hot pursuit and challenging him to come and have a taste of it.

The neighbours, peering round the kitchen curtains, smiled indulgently at seeing her spirits restored.

'That's what I call real mothering,' observed Grandad, downing a pint in the Turk's Head.

Like Mother, Like Daughter
by Barbara Roberts

Leah's sandalled heels kicked gently against my skirt. She sat astride my hip as comfortably as her mother used to do. We waited at the garden gate, the three of us, mother, daughter, grand-daughter, like a sculpture group, lit by the spotlight of the morning sun.

There was a moment of silence when Carrie looked at Leah safe in my arms, and I looked at Carrie, a ring of loving admiration holding us together.

'There's fresh coffee in the pot, Mum, if you prefer it.' Carrie brushed back her hair for the umpteenth time.

'No, thanks. Instant'll do. Look, do go or you'll be late.'

'Don't forget she likes Ribena with warm water.'

'I know. I've looked after her before, remember.'

Carrie grinned. 'Sorry, Mum. I'm a bit twitchy, aren't I? Not used to being out for a whole day.'

'You look as if it's done you good already.' I noted the sparkling eyes, the careful make-up. A new jacket, too, by the look of it. 'Go on, enjoy yourself while you've the chance. And don't worry about Leah. We'll have a lovely time, won't we?'

Leah buried her head against me, without smiling, and stuck her small pale thumb into her mouth.

Carrie opened the gate and paused, jangling the keys to my Mini in her hand.

'Right, I'm off. Mick won't be home till late. One of

his Parents' Evenings. And there's – '

'Get on,' I chided. 'Alison will be waiting for you. Give her my love, if you aren't too busy chatting to remember. You'll have so much to catch up on after all these years.'

And then she was into my Mini and away, her arm like a flag waving through the open window till she was out of sight. Leah waved her fat little hands stiffly from the wrists and then struggling from my arms, stuck in her thumb again, before running uncertainly but swiftly back into the house.

My daughter's house. Surprisingly I had rarely been alone in it. Strange being in another woman's kitchen, tidying, putting away the dishes, wondering where she keeps the butter. In the fridge, or on the pantry shelf as I do? After all, daughters are supposed to keep house like their mothers. Do I put rubber bands round door handles because my mother did? I looked at the pantry door and smiled. There were two fat brown rubber bands. Her mother's daughter ...

But not altogether.

The pantry was filled with tall glass jars, spicy brown with the sort of lentils and peas that I admired in the health food shops but wasn't sure how to cook. Jars of homemade jam, neatly labelled and dated (oh, not like me at all). A row of rough pottery containers that a colleague of Mick's had made them for a wedding present. I lifted a lid and looked in. It was filled with pale brown dusty stuff which smelled like a haybarn. Probably very good for you. Pure fibre like a coconut mat mashed up.

'Gan, Gan.' Leah pulled at my skirt.

'Now, poppet, what is it? Shall we leave the clearing up and go in the garden?'

'But you haven't seen the house yet. My house.'

'Yes, I have, Leah. I've been here before. You know,

I came at Christmas with Grandad.'

'But you've not seen *my* house,' she insisted, stamping both her feet together like a baby kangaroo. 'I've got a special house, all of my own. Come and see.'

She pulled me along through the narrow hall with its clutter of Wellingtons and heavy waterproofs to the foot of the stairs. Under the staircase was a little cupboard with a straw-coloured painted door, stencilled all over with a riot of red poppies. Last year Carrie had been into stencilling furniture, buying cheap pine chests at sales, bathroom mirrors, boxes. Her house was full of enthusiasms, I thought. It was like a library of past loves.

Leah pulled open the door and, hunching down, hopped like a brown rabbit inside the dark cupboard. I leaned in and saw she was sitting on a little rag rug. It had been mine once. Then it had lain by Carrie's own white bed in her pretty bright room at home. Now, smaller, as if it had been shrunk by loving, it lay on the floor of Leah's House. A teddy sat at one side, a fat furry lion on the other. Leah began to set out tea cups no bigger than the poppy flowers on the door.

'It's tea time. We're having tea. Come in, Gan.'

So, my knees cracking, I knelt down and took tea in Leah's House, drinking a tongueful of warm water from the tiny cups that smelt of nail varnish.

We fed Teddy and Leo and each other, and talked.

I actually called her Carrie. Just once. She looked at me seriously, her head tilted. 'Don't you know my name, Gan?'

I hugged her, awkwardly, my knees feeling suspiciously rigid. 'Of course I do, silly.' I was wondering if I'd ever get up again, to tell the truth.

Later we made the beds together, throwing pillows at each other, giggling. Her little bed first. Then the big double bed in Carrie's and Mick's room. A big brass bed, whose knobs rattled as we walked across the uneven dark-stained floor. I found it almost too personal a task. Pulling the rumpled sheets tight across the mattress with its deep soft body shapes in it, picking off a hair on the pillow. His or hers? I didn't even know which side they slept on. I glanced at the bedside reading and felt like a spy. Margaret Drabble. Yes, Carrie's side. But then, *Patchwork for Pleasure* and Dick Francis, on the other table, with Kleenex and a jar of hand cream. Hard to say. But the whole room was a bit of a jumble, really. Clothes about. Scattered shoes.

Their wedding photograph on the old chest of drawers. Both laughing, her veil wind-blown like a halo of light. And a snap of Leah at six months, grinning from her pram. What a lot of joy there was. Smiles, laughter. A happy house.

Leah and I sat in the garden and had our elevenses, which she called 'sevenses. Ribena, with warm water, and Nescafé in a thin china cup which I'd had a job to find. Carrie was into mugs, it seemed. Quicker to wash up.

Lunch was all on a platter in the fridge, covered with clingfilm. 'I don't want you to have to *do* anything, Mum, except look after Leah. Have a nice restful day,' she had said.

And, 'It's such a treat for me to know I can leave her. I never get more than an hour or two on my own.'

What a pity they didn't live nearer. It had to be a special occasion. How nice for Carrie to see Alison again. Must have been six years ago, at the wedding, when they last met, with Alison dashing off afterwards to Saudi Arabia to teach in that English School. They would be talking nineteen to the dozen just as they used to when they were both in navy blue gymslips. Living it up in the Metropole Hotel, with prawn cocktails and wine, and brandy afterwards in the lounge, two married women with children of their own.

I had to admit to feeling a little tired after lunch. It was quite a relief the find Leah nodding in my arms as we sat on the swing in the tiny overgrown back garden.

'She does like a little sleep still in the afternoons. But don't push it,' Carrie had said.

'*I* like a little sleep, too.'

So we took Teddy and Leo out of Leah's House and put them into bed. Leah snuggled down. I drew the curtains against the bright afternoon sun, sang, as well as I could remember, one or two nursery rhymes to her, and tiptoed out.

The sitting room was on the north side of the house, cool and quiet. I slipped off my shoes and lay on the settee. Idly I picked up the book beside me: *Sonnets from the Portuguese* by Elizabeth Barrett Browning.

I should have guessed then. That passion. Those haunting words of love. 'How do I love thee? Let me count the ways.' But I didn't. I thought only, How nice this is. This house. This quiet room, full of books and knitting and patchwork cushions. With a child upstairs and a sunlit garden with a swing in it.

The shrilling phone made me jump.

I grabbed it quickly so that it wouldn't wake Leah.

'Hello? No, it isn't, actually. It's her mother. Yes, people say we do sound alike.'

I laughed.

'Who did you say? Alison? But ... didn't you see her? She was meeting your train at Darlington.'

There were words at the other end of the line, but I couldn't really hear them.

'Yes, it's nice to talk to *you* .... It *has* been ages .... The wedding, wasn't it? Gracious, time flies, doesn't it?

Carrie will be so disappointed to hear she's missed you. Only in the North for a couple of days, you say? Give my best wishes to your mother. I *do* hope she makes a good recovery ....'

I was summoned to another tea party in Leah's House.

My knees and heart aching, I crept into the gloom of the cupboard. Leah was chattering about Teddy who had fallen out of his chair and hurt himself.

After I had inspected his bandaged leg, she wrapped him tightly in a piece of old shawl and laid him down on the rag rug.

'Teddy would like some strawberries, Gan,' she said, stroking his tummy. 'He won't eat anything else when he's poorly sick.'

'What about kissing him better?'

'I've done that. Lots of times. Kissing doesn't make people better.'

Oh, Leah, I know, I know.

I eased myself backwards out of the cupboard.

'I'll go shopping for the strawberries,' I announced.

Pretending was easy for me. After all, it is only the acceptable face of lying and I'd had plenty of practice at that. In the sitting room I searched in my handbag for the tube of Smarties I had brought for Leah. I tipped them into a saucer and crawled back into the heady world of make-believe.

'The juiciest strawberries the greengrocer had,' I said as I showed them to Teddy.

'Those aren't strawberries.' Leah's little mouth, as pert as a cherry, turned away from the offering.

'We'll have to pretend then, won't we? Teddy likes them, don't you?' I pushed an orange Smartie under the soft rubbed nose. 'Yes, you see, he loves them.'

Leah seized the saucer and sorted out the red sweets.

'He only likes the ripe ones,' she said, lifting her firm little chin at me.

Ah, Leah, you, too, know the trick of pretending only when it suits you.

The ritual went on. Leah did not seem to notice that my hands shook, or that I kept looking out towards the front door, my ears straining for the sound of the Mini.

What would I say?

'Alison rang. She's home for two days. Her mother's had a stroke. Slight, they say ....'

And watch her crumble, my beautiful, bright-eyed, bushy-tailed daughter. Caught out. Found out. Her secret .... What secret?

I twisted my wedding ring. An old habit. And then stopped myself, and gripped my hands tightly together. I wasn't praying. I was struggling to work things out, knowing that what I did, or did not do, was going to be very important to all of us. Carrie. Big, shaggy, gentle Mick. Adoring, innocent Mick.

Like mother, like daughter, did they say?

Oh dear, I hoped not. I wanted it to be better for her. It all *seemed* so right. Not a lot of money, but a loving husband, a pretty little house, security.

And Leah. Pretending in her house under the stairs, just as Carrie used to do.

But did you hand it all on, secrets, too, like a congenital disease?

You can see rubber bands, but can you see heartache? Does a child know when her mother is yearning for something else? Someone else. Someone else's.

Carrie could not have known, could she?

'More tea, Gan?' Leah's tiny teapot uttered its stream of water like a string of tears into my red plastic cup.

The door opened and Carrie stood there, her face glowing. Her eyes shone with a rare light. She carried paper bags full of cream cakes and soft Brie and watercress. There was a chocolate mouse for Leah and a bunch of pale salmon-coloured pinks for me.

'Did you have a good day, dear?' I said as I poured tea in the kitchen.

'Fabulous. Superb lunch. Sole meunière. The Metropole's looking up.'

She sipped from her mug and then looked up at me, her face lit by a wide smile.

'Thanks, Mum. It was good of you to have Leah for a whole day. Oh, and by the way, Alison sends her love to you and Dad.'

'How nice of her,' I said, and turned away to the sink to refill the kettle.

Cherry Ripe
by Pat Earl

Charlie Puddington was fed up. Usually he got on well with his brother and there was seldom a cross word between them. But today it was different.

As he stood looking out of his kitchen window with a mug of tea in one hand and a biscuit in the other, his mind was a jumble of disturbed throughts. Of couse it was all Tom's fault, arguing about picking the cherries and going on about people getting old.

Outside the birds were singing and the sun shone in a cloudless blue sky. But there was a certain stillness in the air that warned it was building up to be yet another hot and humid August day.

The pretty garden in front of the cottage was a mass of colour, and each year it was the talk of the village. But although Charlie and his brother worked hard to keep it neat and tidy, it was now getting too much for them.

Hollyhocks and foxgloves, buddleia and mock orange, pinks, antirrhinums and lavender, all jostled for position with fuchsias and roses, honeysuckle and summer jasmine, on either side of the short gravel path which wound its way down to the white picket gate.

Charlie dipped the biscuit in his tea, let it soak for a moment or two, then put the soggy end in his mouth.

'Modern rubbish!' he exclaimed in disgust as he spat the half chewed remains out through the open window.

Why did Tom have to keep changing things! Ginger nuts were the only biscuits he liked. They had body in them had ginger nuts. You could dunk them in your tea and they held together. Not like these other things; as soon as they got wet they just fell apart. Charlie threw what was left of the offending biscuit out into the garden.

It might have been the biscuit, it could have been the quarrel, but most likely, he thought, it was his rheumatics that were making him feel so irritable. Whatever it was, the day had started badly and something told him it could only get worse.

The front door slammed and Tom hurried crossly down the garden path. Charlie watched his brother close the gate behind him, and set off along the sunny lane towards the village.

The trouble had begun earlier that morning when they were having breakfast together.

'Them cherries needs picking,' Charlie said.

'Um,' grunted Tom.

'If summat isn't done about them soon, weather will break and they'll be spoiling on the trees. Or birds will have 'em.'

Charlie took a loud sip of tea while he waited for his brother to reply. But Tom said nothing. 'Well? what we going to do?' Charlie persisted crossly.

'I'll tell 'ee what you'm not going to do,' replied Tom.

'You b'aint going up them ladders this year, not never no more, and that's a fact.'

'What d'yer mean?' demanded Charlie, glaring angrily at his brother, scarcely able to believe his ears.

'At eighty-two you'm too bloody old to go prancing about up ladders. And you know what Doctor said about them dizzy spells of your'n.'

'Doctors!' snorted Charlie in disgust. 'Then how we going to get the fruit picked? Just you tell me that.'

'I be going down the village later. I'll have a word with Vicar. He'll come up with summat, never you mind,' Tom replied.

Charlie knew that it was useless to pursue the subject when Tom was in one of his moods. So he let the matter drop and they continued their breakfast in silence. They had not spoken since.

The little orchard stood in a plot of land behind the cottage Charlie shared with his younger brother. He was just thirteen when he helped his father to plant the trees. In a way they had grown up together. To him they were more than just fruit trees, they were like old friends. Now, even though they were neglected and well past their prime, they still produced good crops. Each year Charlie and Tom picked the fruit and sold it to the local greengrocer.

Charlie waited until his brother had disappeared from view down the lane, then he closed the kitchen window.

'Doctors! Vicars! Musn't go up ladders! Getting old!' he muttered crossly as he mimicked what Tom had said.

The more he thought about it, the more determined he became to make a start on picking the blasted cherries himself. Anyway, he didn't fancy a lot of strangers rampaging around his orchard, doing more harm than good. Like as not they'd never have picked a cherry before in their lives, and you had to know what you was at, picking cherries.

Some five minutes later, dressed in his working clothes and wearing an old Panama hat to keep off the sun, Charlie Puddington stumped out of the cottage and down the back garden to the old potting-shed. The shed door was reluctant to move on its broken hinges, but with an effort he managed to force it open. It was quite dark inside, and he had to wait a few moments until his eyes became accustomed to the gloom.

'I'll show 'em I bain't too old,' he mumbled defiantly

as he struggled to get the long wooden ladder out from behind a rusty old bicycle. But a pedal had become entangled with one of the rungs, and in spite of all Charlie's efforts it just would not budge.

Then, suddenly and inexplicably, the bicycle and ladder parted company, catching him off balance, and he fell back against the side of the shed. Although he had not hurt himself, it certainly did nothing to improve his temper.

'You did that on purpose,' Charlie complained peevishly to the ladder as he dragged it outside and dropped it on the grass.

By the time he had carried it down to the bottom of the orchard he was short of breath, sweating, and even more bad-tempered. Choosing the tallest tree in the far corner by the hedge, Charlie looked for a good strong branch then eased the narrow end of the ladder up into the fork with the tree.

After making sure it was quite safe, he leant against a ramshackle old hen-house in the shade of one of the trees, and rested for a few minutes until he got his breath back. As soon as he had recovered he went back to the shed and collected three dusty wicker shopping baskets.

Slipping the handle of one of the baskets over his left arm, he climbed slowly up the ladder, in among the cool leafy branches of the tree. A few moments later he emerged through the green canopy out into the hot mid-morning sunlight once more.

Charlie settled himself down and made himself as comfortable as possible, then began to pick the juicy red-black cherries which he put carefully into the wicker basket. It was a remote and peaceful world perched up there high above the orchard. A world Charlie had always enjoyed and which he found soothing to his nerves.

He must have been working for a good hour or so, he

had filled one basket which he had taken down and was halfway to filling the second, when he decided that it was time for a rest.

He had a wonderful view of the countryside. Straight ahead he could see the lane leading up to the cottage. To the right the main road wound its way up the hill past the Dog and Ferret, which he happened to notice was open, then continued up past the church and war memorial, right through the centre of Muddlewick village. While over to his left, in the hazy distance between two hills, Charlie could just make out the tall spire of Hillchester Cathedral.

A large blackbird came and settled on a nearby branch, and started to attack the fruit with its yellow beak.

''Op it!' said Charlie, but the bird took no notice. 'Shoo! get out of it!' he shouted, rustling the leaves.

The bird looked up at him, cocked its head on one side enquiringly, then continued to peck away at the fruit once more. Determined not to be outdone, Charlie grabbed hold of a branch with his left hand to steady himself, then with his free hand took off his hat and sent it skimming across the top of the tree towards the bird.

'Now 'op it!' he shouted.

This time the bird flew off, settled in the tree opposite, and continued its meal in peace. Charlie looked down to see where his hat had landed. It was lying on the grass just a few feet from the bottom of the tree. He decided to let it stay there, no point in making a special journey. It could wait until he had filled the basket.

As he worked the sun seemed to be getting hotter and hotter. He could feel it beating down on the back of his head when he stretched out to pluck at the cherries. He began to wish that he had gone down to get his hat. Still the basket was almost full; another ten minutes and he would be taking it down anyway.

The dizziness came on him suddenly, and at the same time he felt a stabbing pain in his chest. The pain got worse, it became so bad that Charlie felt certain he was going to die. Not that he was afraid of death, but at that particular moment it was not convenient. He was just not ready for it. Of course he realised that it was his own fault, he had brought it on himself. At eighty-two, and after all the warnings he had been given, he had no business to be up a tall ladder, on a scorching morning in August, picking cherries.

The giddiness had come on him quickly, and his vision had become so blurred that he could not even see the ground. All he could do was to hold on tightly to the ladder and wait for things to get better – or worse.

'All right, all right, just a minute,' Charlie grumbled irritably to his Maker beyond the cloudless blue sky above him.

Gradually the pain subsided, and the mist cleared from before his eyes. But the dizziness and the pounding of his heart prevented him from moving. He could see the cottage quite plainly now, even the thin patch in the roof where the starlings had robbed the thatch. He felt sad that he was probably looking at it for the last time.

Further up the village he could just see the Dog and Ferret. The thought of never spending another evening drinking with his cronies brought a lump in his throat and tears to his eyes.

'Just a minute, just a minute,' Charlie muttered as he cautiously began to ease his way down the ladder, one step at a time.

He certainly did not intend to die in his present position, and was determined to reach the ground. He was not going to give anyone the satisfaction of saying, in spite of all their warnings, that he had fallen off the blasted thing!

By the time he had got to the bottom the pain had

eased, but he was short of breath and very shaky. He retrieved his hat then staggered back into the shade of the tree, thankful to sink down on the cool soft grass. Sitting with his back resting against the tree trunk, and gently fanning himself with his sweat-stained hat, Charlie Puddington waited for death.

Funny it should happen here, he thought drowsily as he remembered that other important event which had taken place in the same quiet corner of the orchard. It was here beside a young tree that he had courted Bessie Laxton.

She was a big strong girl of twenty-three was Bessie. A smile of satisfaction spread across his face as he recalled the incident. It was as clear to him now as though it had happened only yesterday. He was barely seventeen at the time, that was nigh on sixty-five years ago. Of course there had been other girls since but only one Bessie.

'Bessie Laxton, the first and the best,' he sighed contentedly.

Gradually the world seemed to be slipping, slipping slowly away. There was no point in resisting, no point in holding on, he was quite content to depart this life with cosy thoughts of Bessie to accompany him . . . .

It was not the heavenly choir, nor the heat of damnation that aroused him. It was the sound of clanking metal. Charlie Puddington opened one eye, and cautiously checked his destination. There in front of him, holding the rusty old bicycle from the shed, stood brother Tom.

'Thought you was a gonner this time,' Tom announced cheerfully.

'Ah, well, never you mind about that,' replied Charlie, annoyed at having been cheated out of his great adventure. 'What you'm done about them cherries?' he demanded, jerking his thumb upwards at the tree.

'See you've been at 'em, you old fool,' observed Tom.

'Vicar's sending some students over s'arternoon. Reckons they'll do a proper job, he does.'

Charlie grunted his disapproval. 'What you doing wi' that old bike then?' he asked thoughtfully, rubbing a weather-beaten hand over his stubbly chin.

'After I'd fetched Doctor, I was going to put you across it and wheel you up to cemetery.'

'Ah!' replied Charlie, struggling to his feet. 'Now just you 'old her steady while I gets me leg acrost. Then you can give us a shove up to the Dog and Ferret. If we hurries, us'll get one in 'afore closing.'

Relative Freedom
by Katherine Parry

Marian Leigh, still tightly holding on to her composure, looked at her son and his new wife as their pre-ceremony nerves loosened with the wine, the jokes and the music. She wished she could feel at ease too.

John looked very handsome in his dress suit, she decided, although she had thought it an extravagance when the expensive white wedding was first proposed. It was not as though Liz's family were rolling in money. Far from it – her father was a small builder with a large family, trying to make ends meet. But nothing was too good for 'our Liz', from the full church service with peal of bells to the lavish sit-down reception for one hundred and fifty guests.

In the end Marian's husband, William, had paid half the bill. 'After all,' he said, 'we've only got one son. He has two more daughters lined up. Although if they all get a send-off like this, he'll be bankrupt.'

Marian could not help thinking that some of the money would have been more usefully employed providing a more substantial bank balance for her son and daughter-in-law to start their married life with. John had only recently been made Head of History in the large comprehensive where he worked. Liz was a secretary, but of the modern sort which appeared to be a shorthand-typist with salary to match.

Marian thought of her days as a 'real' secretary, what she supposed would be called a personal assistant these days. She had worked for years until her retirement eighteen months ago, when William had decided he had had enough of travelling around Europe sorting out problems for his marine engineering firm.

He looked good on it, too, she decided. He was losing his paunch now the business lunches had stopped, and he looked tanned and fit after getting the garden into shape. She wished she felt as sure of herself as she did of her husband and son. She had aimed for the graceful, elegant look and felt she had achieved it. Quite fortuitously the tawny orchid buttonhole exactly complemented her cream silk suit, amber beads and earrings, which pleased her. She was uncertain about the expensive hat, had been immediately she had taken it home, but could not bring herself to buy another. She had decided to end the nagging doubt, as soon as she left the church, by removing it.

She wished she could dispel her misgivings about the marriage as easily. Was it because John was setting up on his own? But she was used to his being away from home, and hated possessiveness in any form. She had fought against it as a daughter and had determined never to live her life through her son.

Why then was she feeling like the archetypal mother-in-law? She looked at Liz and could see why her son was attracted. Her dark brown eyes, long black shining hair and tanned skin showed to their best advantage as she stood next to John's fairness. At least a few dark genes would not come amiss in the family, Marian thought, as she moved over to Liz's mother and father, Jan and Al.

'Jack's bearing up all right, then.'

Now what did that imply? thought Marian. Did they expect him to collapse into an ineffectual heap? She smiled at them and scolded herself for not feeling more charitable towards Jan and Al, but immediately she wondered why it had to be Jan instead of Janet; Al instead of — what? She must ask sometime. And why, oh why, had it got to be Jack instead of John? Everything, it seemed, had to be reduced to the lowest common demoninator.

Yes, she admitted to herself, she did feel irritable and touchy, and must stop it.

'Liz looks lovely, doesn't she? I thought the service was beautiful, didn't you, Jan? The sun shone for them too. I'm sure they are going to be very happy.'

Jan looked knowing. 'Let's hope so anyway. I can't see Liz looking after a home, myself. She keeps her own room tidy, I'll grant you that, but she's no good in the kitchen.'

Marian searched around for a safe remark.

'Well, I expect that will alter when she has a home of her own.'

Jan and Al looked at each other in smug superiority.

'Well, she'll do as she wants, that's for sure.'

Feeling that she had reached a dead end, Marian was relieved when William, John and Liz joined them. She looked at Liz and wondered at her mother's remarks. She had always been so quiet and demure in her brief visits to her prospective parents-in-law's home. They had tried to get her to talk freely but had concluded that she was young and shy, and perhaps felt a little overawed by their life-style in the Home Counties compared to the rough and tumble of her Northern working-class home with her five brothers and sisters. Marian still did not know what made her tick, and this perhaps was why she felt — what?

Apprehensive, I think, is what I feel, she decided. As if I have to be very, very careful about what I say and how I act towards Liz.

She had tried to draw Liz out and give her confidence

but there had been very little reaction. Now her Mother had presented an entirely new facet of Liz for Marian's assessment. Was the quiet girl with sensitive feelings really a young woman of determined ideas? Was the gauche barrier of silence really a steel shutter that came down to keep out unwanted encroachment?

I must stop this, thought Marian. After all, John has known her for a year, and of course she has talked to him, if not to us. He looks happy and sure of himself. His prospects are good. She has a job, and living up North they've been able to buy a small house, so what is there to worry about? She decided to refill her glass and drink to the future. Who knew? She might yet be the perfect mother-in-law.

Three Martinis and a lot of chat later, she was ready to leave when William said it was time to go. Liz and John had already made their traditional exit, and they themselves had to make long drive back to Surrey. ...

Since then the years had flown past, she thought as she looked out at the garden.

The forecast had said rain in the afternoon — and there it was, an undeviating drizzle. But good for the plants. That morning William had shaved the lawns while she put out some bedding plants; Ten-week stocks, ageratum and lobelia in the borders; Nicotiana, Virginia and night-scented stocks near the house so that, as the seed packet promised, 'The scent would provide indoor fragrance'.

William had discovered a hitherto unknown talent when he had invested in a small greenhouse. They no longer had to buy expensive plants from the garden centre, and Marian loved watching him as he carefully pruned and watered the sturdy seedlings. In a few months he would hover with watchful pride over the reddening globes of tomatoes and the rich curled heads of chrysanthemums.

The cheesy smell of the soufflé, nearly ready in the oven, and the tang of the oniony salad completed her sense of satisfaction as she called William in for lunch. They both had time to stand, stare and savour now, and she was well content.

Except, of course, for John. She tried not to think about him too much as she could do nothing. It was, in fact, three years ago this week that she had stood in the flower-decorated reception room of the Mitre Hotel. The sun had shone that day and the heady mixture of wine, good food and scented blooms created an ambience of well-being and high expectations. She had resolutely put her doubts out of her mind and enjoyed the chat, the dancing and the pleasure of watching John's happiness.

She had tried her best then and afterwards to be nice to Liz and to make it clear that she did not want to hold on to John; just as she had tried to be friendly to her family, taking an interest in their numerous relatives, inviting them down to stay. In short, generally going about wagging her tail, trying to please.

Of course, it did not help when forthright Aunt Eva May, winkled out of Cornwall for the wedding, had said that she could not get two words out of Liz, and all her family talked about were kids and cars.

This unpleasantly coincided with Marian's own feelings and her discomfiture had been compounded by overhearing a forthright exchange between Jan and her sister.

'Liz'll have to watch *her*, you know,' said Jan.

'How do you mean?'

'Well, he's an only child and you know what that means.'

'What — he's a mummy's boy?'

'Well, there's that, of course, but my worry is that *she*'ll interfere. She's got nothing to do now she's retired. You can bet she won't leave them alone.'

Now, Marian felt again the sense of cold apartness that had come over her when she realised they were talking about her. Why were people so unkind? This prejudice against the only child. If one wanted to generalise, what about the large family with the bossy eldest, problem middle and spoilt youngest – and as for herself with nothing to do!

Marian thought of her pleasure at being able to indulge at last in her interest in the past. The fascination of unearthing old wills and records, looking at old buildings, and meeting people of like interest took up nearly all her spare time. That was apart from the time she spent on the house, garden, the theatre and their very good friends.

But don't think about it, she reminded herself. There was no point in reliving the past. It was all over now and she would probably never see Liz's family again. Nor, she sighed, was she likely to see her granddaughter, now eighteen months old and from the photographs growing into a delightful little girl, fair like John but with Liz's dark eyes.

John was still up North in the house on which William had put down the deposit, as a wedding present. But Liz had gone back to her mother, taking Julie with her.

Marian thought, too, of the few fleeting visits they had made. They had always stayed at a nearby hotel and their visits were never more than a couple of days because as William had said, 'I just can't relax there.' She had admitted that she felt like that too – even John, who was always so open with them, seemed tense and reserved on their visits North.

They had noticed that it was he who prepared the few meals they took at the house, and that it was he who dashed to the shops to get something that had been forgotten.

Liz still never said much to them. It was mostly a question and answer routine. William would say, 'How is your job going, Liz?' She would give a laugh and say, 'All right.'

It was in an effort to extend the conversation at one uncomfortable coffee-time, that the talk grew into a discussion of women at work and Women's Lib. And it was then that they heard for the first time something of what Liz was thinking behind that calculated reticence.

Women were as oppressed as blacks, she said. Her mother had waited on her brothers and her father hand and foot, and she certainly was not going to do that.

John had laughed at this and Marian smiled too, but began to wonder if it was really funny when Liz went on to say that her work was as important as John's, and that she certainly was not going to leave it, even if John did get a deputy headship in another town.

They wondered where this left John in the promotion stakes but consoled themselves on the way back in the car by deciding that Liz's views would change if and when they started a family. John had told them they would like children so presumably Liz didn't mind giving up her job for that.

But as it turned out, she did. She worked until she was seven months' pregnant and went back to work when Julie was two months old. Marian felt quite bitter when she thought of her granddaughter farmed out to a childminder.

She had been up there only once after the baby was born. She had seen the mess, the muddle and the perpetual pressure to get off in the morning; to shop, get the meals, mow the lawn, repair the fence, fix the doorbell, put up shelves ... And it seemed to Marian that it was not just the odd jobs John was doing but most of the housework as well. He looked thin and tired. She knew that he was trying to study for further qualifications but was not surprised when he told her that he was dropping that for the moment.

'Does Liz have to go to work, John?' she asked. 'You would be a bit short for a while, I know, but the pressure would be off you all.'

'You don't understand, Mum,' he said. 'She won't stop at home. You've heard her say her job is as important as mine. But I don't know, it seems to me we're not doing any job properly! I can't carry on with my studies. We're scraping in to work with a minute to spare and leaving as soon as time is up. And as for Julie — I don't like it!' he said. 'And I can't see that it's necessary. You managed to stay at home with me and carve yourself out a career — and cook,' he said, looking like a small boy again. 'I'm fed up with fast food. I tell you, this Women's Lib has a lot to answer for.'

It all seemed like a bad dream now. Marian sighed as she cut into the golden brown soufflé. She watched William tuck into his lunch and wondered how John was managing, left alone up there. He had visited them three months ago and seemed to be coping with his new life style but the cheerful nonchalance he had had before his marriage turned sour, was replaced by a wary self-restraint.

He had been to see Julie but didn't talk much about the visit, and they hadn't pressed him although they were longing to know how she was growing up. She was walking now and beginning to talk. But we have missed all that delight, thought Marian. She hoped Liz would let her visit them when she was older but had her doubts. Her own granddaughter would be a stranger.

It was then the telephone rang, not the usual time for their friends to ring.

'It'll be a wrong number,' said William.

'Hello, Dad, I'm in London for the day. If it's all right with you I'll pop along this evening about seven'.

'It's John. He's coming about seven,' called William. 'And I expect he'd like a meal — is that right, son?'

'Oh, yes, if that's all right with Mum, but I've got a friend with me.'

'No problem,' said William. 'See you soon. He's bringing someone with him, Marian.'

'Did he say who?'

'No, but I expect it's one of his colleagues. He said something about a meeting, and fitting in a visit to the Wallace Collection.'

Just after seven o'clock Marian was in the kitchen when she heard William go to the front door. They had arrived, so she could put the veal escalope in the oven to keep warm and chop the tomatoes and cucumber ready to cook quickly and spoon over, after they had had a drink.

She could hear John's voice and William saying, 'And who is this?'

'I'm Dana,' Marian heard as she went into the hall, and there instead of the young man she had expected was a girl. She was striking with her close-cut black hair, white skin and the bluest eyes.

'Dana is in our Art Department, Mum.'

'Lovely to meet you,' she said. 'I was so pleased when John said I could come to supper. He told me what a wonderful cook you are.'

Marian smiled and started to say that she had better taste it first but Dana was away into the sitting room, and before they could get a drink into her hand, admiring the John Brunsdon etching.

'I love the bold sweeping lines, don't you? And what a lovely room this is'.

William and Marian sat intrigued by this self-assured, talkative young woman. They nodded and smiled while she and John bubbled with what they had done, who they had seen and what they had thought. How different from those times with Liz. There was no desperate search for something to say now.

Marian let the talk wash round her. What a relief to see John so lively and full of fun again. It was when she was dishing up Baked Alaska — John's favourite — that she began to listen properly.

'Of course, I doubt if I'll get it because Stephen Winters, another art teacher, is after it — and although he has no more qualifications and experience than me, I'm almost sure he'll get it'.

Marian gathered that Dana was applying for the post of Head of Department and objected strongly to what she considered the school's tendency to give senior posts to male applicants.

'I'm afraid that does seem to have happened,' John confirmed.

Dana went on, 'We're all on an equal footing when we're students, but where money and status are involved the old prejudices materialise. And not all women disagree with it either. There are still some who don't realise that our expectations and rights in the home, as well as at work' — she looked hard at Marian — 'have altered the power structure between the sexes.'

Marian stared at William and knew that he, too, was thinking that this all sounded very familiar. But Liz's rebellion had held the weakness of personal resentment while this girl, Marian thought as she listened to her reasoned arguments and talk of something called the National Women's Register, was very convincing. Even John who, Marian remembered, had said he had no time for Women's Lib, was listening without raising any serious objections.

'All we ask is that we should be equal, and free to fulfil ourselves as we want,' said Dana.

Well, perhaps you're right at that, thought Marian.

She looked at John and saw him as a stranger might:

a grown man who had made one mistake and might make another.

Suddenly she did not want to be part of it any more. The world was changing. John had to come to terms with its problems in his own way. She would no longer subject his life to her close concern.

Marian got up to open the window, looking out at the wet grass glowing in the evening sun. She was suddenly acutely aware of the vibrant reality of everyday things, and felt at one and at peace with the garden, her home and her life. It was her universe and she felt it was good. She stood there for one long contemplative moment and then joined the others when she heard John's call.

'Coffee's ready, Mum.'

After that it was not long before John and Dana left. Marian and William waved goodbye as the car halted momentarily at the corner of the avenue, and then slowly walked into the house.

William watched her as she stood motionless in the hall.

'Now then, dear, before we wash up, I'll make you a nice cup of tea.'

He came over and held her close.

'You're not going to agonise over John, are you?'

Marian laughed. 'Not any more,' she said. 'I'm just appreciating my home, and you, and our life together.'

William gave her a long look.

'You've finally let go, haven't you?'

'Yes,' she said. 'I'm free at last.'

Ianto Clown
by Ivor Middleton

They sent for me from the Red Gate. Ianto was drunk, all efforts to send him home had failed, and as always I had to go. Raining pouring it was too, and I cursed Ianto and the weather.

The rain was being driven off the sea a few short miles behind me, by a strong gusty wind towards the dark mass of the Rhondda's ahead. Up in one of the valleys a colliery had emptied its coke ovens and by its light I could see, as though a giant hand had shaken a sheet, the rain cascading forward in huge corrugations.

I got to the Red Gate and went inside. The place was blue with tobacco smoke; my eyes smarted and my lungs protested. I was deafened by the noise of a dozen conversations; some had almost reached the fighting stage. Music Pryce was there in a corner with his choir, trying to get them to render something that would soothe the valiant hearts and lead them into sweeter thoughts. Ianto was standing against the bar singing the two-line refrain of his favourite hymn. Will Dai, the landlord, came from behind the bar at the double when he saw me.

'Thank God you've come, Trefor,' he said. 'The flamer has turned the place upside down. He's busted Tommy Tutt's face and they've taken the poor dab home, so get him out of here quick.'

'He's all right now,' I protested, 'he's all right now he's singing that old hymn.'

'Look, Trefor, I don't want the flamer in here now or ever, that's plain enough, isn't it?' I thought he was going to have a go at me the way he stuck his fist in my face, but it was only to emphasise his point.

Ianto, as always, was glad to see me, and as usual it was only after it was confirmed over and over again that indeed we were bonded thicker than any father and son that I was able to get him to the door. He had got the *hwyl* with the hymn now, and the tears were streaming down his face. Later he would tell me that he would reform and go to Chapel again. He placed an arm the size of an oak branch around my shoulder and we staggered down the streaming road which was in stern competition with our river Ely in sending water down to Cardiff Docks.

It could have been Ianto taking a deep breath to render with greater poignancy another refrain – anyway, we fell in the gutter. Luckily I fell clear of him, just beyond, and I could see the bow waves breaking over this stranded whale. There I was on all fours trying to move his legs, which were bent under his huge frame, in the hope that he would be able to stand up again. The rain was coming down in torrents and the only light was the dancing gaslight that proclaimed 'The Red Gate', outside its door.

'Ullo, what's this by here then?' The man bent down, peering at the heap in the gutter. 'Can't make out what it is,' he muttered. 'Oh, I see now, Ianto it is.' He moved down to where I was on my knees. 'Some boy, don't know who he is, I'm sure,' he said absently. Then, no longer interested, he went on his way.

'Can't understand why Harged Evans allows her boy to go about with old Ianto, but then, soft she is with him, he's the baby – we're all soft with our babies, in't we?'

The two women walked away, muttering at my mother being so soft with me.

'*Ach y fi*, old Clown, drunk again! Have to get a rope and tackle to get him from there, *bach*. Let the flamer drown, and go home, boy.' Big man in Bethel Chapel he was, who kept his Christianity for Sundays and week night prayer meetings.

'Eh, no good boyo, is it, then?' Maggie Scrag End it was, with Will, her dead husband's cap on her head; her frail figure draped by a coat that reached down below the top of her high laced boots, and the inevitable black shawl around her shoulders, dripping at the corners like a nine times drowned cat.

'*Duwedd*, Trefor! Won't shift him from there, will you boy? What are you going to do?'

Hell, I thought, if you can't be more help than that, it would be better if you were to clear out of the way. I looked at her.

'You lift him up, Maggie, then I'll do the rest.'

'Don't talk soft, boy, I can't lift him up, you know that.'

'Well, I can't lift him either, but we had better try, or the flamer will drown down there.'

'Aye, there's awful it would be if he drownded,' agreed Maggie.

Mixed with the gurgles of the half-drowned Ianto came the refrain of the hymn.

'Loves that old hymn he does,' said Maggie.

In our efforts to get him into a sitting position, Maggie had fallen into the gutter. I could hear her swearing as she got up.

'There's all wet I am, Trefor. What are we going to do?'

No good going back to the pub for help; all we could expect there was ribald remarks and useless advice. Maggie had a brainwave.

'Stay where you are, I won't be a minute,' she said.

'You had better not be,' I replied. 'If you don't do something, we'll both be in Cardiff Docks.'

Anyway, true to her word, Maggie was back in no time between the handles of a wheelbarrow, and with a stout rope around her shoulders.

'Now, Trefor, if we put this old barrow on its side, we'll try to ease him into it then you can wheel him home, isn't it?'

'Good idea, Maggie *Fach*! What do you think I am? Lew Treferig's carthorse? How do you think I'm going to push this lot up the Bryn?'

'Try we will, boy *bach*. Put this rope around your shoulders you, and I'll try to hold the barrow off the ground.'

We got him into the barrow, and with heads well down into the wind and rain we started our journey. Ianto always wore his old bowler hat, except for work. After this had fallen off a few times, Maggie picked it up and put it on her head.

'I can't see a thing, Trefer *bach*, but you pull boyo and I'll follow,' she yelled into the wind.

Ianto was complaining that his head was bumping into my behind, but I told him that I didn't mind and that he should be grateful for a soft cushion.

Strength of an elephant, Maggie had. With plenty of stops to ease our lungs from bursting, we hauled, pushed and shoved. A ten-minute walk it was in the ordinary way but it took us two hours, with the rain coming off us in clouds of steam. Going down the cinder path was not too bad, but there was a ditch one side, a tiny tributary of our river. The other side was grazing land, and I had wild ideas of harnessing a cow to do the hauling. We kept well to the field side away from the ditch, but two or three times we ran on the grass, then we had the rigmarole of tipping him out of the barrow and the agony of putting him back again. At these times, Maggie's chest would be playing a chorus from the *Messiah*, and there was not enough air on the Bryn to fill my lungs.

It was when we left the path to go up and across the Bryn that we had to abandon the barrow. The wheel kept digging itself in the soft earth.

'Now, Maggie,' I said, 'any more ideas?'

She was slumped across Ianto in the barrow. Her chest had finished the Hallelujah Chorus, but she was still with Handel, wheezing out the discords he was so fond of. Wonderful is the strength of youth with desperation to drive it.

Ianto had stopped singing and was now repeating like a clockwork parrot, 'Wet I am, boyo. Soaked I am, *bach*.'

I threatened him with one on the jaw if he didn't shut up. It was my idea for what it was worth; I got the rope off the barrow and tied an end under each armpit and over my shoulders.

'Now, Maggie, try to keep his head off the ground and I will pull.'

Poor old Maggie, on all fours she was as we went inch by inch towards the hut. Her chest had started again; this time it sounded like the Amen Chorus.

Duw, I prayed, let it not be Amen for the poor old dab too! We reached the hut and propped Ianto against the side, there was no guttering and the rain came down on him in a steady sheet.

'Get me inside, Trefor *bach*, drown I will here,' he pleaded.

Poor old Maggie was on her knees, her chest gurgling and sounding like the blacksmith when he was trimming the horses' hooves with a rasp after shoeing. I lifted the latch and went inside. I knew the layout, of course, and found the matches and lit the lamp. As always, it was clean but a bit untidy: the copper kettle was shining on the hob of the unlit fire; under the mantelshelf was suspended a brass rail off two bosses. This was where Ianto dried his washing in winter. Maggie staggered in and sank wearily down on the old three-legged stool.

'Let me get my breath you,' she wheezed, and after a short rest she got up. 'Light the fire, Trefor.'

So saying she pulled two chairs up to the fireplace, and taking off her coat draped it over one of them; her shawl she put over the brass rail.

'Off with your coat, boyo.' This she draped over the other chair.

'Paper you.' I found some and gave it to her.

She swept the kindling wood off the hob and lit the fire.

'I was going to do that,' I started to say. She ignored me.

'Soon have a bit of shape here in a minute.'

'But what about Ianto,' I protested.

'Oh, he's safe enough outside, can't get any wetter than he is. Let's get it warm here first. Bring me that bath I saw outside.'

'What do you want a bath for?'

'We are all going to have a bath when that old water is hot enough, or catch our deaths we will.'

On one side of the fire a capacious boiler had been built in; on the other side a deep oven. It wasn't long before the bubbling of the water was accompanying Ianto who had started singing again. Maggie got hold of a pan and started ladling the hot water into the tin bath.

'Take these old coats back there, Trefor. Now let's have him in here.'

We dragged him in and set about undressing him. When we got to his underclothes, I said, 'All right, Maggie, I can manage him now.'

'No, you can't. Look, he's all over the place. You keep on holding him.'

True enough, he was stamping about like a stallion. I had to give him one; he was making ribald remarks, telling Maggie what a treat was in store for her. I told him sternly that if he didn't stop it, I would put him outside in the wheelbarrow again. He spilled half the water protesting that it was too hot. Maggie gave him a slap. Rubbing the soap well into the flannel, she doused it liberally with water and poured it over his head, rubbing vigorously. Then she washed his back and chest.

'Now *fach*,' I said, 'I'll manage the rest.'

'No,' she replied. 'I'm going to see the poor old dab bathed and put to bed tidy.'

I was getting alarmed.

'Maggie ...' I got no further, she looked at me.

'Don't be *twp*, boy. Married I've been, know what a man is I do. You just hold him.'

Ianto said, 'Leave her alone, Trefor, she's got a nicer touch than you.'

Surprised, I looked at him. He had spoken quietly and seemed to be quite sober. Maggie looked across and smiled. The lights were dancing in her eyes; her flushed cheeks brought her face alive and she looked a slip of a girl again. Tenderly, she washed between his legs and then down to his ankles. 'That will do,' she said quietly, and she reached over and took hold of the rough towel and dried him.

'Sit you on the bed, *fy anwyl i*, and I'll wash your feet.'

She dried them and, still on her knees, they looked at each other. Ianto held out his arms and she went hungrily into them.

'Oh, Ianto, there's lonely I am! *Fy nghariad*, I want you *cariad*. Oh, I do want you.'

Quietly Ianto answered, 'I am lonely too, Maggie, lonely in this old hut. It wants a woman around here it does.'

He bent his head and kissed her.

'Oh, Ianto,' breathed Maggie, 'we'll be together now. We will be what the sun is to the flowers, alive again.' She turned the bedclothes back and helped him in. 'Go you now, Trefor,' she said, 'because whatever the rest will think, Ianto and me will be together for always now.'

I picked up my coat and went quietly home. I was crying. The Chapel would banish Maggie with Ianto, but I knew what they had found. Salvation.

Glossary

Fy Anwyli:	'My dear', but much deeper in feeling than English
Bach:	masculine diminutive, sometimes a term of endearment
Cariad:	Love
Fy Nghariad:	mutation of 'cariad', again with deep feeling
Twp:	daft or silly
Cwch:	to cuddle, (sometimes to hide)
Hwyl:	fervour
Ach y fi:	expression of disgust. N.B. 'F' sound as English 'V'

Lady Luck
by Eva Lomas

My Great Aunt Emily was quite a girl. In fact, as her mother put it, almost quite a boy, for she insisted on wearing knickerbockers!

And this in the year 1910!

Not, you understand, all the time. Mostly she just wore knickers — under her skirts, of course — but when she was cycling she wore knickerbockers, tan-coloured ones.

Oft of a summer's morn, after putting away three slices of bacon, two fried eggs, several slices of toast and marmalade and two cups of tea (my Great Aunt Emily was a big girl), she would pack a few sandwiches, pop them into the basket on her handlebars and cycle forth, flouting convention and flaunting her tan-coloured knickerbockers. There were few female cyclists in those days and even fewer wore the new cycling gear.

I know all this about my Great Aunt Emily because I have her diary, and a very educational book it has turned out to be. It could quite easily be called 'How to get your man in six easy stages'. I don't suppose she had ever heard of Women's Lib but she certainly made her mind up about which man she wanted, and she got him; whether it was by fair means or not is a debatable question, but maybe she thought the end justified the means.

Have discovered that that nice Mr. Henry Montague goes to market every Saturday and Tuesday. Must make sure I am there, too. We conversed for a moment or two this morning – he seems to be rather shy. He has the broadest shoulders of any man I have ever met.

The Henry Montague referred to in the diary kept a smallholding about two miles distant from my Great Aunt Emily's home. Now two miles there and two back is a nice cycling distance – a fact which suited my Great Aunt Emily's purpose admirably.

Have persuaded Mama that the taste of Mr. Montague's tomatoes is much superior to that of tomatoes bought in town, and have volunteered to cycle over every other day to his house to purchase fresh ones from him. N.B. Must remember to look up something about chickens and pigs so that I can converse intelligently with him about them. He has the most remarkable brown eyes.

Entries like this continued for some time. When the tomatoes ran out it became eggs. Great Aunt Emily didn't record what happened when the hens stopped laying but no doubt she managed to persuade Mama to buy something else from Mr. Henry Montague.

Gradually '*Mr. Montague*' became '*dear Henry*', and with what rapture must she have recorded: '*Today dear Henry asked me to accompany him to a dance on Saturday night.*' She goes on to describe the sprigged taffeta she was intending wearing – evidently knickerbockers weren't the in thing for dances. And when he came to collect her for the dance: '*My dear Henry had picked me a bunch of aconites.*' One of the big spenders! '*Oh, how tall and splendid he looked tonight. We shall make an ideal couple as we walk down the aisle together and I intend to be an excellent wife to him.*'

Apparently dear Henry's generosity knew no bounds for a few days later we read:

Met dear Henry today. Think he is beginning to care as he gave me a dozen beautiful brown eggs. Wonder how soon he will 'speak'.

If my Joe gave me a dozen beautiful brown eggs I should think that he was suggesting an omelette rather than holy matrimony, but then times change.

And the following day:

Saw dear Henry talking to Father last night. They both glanced in my direction several times. Could he have been asking for my hand? Oh bliss!

But alas:

Decided to take the bull by the horns and ask Papa what he and Henry were discussing. He said, 'Pigs, and how to fatten them.' I shall never speak to Mr. Montague or eat bacon again.

But naturally she didn't mean it, and very soon she was chatting up dear Henry again and quite probably eating bacon, although this is not actually recorded.

But despite dear Henry's little gifts and invitations to dances, no proposal of marriage was forthcoming, and this began to worry my Great Aunt Emily not a little.

She took to cycling off alone – in her tan-coloured knickerbockers, of course – and sitting by the river, 'sighing and yearning for her beloved' as she put it in her diary, but actually I think she was planning her next campaign.

Now my Great Aunt Emily also had a Great Aunt Emily, a very wealthy spinster who had taken a great interest in her namesake from the day she was christened (as indeed her parents had hoped when they chose the name). And so, as they said in those days, my Great

Aunt Emily had 'expectations'. Not that I had any 'expectations' from my Great Aunt Emily. Indeed she spent so many years being 'a good wife' to Great Uncle Henry (as she had promised) that by the time their possessions had been divided amongst their many offspring, there was certainly nothing left over for great nieces.

Well, one morning when my Great Aunt Emily had taken herself off to the river, her Mama looked through the window and saw their rich relation coming up the drive. Immediately she had a vision of her daughter arriving home in that ghastly outfit and all that wonderful wealth disappearing into some other great nieces's pocket. Fortunately dear Henry had just walked in at the back door and, in a flash, she had rolled up one of my Great Aunt Emily's skirts, thrust it into the bewildered Henry's hands and despatched him to find her daughter with the instruction that she was to put the skirt on over her knickerbockers, and on no account to allow them to show when she arrived home.

Dear Henry ambled off riverward and at length came upon his intended — well, she intended him anyway. She, having partaken of her sandwiches and an apple, had lain down on the bank of the river and was now fast asleep. Henry lay on his side close by her and, propping his head on his hand, gazed into his beloved's face — for, truth to tell, he was more than a little fond of her. How long he gazed I don't know but eventually my Great Aunt Emily stirred, sighed, and opened her eyes.

So amazed was she to find a face within inches of her own that she sat bolt upright, knocking dear Henry's arm from under his head as she did so; whereupon he slid slowly but surely down the bank and into the river.

Fortunately the river was not very deep at this point but even so he got soaked to the waist and looked a very sorry sight when he had climbed back up the bank. The cold water brought him to his senses and he remembered the skirt and Mama's message.

My Great Aunt Emily grasped the situation at once (she was a bright girl), suggested that they go into a nearby barn so that, after putting on her skirt, she could remove her knickerbockers and let dear Henry wear them instead of the soaking trousers he now had on.

Back at the house Mama had grown worried at the non-appearance of her daughter and had sent Papa hot foot after her. He, seeing my Great Aunt Emily's cycle propped against the barn, thought she might be in there and, without stopping to knock, walked in just in time to catch dear Henry literally with his pants down, and his girl friend adjusting her skirt.

Papa's mouth fell open, the colour of his face changed through red to purple, and he started spitting and spluttering to such an extent that a poor little field mouse cowering in the straw was drowned on the spot.

To cut a long story short, Papa insisted that dear Henry make 'an honest woman' of his daughter, and when the betrothal appeared in the local gazette the following week nobody was surprised.

The next entry in my Great Aunt Emily's diary is interesting:

How strange a part Lady Luck plays in our lives, for, had dear Henry been standing where I was and I in his place when he climbed out of the river, it would have been he and not me who saw Father in the distance coming up the lane (dear Henry's eyesight is quite as excellent as mine), and most assuredly I should never have got him to go into the barn with me, let alone remove his trousers, had he known my father was anywhere near.

Choc Drop Gran
by Iris Taylor

Mrs. Regan lay in her single bed, waiting for her cup of tea. She had heard the creak of floorboards above and smelt the slight burning of Hilda's toast.

She was glad that she still had her senses of hearing and smell unimpaired, and adequate sight. She woke early but enjoyed the morning sounds: the milkman's clatter, the thin whistle of the postman and the plop as the papers shot through the front door in the hall next to her bedroom.

When her dear Edward had died two years ago, she had wanted to die too. She used to say so to her only child Hilda, but it made her angry. Mrs. Regan couldn't think why because Hilda would be much happier when she was gone and it was foolish to pretend otherwise.

Everyone said that she and her daughter had worked out an ideal solution, turning Hilda's house into two flats with her upstairs like an avenging angel and the open staircase joining their two lives.

Hilda had had a brief wartime wedding, so brief that she had still a sharp spinsterish air about her. Her great efficiency made her critical of the forgetfulness and slovenliness that Mrs. Regan felt coming over her own life.

Her bedroom door was flung open, the curtains whisked aside, and the tea put down and the electric fire switched on in the routine first-class order of a good hotel. But there was no kiss, no lingering chat while she drank her tea. Hilda was always in a hurry. True, she went out to work, but Mrs. Regan often longed to say she would willingly forgo the tea for just a few words to start her day in a friendly fashion.

But this morning Hilda did fling out: 'They're coming for the weekend', and Mrs. Regan knew that inside her daughter was smiling.

No need to ask who she meant. The one reminder of Hilda's brief alliance was Ronald. He held in the palm of his scheming pudgy hand all the love that Hilda was capable of giving.

Mrs. Regan's brief 'Oh, good' was swiftly checked.

'Goodness knows where I'll put them, though ... now. Sheila is too big to share their room.'

'Surely she's only six?' Mrs. Regan sometimes forgot. She wanted to be reassured. But Hilda had gone and her own long lonely day had begun.

She said a little morning prayer in bed now. A brief 'God bless dear Edward', and 'Don't let me be too stiff today'.

Her arthritis bothered her a lot these autumn mornings and it took her a long time to uncreak herself. Hilda threatened her with the doctor or a home help if she ever mentioned her infirmity. Poor Hilda, she was so flawlessly efficient it must be hard for her to watch the decrepitude of old age at close quarters. Almost harder than going through it.

I believe I frighten Hilda, she thought. And she had to chuckle at the idea that her frail reflection in the mirror could cause fear to muscular, bouncing Hilda.

She was glad that today she could move easily because she had a lot to do. With Ronald coming to stay, Hilda would be on the warpath ... dusting and polishing both her own flat and her mother's.

'Really, you keep a handkerchief in every vase!' She always complained at her mother's habit of pushing things out of sight. Hilda like to tidy away all the odds and ends that Mrs. Regan liked to keep within reach of her chair: the strawberry pincushion Hilda had made at school, the nail scissors shaped like a stork, the unfinished crossword. Hilda put them where she could not find them. This time she was determined to tidy up herself before Hilda began the invasion.

She dusted the row of small frames on the top of the piano no one ever played. She studied Ronald's wedding group. She and Edward looked almost as gay as the bride and groom. She remembered Hilda's bitter comment 'How did she dare to wear white?'

But she had asked no questions, even when Hilda was busy explaining to all the neighbours that Sheila was, of course, 'a premature baby'.

She tried to tell Hilda that it was sometimes the silly innocents who made foolish mistakes, and Ronald's had turned out to be better than he deserved. But Hilda had never forgiven her daughter-in-law for knocking her idol from his perch.

When Sheila had been small they often came for weekends, leaving the child with the two grandmas while they went to a party. But they had not been for a year and Mrs. Regan wondered if Sheila would remember her.

She made herself a snack meal at midday, and with the aid of her sticks managed to get into the garden. The early mists had cleared and the autumn sunshine warmed her bones.

Hilda loved her garden. She had always spent long hours tending her plants. Only now she told the neighbours: 'I must make a nice garden for Mother to look at.' And the neighbours looked over the fence and said: 'Your daughter is always thinking of you, isn't she?'

In the winter Hilda bought flowers from the florist's every Saturday handing them over with a tart: 'I believe in flowers when you are alive', so that Mrs. Regan could see her own flowerless grave stretched before her.

She cut a few late roses with her stork scissors, giving the velvety buds a little kiss and being rewarded with a thorn prick for her foolishness.

Hilda came home about six o'clock, bringing some frozen fish and peas which she carefully halved, leaving her mother to cook her own meal and scolding her a little for not leaving the cleaning to her.

Martyr-like she banged about upstairs long after Mrs. Regan had retired to her electric blanket and the comfort of her transistor radio, but not before she had sprayed her bedroom with an aerosol. For when she had suggested to Hilda that Sheila could have the camp bed in this downstairs room, Hilda had been horrified.

'What? A child with you in your room? Whatever next.'

Mrs. Regan wondered if she was rotting or unclean. Perhaps she smelt, and even the outspoken Hilda didn't like to tell her.

When the family arrived the next day, they all trooped upstairs to Hilda's flat. She could hear Ronald's laugh, and Sheila's running footsteps overhead shook her electric light fitting. The smell of Ronald's cigar floated down the staircase. Mrs. Regan sat and waited.

She heard a crash, a slap, and Sheila's sharp cries, and wondered which of Hilda's ornaments had gone this time. The pattern was as before. Soon Sheila would creep away and come down to see Choc Drop Gran.

Hilda preferred to be called Nanna, which her mother thought sounded like some old goat. When Sheila was learning to talk she had been puzzled by 'Great-grandmother', and she always thought of the tin of chocolate buttons that Mrs. Regan kept. So Choc Drop Gran it had become.

Her door opened and the child ran into her arms as if she had seen her only yesterday.

She was a sharp little thing, independent yet clinging as children who sense they are unwanted by one parent often are. But she never showed her tantrums or her spite to Mrs. Regan.

She snuggled into the large armchair, clutching the tin of chocolates, eating them now as if this was a long established ritual revival. She had forgotten nothing. The contents of the glass-fronted cupboard had to be inspected next. Sheila loved the old Coalport china and had to hear again where it had come from and who had brought it back from which holiday.

A curl from Hilda's first haircut in a glass-topped box, and a yellowing pair of her bootees, always brought on a fit of the giggles.

An hour passed all too quickly and then Mrs. Regan was hauled upstairs by Hilda and Ronald, one slow step at a time, to take tea with the family.

The gate-leg table was out to its full extent, loaded with boiled ham and salad, tinned fruit and cream, and in the centre a large iced cake.

'Oo,' exclaimed Sheila. 'Is it a birthday party?'

'Silly girl,' said Hilda, 'you can have an iced cake without a birthday.'

Sheila pouted and went in to the shelter of Mrs. Regan's protecting arm. 'I'm seven at Christmas,' she whispered. 'How old are you, Choc Drop?'

'Don't be rude,' said her mother. 'And stop that silly name. You're a big girl now.'

Ronald winked. 'Well, over the three score years and ten, eh, Gran?'

'What's three score and ten mean?' asked Sheila.

'Don't they teach you anything at your school?'

snapped Hilda, bringing in some more cakes.

After tea, during which both Sheila and Mrs. Regan were blamed for not eating enough, Ronald and his wife went off to wash up while Hilda fussed with the carpet sweeper.

Mrs. Regan was installed in Hilda's armchair. Sheila was in disgrace for spilling her tea.

'Come here, love,' she called, scrabbling in her large handbag until she found a pencil and a notebook. 'Show me how you can do a little sum,' she said. 'Look now. A score is twenty. Well, next time I have a birthday I shall be four score.'

After a lot of pencil biting, Sheila came up with the answer. She danced round the room. 'Choc Drop is eighty, Choc Drop is eighty,' she chanted.

'Be quiet,' said a voice from the kitchen.

'I'm going to give you a present in advance,' said the child. She flung her arms round Mrs. Regan and gave her a resounding kiss. 'It's not much of a present,' she said.

Mrs. Regan was expecting a pretend present, clutched in an empty hand. She had played this game before.

'Tell me what it is,' she said.

The child hugged her again and lifted up a grey curl to whisper in her ear.

'It's a lot of love, that's all.'

'Do you know,' said Mrs. Regan slowly, 'that is just what I've always wanted.'

'Sheila,' snapped Hilda, returning to the room. 'Don't whisper, it's rude.'

But Mrs. Regan was putting her pencil back into her bag. Sheila's little teeth marks were on it. It would go beside the curl and the yellowing bootees.

'Thank you, darling,' she said. But she was not looking at Hilda.

The Traitor
by Glynne Jones

When I saw him first my heart filled with pity. It was a foggy morning in late-November, and it was the hurt, lost expression in his eyes that made me notice him as he brushed past me on the pavement in Lambeth Palace Road. I was walking towards Vauxhall and he was going in the opposite direction, keeping close to the wall with his head down as if trying to pick up some cold scent. Although I was intent on getting to my destination, I stopped and looked round after him. Maybe he had sensed human compassion, for he had stopped too and was looking in my direction. I walked on, thrusting my hands deeper into my overcoat pockets; I had no mind to be saddled with a stray dog.

Half a minute later he passed me again, this time from behind. He trotted on a little way ahead, glanced casually over his shoulder, stopped and waited. When I was nearly up to him he started off again. I slowed down. He stopped, and this time waited for me to pass him before starting off again. When these manoeuvres had been repeated a few times there was no doubt about it: I had been adopted.

I crossed the road to the Albert Embankment. He came after me. There I made a stand and tried to send him home. It was hopeless. I waved and shouted at him, but he most obviously had no home. He just stood there patiently, well out of range, wary and without understanding.

He looked comic standing there, large and hairy and conforming to no known breed. He had the coat and markings of a wire-haired fox terrier, white and black with brown ears, but he was too large and podgy. He looked strong and well-fed, with a bull neck and powerful shoulders, but his general hairiness made him look clumsy. Collarless, dirty and bedraggled, but too large to be pathetic, he looked as though he might have escaped by sheer strength from a dogs' home or from one of those places where waifs and strays are painlessly destroyed.

I stopped trying to drive him away. The poor dumb brute: who knew what saga lay behind his appearance on the streets of London, or the wild hope in his heart as he rushed madly out into the foul foggy air of liberty and freedom once again? His hope of meeting with some friendly gesture must have faded long ago, but he had not let that daunt him. He had settled down to his tireless search, seeking the way back to some gloomy hovel that he knew as home. The roar of the buses and the terrifying clangour of the trams frightened him and he kept close to the wall; but he kept on searching.

I walked on and the dog followed. 'Followed' is hardly the word; rather did he move along with me, making me the base of his operations — now running on ahead, now lagging behind to investigate some new scent. On we went, past the empty flowerbeds and up the slope to Lambeth Bridge. Passers-by gave the dog a wide berth. Some looked askance at the dirty, untidy creature and curiously at me; others glanced at him with a smile. But no-one stopped, no-one had a kind word. They were all too busy about their own affairs.

At the foot of the bridge he stopped and waited for me to come up to him, and then sedately trotted along by my side to the kerb where we waited our chance to cross. When the lights halted the stream of traffic thundering down from the bridge, I crossed quickly to the island in the middle of the road. I was amused and impressed to see how competently my new follower made the crossing. He kept very close to me, hurried when I hurried, and stopped when I stopped. But he did not like the look of the huge red monsters that seemed to charge straight at us before swinging left with a snarl and a roar up the incline of the bridge. His hindquarters trembled and there was a frightened look in his eyes as he looked up at me.

My calm must have reassured him, for he promptly sat down, edging closer so that his shoulder was touching my leg. I hadn't the heart to draw away, for this blind trust moved me. It was as complete and unquestioning as that of a little child. When the lights changed again and the last half of the road was clear we crossed to the other side.

The spacious freedom of the wide pavement on the other side was reassuring, and he ran on again. As he ran he still kept his nose down, as if even now he expected to pick up at any moment a familiar and friendly scent from the cold stone of the London pavement. His disreputable hindquarters shivered with the cold. It must have been a long time since he had last eaten. He still glanced back at me every few seconds to make sure I was following. What was it that drove him on with the search, kept alive the hope that happiness lay somewhere ahead if only he could find the lost trail? Lost, cold, homeless and hunted, but forced by his very nature and circumstances to attach himself to some human being, he still had some blind urge at the back of his mind, driving him on.

The patient misery in his eyes made me stop at last. I called to the dog. He came to me, obedient but wary. I crouched down and called him close to me. I put my hand on his head and made comforting noises. He remained quite still and I could almost feel the ecstasy of gratitude surging within him. When I took my hand away he put both his paws on my knees and frantically licked my wrist, looking up into my eyes. There was something new in his gaze now, and my heart turned over inside me. I straightened up and walked on, with the dog trotting beside me.

The traffic was farther away from us now. The river gleamed dully in the grey light. Along the Embankment the beautifully proportioned lamp-posts loomed singly, each one wreathed with its lovely bronze porpoises, streaming with moisture as they greenly writhed out of their native element. Across the river a tug hooted mournfully as it felt its way cautiously forward to the arches of the next bridge. The muffled rumble of the traffic seemed far away, and the busy click of the dog's pattering feet sounded loud in my ears.

He was away in front again. He was inquisitive and not very intelligent. Somewhere opposite the Tate Gallery the pavement was up, and a portion of it was fenced off with metal posts and high chain-link fencing. The dog found a gap in this fence and nipped inside, busily exploring until he came to the wire at the other end barring his progress. He stopped, puzzled by this senseless hindrance, just as I walked past on the other side. The wild panic in his eyes as he scrabbled at the wire and found he could make no impression brought me to a halt. I walked back to the gap and waited. He came running back, found the gap again and hopped out, throwing me a quick look of thanks.

I was beginning to wonder what I was going to do with him as we walked past the few dingy shops to the foot of Vauxhall Bridge. The lights were green and we crossed to the island. There was a break in the traffic which normally swished round Bridgefoot and the dog loped quickly across. Evidently he was used to crossing roads and knew how to seize an opportunity. On impulse I turned back and crossed again to the Albert Embankment. Just then the traffic lights changed and I crossed left to the other side of the road near the archway under the railway bridge. The dog could not follow, for there was now a river of traffic rolling down from the river bridge as well as an endless stream filtering to the left and up over it.

I was near the end of my journey and felt relieved to be free of what had looked like becoming an obligation. After all, what could I have done with him? I couldn't keep him with me, and where could I have taken him? He would have been the most awkward liability, and why should I saddle myself with another one? These questions had been settled by the dog's own stupidity.

I stood on the corner, justifying myself and watching the dog to see what he would do. I could only judge of his despair when he found that the now familiar figure was no longer with him. He was trotting backwards and forwards on the pavements, looking up at everybody he passed. He looked back across the road to the island, but a stream of hostile traffic made that impossible. After a few moments of agonized searching he headed north with his head down again, trying to pick up that forlorn scent. He trotted away on the pavement, steadfast as ever, up over Bridgefoot and away over Vauxhall Bridge, over the river into the fog to suffer God knows what further hopes and heartbreaks.

I watched him go; then, digging my hands deeper into the pockets of my overcoat, I walked into the thundering darkness under the railway bridge.

Greenfingers
by Nell Arch

Min hovered protectively over the small green plant in its white plastic pot. Crooning soft words of encouragement, she carried it tenderly over to the kitchen window-sill, its tiny fronds trembling as she set it down.

She had been rather surprised when Dennis had told her that his secretary had sent it to her. She had never liked Rita. Too flashy by half, she always thought, with her tight tee-shirts and slit skirts. Not the generous type at all, but nevertheless she took the little stranger to her heart.

The small flat was filled to overflowing with plants of all kinds. African violets, mother-in-law's tongue, busy lizzies ... she had them all. On tables, shelves, in every corner they grew and flourished under her loving care. On the kitchen window-sill the little plant settled down, flanked by a Coleus on one side and a maidenhair fern on the other, its leaves unfurling and reaching out to the sun, like tiny fingers. To Min all the plants vibrated with life. They peopled her world, and she felt at one with them.

Min was shy, which probably explained her attachment to plants. Dennis had tried in the early days of their marriage to encourage her to meet his friends, but on the few occasions that she made the effort it was not a success. She had little to offer in the way of conversation, retiring into her shell at the approach of a stranger. Her name would arouse a little curiosity at first, but having reluctantly explained that her mother was mad about mythology and had christened her after Minerva, the goddess, interest would flag and once again she would find herself alone in a corner, whilst Dennis would drift towards more congenial company.

As time passed she would make excuses whenever an invitation came their way, and eventually it became quite normal for Dennis to go out on his own. She gave no sign that she cared and he seemed resigned to the situation.

The morning after Min was given the plant, her mother called in for her usual cup of tea and a chat. As far as Min was concerned it was not always a welcome visit, but Min being Min would never say anything to discourage her. Her mother was not very impressed with the new addition.

'Scraggy-looking thing,' were her first words as she peered through her glasses at the tiny green object. 'What's it called?'

Min had to inform her that she had no idea.

'Fancy Rita giving you that. It looks as if it's dying to me.'

Min found herself defending it, feeling sure in her heart that the plant understood what was being said, although she would never dare admit as much to her mother or Dennis.

'Oh, it's not so bad, it's still only a baby.' And she whisked it away, back to its place in the sun, determined to have an encouraging chat with it once her mother had gone.

Her mother had never had much time for Dennis and from the start had warned Min about Rita. 'You know what these secretaries are like. There's something about married men that gets them going. I read an article about it, and they said it was because they were unobtainable.'

'But, Mother,' Min had protested. 'Denis isn't like that, and I'm sure Rita is a nice girl really — although she is so smart and efficient, she frightens me a bit.'

Nevertheless, her mother's words had lingered in her memory, and at every opportunity she would bring Rita's name into the conversation. Denis evinced surprisingly little interest in his secretary's comings and goings, professing to know little of her private life, and as time went by Min gave up, satisfied that no man who was interested in another woman could know so little about her. She would have been amazed to know how much Rita knew about *her*. As is often the case with the boss's secretary, Dennis would frequently unburden his soul during the extended coffee break and Rita was only too ready to supply a sympathetic ear.

Within a week of the plant's arrival, it had grown three inches and Min began to wonder just how big it would be full-grown. Its progress was so noticeable that she found herself watching for each new development, like a mother studies the growth of a new baby. At the end of the month its tendrils were trailing along the window-ledge and over-taking the maidenhair fern. It was then that Min decided that it would look better in a hanging basket. That evening she persuaded Dennis to put a hook above the sink to suspend the basket from, and standing back with her head on one side, she admired the effect of the evening sunlight through the feathery leaves.

Standing at the sink in the morning, she would glance upwards, gloating over the new pale green fingers creeping over the edge of the basket, one long strand hanging well down as though it was holding out a hand to her. Leaning forwards and upwards she gently brushed her cheek against its delicate softness. Suppressing a giggle she glanced behind her, but Dennis was buried behind his morning newspaper as usual.

As the weeks passed the fronds grew at an amazing pace and soon she began to notice how strong it was. Now the stems were nearly as thick as her little finger and were curling round, back and forth like a serpent, she thought, controlling a small shudder. Curious to find a name for it, she searched through her gardening books to no avail.

She began to wish that it would stop growing so fast, but hadn't the heart to cut it back. This had always been a failing with her. She could never bring herself to chop off a leaf or a stem. Soon she found that she was pushing it to one side as she worked at the sink, looping the coils back and up, but sure enough they would slowly uncurl and once again reach out as if to touch her. She no longer lavished so much attention on it, but turned her affection back to her old loves.

In July she and Dennis spent two weeks in the Isle of Wight, having arranged for the neighbour across the hall to come in twice a week to water the plants. In return Min would feed her cat when she went to her daughter's place at week-ends. The weather was perfect and for once Min acquired a light tan, offering her pale body to the sun in a modest one-piece swim-suit. She did not approve of the tiny bikinis which exposed more than they concealed, and would try to find a remote corner of the beach far from the profusion of bare limbs — which it was obvious did not embarrass her husband.

From behind her dark glasses she would keep a watchful eye on him and at the slightest sign of interest would try to engage him in conversation. When the sun became too hot for her white skin, and Dennis was having his after lunch doze, she would explore the local shops, but nowhere, despite the numerous plants in evidence, could she find one that remotely resembled Rita's gift.

During the second week she took a 'bus to a large

nursery outside the town. In the humid atmosphere she prowled, tempted to buy first this plant and then that, darting from one exotic growth to another. There was still no sign of a fellow to her strange acquisition. It was as though she had the only one in the world.

As the holiday drew to a close she experienced a sensation that was an odd mixture of fascination and terror. For once, she dreaded the return home. Would she find that the plant had grown even bigger?

They returned late on the Saturday evening. The kitchen was in semi-darkness. The mass of greenery blocked the window, giving the room an eerie underwater aspect. Hastily, she switched on the light before Dennis could complain. She had a headache from travelling and an argument was the last thing she wanted.

The next morning she sat on the kitchen stool, contemplating the monstrosity. It was a wonder that Dennis hadn't noticed it, and in a way she wished he had. Perhaps he would have cut it back for her. Twice she took the scissors from the drawer but put them back again, unable to make the first cut. Now, when the delicate fingers touched her cheek, she moved away with a tiny shiver, like icy tears trickling down her spine.

It was whilst she was walking around the supermarket that she came to a decision. The plant must go. It was stupid allowing it to take over. Today she would take it down and throw it in the dustbin. Two minutes and it would all be over, she told herself, but her steps slowed as she envisaged the act of destruction and she shook, visualising the moment when she would cram the long arm-like strands into the dustbin. The plant had assumed a human quality and as she gazed unseeing at the rows of closely packed shelves, she knew, beyond any shadow of doubt, that it was waiting for her to make the first move.

Her heart was thudding and she wondered if she was losing her mind. Pretending to study a special offer on baked beans, she considered discussing her fears with her doctor but with a shake of her head dismissed the idea. How could she tell anyone that she was scared of a plant? More than scared, she was terrified.

Putting off the moment when she must leave the shop, she retraced her steps, seeing nothing of the goods on display. It was as though a cine-film was running behind her eyes. She saw once again the strange little smile as Dennis handed her the plant from Rita, Rita who had never bothered with her before. Then she saw her first hesitant step through the door, the dimness of the kitchen, and the moment when she would grab the kitchen knife and chop the plant to pieces.

It was so vivid that she gave a gasp of horror and her hand, making an involuntary movement as if to ward off the plant, flew out, sending several tins from a nearby display clattering to the floor. She came to her senses with a jolt and, bending to hide her embarrassment, with trembling hand re-stacked the tins. The simple act had the effect of calming her, and with a determined step she marched out of the shop. The time had come to make her move, but even so she hesitated as she arrived at her front door.

Hanging her coat in the hall, she collected the steps from the broom cupboard and gently pushed the kitchen door. But something was jamming it from the other side. Forcing it a few inches she peered round the edge. The kitchen seemed lighter than when she had left the house, and as her eyes travelled round and down, her face paled. Gasping, she sank to the hall floor.

Her eyes tightly closed, she could still see Dennis stretched out on the floor, his face contorted with agony, sinewy fronds cutting deeply into his neck. One hand was reaching hopelessly towards a kitchen knife lying near his lifeless body.

It was obvious that the struggle had been long and

hard. Her brain was speeding in circles as she finally forced her way into the room. A little calmer now, she studied the situation.

Loosening the strands from about Dennis's neck, she gently replaced the plant on its hook. Was it her imagination that a litle green finger caressed her cheek as she turned to place an upturned kitchen stool near the body before 'phoning the doctor?

The Year of the Rabbit
by Bruce Cameron Firth

We should never have caught him up. Jim and I played a perfectly ordinary game of golf, always hoping to get the score for eighteen holes down to a hundred, but seldom making it. And we knew the little etiquettes of the game. We never loitered on the course, except on very rare occasions when there was no one in sight behind us. Then I might even allow myself the luxury of a few unofficial practice shots. So we generally kept up with the rate of play of other users.

It was Jim the considerate who asked him to join us and, to give the man credit, he was reluctant to do so. He described himself as a rabbit, and maybe it was that which first made him such an attractive proposition to Jim.

'We're not exactly hares ourselves,' he said. 'And golf was never meant to be a solitary game. Join us for the last nine holes.'

Well, he did join us. I've never spent so much time searching for lost balls as during that homeward stretch, and we had to let one couple and a foursome go through us before we eventually arrived back at the club house.

That was not so bad. It reminded me of my own tentative beginnings when Jim first invited me to play with him three years ago. I had never played regularly before, hardly knew the rules, even; but I did enjoy those Thursday afternoons.

The Deepdale course could have been designed for beginners. It had wide, open fairways, a number of elevated tees from which my occasional good drive could look as if it were sailing away as well as anyone's, and only two streams to cross. Everyone at the office knew that on Thursday afternoons I was not available, and when I arrived at the Club House soon after noon Jim was always waiting for me. He would watch my every ball, and I relied on the fact that when I lost track of it, Jim would know and go straight to it. He did sufficient coaching to be of assistance without interfering with my enthusiasm, and was patience itself while I gradually acquired a swing which was something like reliable.

Jim had retired many years before and played regularly on many different courses with many different people. Nevertheless, he had the ability to make me feel that our afternoons were special. At the seventh hole, before the first stream, his flask would come out to fortify me, and at the short thirteenth he always asked if I had a drop to help him to a birdy. On the occasion when he took five at that very hole while I got down in my first par three, he took Jean and me out for dinner.

That started a social arrangement between us which lasted right up until the argument. On Thursday evenings Jean and I would go to dinner with Jim and his Lovely Lucy, as I always called her. We would generally play a rubber of Bridge afterwards. Then, most Sundays they would come to us for lunch, after which we would play garden games if the weather was good or have putting practice on the carpet if it was not.

We got to know one another pretty well, and the ladies often remarked on the way our differing personalities complemented each other. It was true. Jim was patient and understanding. I was always anxious to get going, never took time to steady myself at the start of a stroke, and could never understand why most players appeared to saunter around the course studying each hole as if it were a work of art before attacking it. Jim was the most considerate person I had ever come across, while I considered that if I did not look after my own interests no one else would. Jim was calm and deliberate, where I was rash and often intemperate. He seemed to have time to enjoy life, whereas I was always too anxious to get on with it and seldom made time to enjoy it properly. Fortunately, there remained sufficient common ground between us to make the time we spent together extremely pleasant.

Eventually I was pressing a score of a hundred as closely as Jim was, and I became relaxed about his proclivity to let other players join us for the odd round or part of a round. I even became a member of the Club and used my privilege to invite Jim and whoever else had joined us into the Member's Bar for drinks at the end of a round. That would set us up nicely for the evening meal at Jim's place. He seemed to enjoy the whole ritual as much as I did.

Blake was good-looking and affable. He had taken a very early retirement, and here he was at fifty-two, with all the time in the world to play golf where and when he would, choosing to muscle in on our Thursday afternoons on the course. He was a powerfully built man, much taller than either Jim or I, a fact which should have given him a decided advantage. But nothing seemed to make an impression on his appalling game. And nothing seemed to curb his noisy enthusiasm for it, nor the infinite pains Jim continued to take to help him. I'll help anyone once, or twice even, if I see some merit in it. But this man took liberties all the time, excusing them on the grounds that he was new to the game even after he had been wasting our time for a year.

It took him ages to learn to keep quiet when we were teeing off. He never appreciated that his infernal whistling as he strode down the fairway was disconcerting to players teeing off elsewhere. He was like me in never wanting to wait his turn to play, and that disconcerted me. If he did not like the lie of a ball he would move it. Most of his drives went anywhere, and then he would bring out another ball to try again, often with even more disastrous results. And he laughed at everything, particularly when he came to one of the streams. He hardly ever got over one. He would whack a ball off the tee, straight into the water.

'Ha, ha, ha,' he would laugh. 'Good job that was only a practice ball. Watch this one go.' We did. We watched it follow the first one. 'Perhaps the tide will have gone out by the time we get back,' he would say.

After yet another failure he would declare that no hole is worth more than three lost balls and then walk over the bridge chuckling to himself and carrying on as if nothing had happened. There, too, he would occasionally stop to draw our attention to the beauty of the place.

'Look,' he would say, 'did you ever see such a haven in the midst of our concrete jungle? And what about the smell? Isn't the fragrance of the pines and the shrubs overpowering sometimes? It's almost as good as the smell of the last week's cuttings in the long grass when I'm thrashing about for one of my lost balls.'

That would make him laugh again. I had difficulty hiding my impatience.

It all came to a head one day when we were wasting another Thursday afternoon with him. I had complained to Jim often enough about how Blake had been taking the edge off our game. Jim, however, was obsessed with his mission to make Blake a reasonable player and would not be deterred.

'He'll wake up in the end,' he would say, 'And when the penny drops he'll probably beat the both of us. You'll see.'

This day, there was rain in the air. Not enough to dissuade us from playing, but more than enough to wet Blake's glasses and make his game even more insufferable.

It soon became obvious that he could hardly see the ball.

'Look, Blake,' I said, 'you can't play with rain all over your glasses. Why don't you enjoy a few drinks in the bar while Jim and I hurry round on our own?'

'Couldn't do that, old chum,' he laughed, 'unless I put them on your account. Don't worry, I'll make it.'

After that he stopped to remove his glasses to dry them for every stroke, but that only held up play for even longer and made no difference to the fact that he needed two or three swipes each time in order to move the ball anywhere at all.

'Look, Blake,' I tried again, 'it really is no good. You can't be enjoying the game in these conditions, and all these delays are making it intolerable for us.'

Jim said nothing, but played his ball a hundred yards forward and moved ahead.

'Relax, old chum,' beamed Blake, 'I promise you it's far worse for me than it is for you. But I'll tell you what – I'll do without the wretched glasses. That should be a laugh.'

From then on he would slip his glasses to the back of his head as he addressed the ball. He had to lean well over to see it at all, and he stood no chance of hitting it properly. It was impossible.

My opportunity came when, after I had driven a superb shot from the eighth tee, he took three strokes and one lost ball to land his replacement ball just behind my own on the edge of the fairway. It was his turn. He put his glasses on the back of his head and lashed out at his ball. It did fly a few yards, but the effort he put into the shot dislodged his glasses, which fell to the ground just as I was stepping up to my own ball. I stood on them, quite relieved to have achieved something which might get to him.

He did not get angry, which would have pleased me. He just picked up the broken spectacles and said, 'I think I will call it a day now. It's a great pity. I've had these glasses more than ten years. I prided myself on looking after them.'

The rest of the round was a disaster. Jim asked me how the incident with the glasses had happened and I lied unconvincingly, saying that it was a pure accident. Perhaps it was the untruth, lying uncomfortably on my conscience, which did it. Perhaps it was the knowledge that Jim must have rumbled me, but I played the remaining holes almost as badly as Blake would have done.

I persuaded Jean to make an excuse for not going to Jim's place that evening. We also called off Sunday lunch.

Next Thursday it was Jim who was not available and for one reason or another we have not played in the three months since.

Now I hear that Jim plays a round with Blake each week, on Thursday mornings. Apparently the prescription for his old glasses was very much out of date. His new ones have made all the difference, and now that he can see properly, he and Jim are both scoring less than a hundred regularly. Some rabbit! I knew we should never have caught him up.

Dancing On The Promenade
by Mallie Aarstad

During the summer holidays when I was a boy, my parents would put me on the train at the Newcastle Central Station for King's Cross. There I'd be met and taken to Bognor Regis where I'd stay with Dad's Aunt Julia for two or three weeks or more. Sometimes it seemed like the whole summer. Other times it went too quick.

Aunt Julia took in lodgers, preferring theatricals for a seasonal long let in preference to the weekly holiday-maker. In the world of the boards, the bush telegraph gave her place a star rating. In after years many an old pro, whether living it up or not, would think back wistfully to bygone days of savouring Aunt Julia's steak and kidney puddings: steamed for hours till the suet outside was white and luscious, the meat within succulent and tender, and the rich brown gravy positively bubbling with joy as it was spooned on to your plate. These feasts and others were in fact made by Aunt Ada. No relation, just the friend who had come to live with Aunt Julia when Uncle Dick died years back. The friend to share all the expenses and do all the work.

Aunt Ada was mostly to be seen in the kitchen, baking bread, bottling jam, whisking whites of egg in a blue-lined bowl till they stood stiffly like the peaks of Everest. Few could resist the various savoury or nut-sweet and coffee smells that would come wafting along the passage and would take a peep around the kitchen door ... as quickly to withdraw. Not that vague Aunt Ada, paper thin and tall, would not have welcomed a visitor; it was the sight of an almost perpetual mountain of unwashed dishes that was too much of a reproach for someone with time on their hands. I can't ever remember seeing Aunt Ada sitting down.

Aunt Julia was plump and white-haired. She rarely stood. Not that she was incapacitated in any way. If there was no other mode by which she could get to the Playhouse, then Aunt Julia would walk. Bridge occupied her a great deal. Alone she played Patience. She had the slimmest, whitest fingers I've ever seen, and a swift and fluid way with a pack of cards that would have been the envy of any card sharper.

That is what Philip Leman said. He taught me some sleight-of-hand tricks with the appropriate patter to fool my friends when I got back home. The 'Pick a card, look at it and put it back' trick he demonstrated over and over again, but I always felt it rude to look away, even though I knew that in the split second when his eyes held me so compellingly my ace of clubs would be sneaking its way up 'Uncle' Phil's coat sleeve.

On the stage Philip Leman took on different characters. In one act he might come on, cloaked and silent, as Scorpio the Magician, and pull vivid squares of silk from out of the empty air, leaving them to paint the stage with colour. Mute still, he would balance a lighted cone of paper on his nose whilst juggling three balls back and forth. He pointed and gestured, indicating the box he held in his hands so that all could see it was empty. And yet it was not! Such a small box to hold such a multiplicity of objects, ten times the size of their container. A fanfare of sound brought the act to its conclusion, the curtains parting only to let the magician take his applause on a stage now heaped with colour.

Best of all I liked his ventriloquist act. For this he wore a formal dinner suit but his red-nosed and voluble companion wore black and white checker-board tweed, reminiscent of the tic-tac man on the race course. Their conversation consisted of naive and innocent remarks from the dinner-suited gent which his red-nosed companion misinterpreted most scandalously, resulting in peals of laughter from the audience.

Not all of Aunt Julia's lodgers were sociable like Philip Leman but I got seats for all their shows and that suited me. My first question on reaching Bognor was always: 'Who's here now?'

This time Aunt Julia told me: 'You'll be pleased that Mr. Leman is back again for the season and his nephew is here, too ... Jack Chalmers, leading man with the Auriol Players.' Aunt Julia raised her chin. She was quite a snob about her lodgers.

'Such a nice young man,' Aunt Ada breathed, chopping something on the chopping board. Mint, I think it was.

'Anybody else?' I asked, because for letting there was one double room and two singles. Never more than four people, never less.

Aunt Julia put the knave, ten and nine beneath the queen and paused. And pondered. Then, with a quick movement, she lifted a wave of cards from one row to another and said shortly: 'Two young women.'

The chop, chop, chopping ceased. 'They're quiet, Julia. You wouldn't know they were here,' Aunt Ada murmured in slight protest. But I knew what Aunt Julia was thinking and I was with her there: 'Where there's girls there's trouble!' Still, there was Philip Leman and his nephew to give support to Aunt Julia. They'd not put up with any silly nonsense.

Next morning when I saw Jack Chalmers I laughed

out loud. It wasn't like now; in those days a fellow never helped with the housework. Dad would sit importantly to carve the Christmas turkey but it was Mum who washed all the dishes, late at night, alone, after the relations and all had gone. And now here was the male lead of the Auriol Players in the kitchen with an apron round his waist, washing up! Hearing my guffaw he turned and took a swipe at me. I got a soapsud in my eye.

'Serve you right ... and you can get a tea towel in your hands and dry that cutlery,' he said as I made a dive for the door.

But he was OK was Jack Chalmers, and we got along together fine. He had boundless energy and, unlike the usual pro, was up early in the morning for a pre-breakfast swim. I didn't need to be asked twice to join him. When we returned, all bright and breezy, Uncle Phil would look up with bleary, disillusioned eyes.

'Wish I could have come as well,' he would rumble, 'but I'm allergic to water.'

Later in the morning they would go along to the Hall where some electrical job or other might need to be done. 'Fancy coming with us, Dick?' Jack asked one day. My beaming face gave him the answer. I was along with them each morning after that.

There was something very special to me in being in a theatre before the doors opened. I felt puffed up with pride. Except for the odd cleaner after last night's débris, no one was allowed inside other than the performers ... and me! I was one of the elect.

Acoustics sound hollower in an empty hall. Uncle Phil from the spotlight in the circle was perhaps calling instructions to Jack in the wings. I was initiated into the mysteries of the projection room for sometimes a short film would be shown for which Uncle Phil would act as projectionist. Giant reels of celluloid they were, liable to break and leave a blank screen.

If the film wasn't mended within sixty seconds a slide would be shown apologising for the interruption and assuring patrons that service would be resumed as soon as possible. This, of course, was the signal for the youth in the hall to stamp their feet and boo and roar. I used to boo and roar with the rest, and fly paper kites across the hall, until I knew Uncle Phil was the projectionist.

During the morning others of the Auriol Players would drift into the hall to practise, or just for a chat. Aunt Julia's two young women were often there, Clare Eaton, the good-looker, and Mavis, the blight. One day as we were walking along the promenade, putting in a bit of time before savouring 'the dish of the day', Uncle Phil gave me a nudge: his eyes were on the good-looker with Jack, a few yards in front.

'I was married long before I was Jack's age,' Uncle Phil said. 'It might steady him up a bit.'

What a blithering stupid idea! It was a minute or two before I could get the words out : 'What does Jack want steadying up for? He's all right as he is.'

'He doesn't stick at anything, Dick. He's had one or two good jobs ... there was one with a band, much better money than now, and he chucked it. Just like that!' There was a Scorpio the Magician click in the air. 'Completely irresponsible, and you can't go through life like that, Dick,' he admonished me. Uncle Phil, himself a stick at nothing! Perhaps a bit down at heel now, but a wise man at that, the cigarette ash powdering his jacket.

My face stiff with disfavour and puzzlement, I surveyed the pair ahead. There was Jack, all spruce and fit and clean. It seemed to me that Uncle Phil's point of view hadn't all that much going for it if marrying and 'steadying up' meant ending up like him.

Suddenly Clare, in front, gave a loud burst of laughter, stopped walking and broke into a dance routine ... right there on the promenade at Bognor, with people passing by and looking on and smiling. Jack kept time with his hands. It only lasted a few minutes but it did everyone good to see her. Perhaps she mightn't be so bad after all!

A minute or two after this Mavis came teetering up behind us. She passed Uncle Phil and me and laid her hand on Jack's sleeve.

'Oh, I do wish I could paint,' she told him, 'I've just seen what would have made the loveliest picture back there.'

Jack looked down at Mavis with the same kind and sympathetic expression he showed to Aunt Ada. I hurried past to hear the funny story that Uncle Phil was relating to Clare. No one would think of telling funny stories to Mavis, and none of us knew anything about the painting and poetry and sunsets that she fluttered on about. I supposed that if Jack had to marry, Clare, the good-looker, was the better of the two but I couldn't see the reason for all the rush.

However Uncle Phil seemed to have got stuck on the idea. There was no stopping him. 'Where are you girls off to today?' he would beam at them. And then: 'That sounds a good idea. Come on now, Jack and Dick. We've never been there, have we? Let's make a party of it.'

For a man calling himself Scorpio the Magician, and thinking he was the wise uncle, Philip Leman was unaccountably blind. He missed seeing the fluttery eyelashes of Mavis as she drew near to Jack. He missed a whole lot that I could see. It was strange, very strange.

We hadn't gone far this day. Uncle Phil, his inevitable camera poised, had just taken our photo. We'd been leaning against a five-barred gate. A tan-coloured gelding was champing the grass in the field beyond and I rather thought the way the lens was aimed that there'd be more of the gelding than of us. When he said: 'OK, that's it', we took the unnatural grin off our faces and straightened up. Only Mavis remained still, white arms stretched romantically along the five-barred gate.

'I wonder,' she murmured in her 'visionary' voice, 'why that bird is sitting just there!'

All eyes turned upwards to see a solitary crow perched on a telegraph wire. 'Dash it all, Mavis,' Clare burst out caustically, 'the bird has to sit somewhere.'

I couldn't help a shout of laughter which I quickly turned into a choking sound, as if I had got something into my throat and was having trouble clearing it. Mavis's face looked tight and secret. I hoped she hadn't noticed.

We turned to walk further along the road, all of us except Uncle Phil who was leaning now on the gate and muttering something about the joys of the 'simple life'. I knew he'd catch us up in a minute or two and I tagged along apologetically with Mavis.

I thought Clare was looking rather nice today. Plump and natural and not all done up with eyelashes. I'd still a bubble of laughter inside me and I looked on approvingly as Jack took Clare's hand and they put on a spurt and hurried ahead. I felt the bird-watcher at my side quicken and start. And then it happened!

There are a few actions which are uncontrollable: the explosive sneeze, the burst of laughter, and the involuntary impulse which operated my right foot. A second more and I could have had myself under control again, but the foot came out as swift as the laughter. Mavis was on the ground.

We turned back the way we had come, Jack and Uncle Phil in front with Mavis hobbling between them and clutching on to their arms. Clare and I brought up the rear, Clare carrying Mavis's handbag.

Now I ask what can a little fall do? There's an old lady

in number 22 next door to us and she's always falling down and bobbing up again cheerfully.

It was the way she fell, Mavis murmured. She must have twisted her ankle or something, but when Clare suggested a doctor or a bonesetter Mavis patiently shook her head. Time was all that was needed, apparently. Time and Jack's strong arm to help her as she walked. The show must go on. Her dancing routine restricted, she took on old nostalgic singing parts, the spotlight playing on her as she stood on a darkened stage. The silly blinking audience loved it. It made a fellow sick!

I had only a few days left after that, then they all came to Bognor station to see me off. 'Don't forget what I told you about those card tricks ... keep the eyes of your audience fixed on your face and not on your hands,' said Uncle Phil.

Jack wanted to know how far the sea was from Newcastle. 'If we come to play in the North you and I must have our morning swim, Dick.'

'It's Whitley Bay, and there's Cullercoats and Tynemouth too!' I cried.

Clare kissed me goodbye and Aunt Ada gave me a package of eatables to console me on the way. But I was feeling pretty bleak in the train going North that day, I can tell you.

That was the last time I went to Bognor. The following spring Aunt Julia sold her house and went to live in a residential home catering for the tastes of elderly ladies wishing to play Bridge all the morning and conduct an inquest on their opponents' play in the afternoon. Aunt Ada was put out to grass.

No use saying I often thought of my holiday of that summer. I didn't. I remembered the card tricks Uncle Phil had shown me, of course, and the swimming, and lots of laughs and fooling around with Jack, but the girls were dim figures to me now, almost forgotten. It never even occurred to me that my foot's reflex action might have had the opposite effect to what I'd intended, and the girl on whom I had set my seal of approval rue the day Mavis had her fall. For kind and cheerful Jack, washer-up for poor Aunt Ada, would never let the helpless and the weak walk alone. Sympathy could be a stronger bond than laughter. . . .

But nothing is entirely lost to memory. Touch the right trigger and it all comes back. I've a boy now the same age as I was when I went to Bognor, and a girl a few years older. They were both out the other night when I turned on the T.V.

'D'you want the other side?' I asked, but Peggy shook her head. She was knitting a skirt on circular needles and reading from her library book, perched on the arm of the chair, at the same time. So I left it as it was, and after some time she got up to make coffee. She brought me a cup in and I drank it, I think. I'm not sure: my eyes were glued to the small screen.

Only when the last credit titles had rolled away did I switch off. Peggy was shaking her head incredulously as I came back to my chair.

'Well, I once met one of the players on holiday a long time ago,' I said, and told her the story I am telling now.

'She musn't have changed so much if you recognised her after all this time,' Peggy said, but I shook my head and thought back to the film. Of course the years had changed – aged – her, and she had grown heavier in build, yet I could sense an exuberance in her that was just the same. Given the opportunity, Clare might still break into a dance routine on the East coast here and make us laugh as she did all those years ago at Bognor.

The Boiler Party
by Robert Sharpe

It was one of their favourite hymns and the children sang it beautifully.

> *When a knight won his spurs in the stories of old,*
> *He was gentle and brave, he was gallant and bold.*

Mr. Sewell, the headmaster, who with the vicar was leading the school assembly, permitted himself a wry smile at the words of the hymn. He remembered when he had won *his* spurs, serving as a young stoker on board *H.M.S. Belfast* during the war.

With a shield on his arm and a lance in his hand, the children's clear voices rang out.

No charger and lance in those days, he thought. Where were they – Rosyth or Scapa Flow? Anyway, it was boiler cleaning time.

He could hear Buck Taylor shouting across the messdeck, 'Hi, Sewell, you're down for boiler cleaning tomorrow. Aren't you lucky?'

Oh, God! He recalled the dead weight he had felt in the pit of his stomach. It was tough, dirty and strenuous work; or so they said, he'd never done it. Worse was to come. When he looked at the notice board, he was listed with three others to clean internally the auxiliary boiler. This was a small boiler used when the main ones were closed down.

He was dimly aware of the singing going on: *For God and for valour he rode through the land.*

07.30. Outside the Chief Stoker's Office, the notice had stated. Chief Stoker Higginson didn't waste time on preliminaries.

'Petty Officer Clarke is waiting for you down below. The job has to be completed today. Sandwiches will be sent down at dinner-time; you should be finished by tea-time. If not, a meal will be kept for you. In any case, you stay on the job until the Engineer Officer is satisfied. MacLean and Sewell, you two – one of you in each bottom drum. You're the skinniest pair and will have no trouble getting in –' he paused – 'or out,' he added, as he looked them up and down.

Mr. Sewell smiled at the memory. He had only weighed about eight stones then, and his fellow sufferer, a tough little Glaswegian and former apprentice jockey, weighed even less. If anyone could get into the drums they should.

No charger have I and no sword by my side. . . . The words echoed in his head.

MacLean might have been at home riding a charger, but Sewell couldn't imagine him as the gallant knight. However, they didn't lack boldness. It takes a certain type of courage to squeeze through an oval-shaped opening of eighteen inches by ten inches and be confined – imprisoned might be a more apt description – inside a steel cylinder ten feet long and three feet in diameter, and then be expected to do hard manual work.

Sewell had heard a tale on the mess-deck of a man getting stuck in a manhole door. The body swells when panic takes over, and the unfortunate wretch had to be given an injection by a hurriedly summoned doctor, to quieten and relax him sufficiently to be dragged clear.

'There's plenty of rags in there for you to lie on, but it's not a bloody bed for you to get your head down,' said Stoker Petty Officer Clarke. With sixteen years' service, S.P.O. Clarke was a man of vast experience and this was his domain, the boiler room, where he joked, cursed, cajoled or bullied, whichever he thought was necessary to achieve the ends required by his superiors.

'Tie a rag over your head and another round your neck,' instructed Clarke. 'This mutton cloth put over your nose and mouth, and tie it behind your neck.' They did as ordered. Clarke went on: 'You can wear these protective goggles. They'll become so misted over that you'll be glad to get 'em off, but by then you should be able to do without 'em. Right, let's 'ave a look at you.'

Clarke had a tuft of dark hair growing high on each cheek bone, just below his pale blue eyes, which now looked them over from head to foot.

'Christ!' he spluttered, suddenly exploding into laughter. 'The last time I saw anything like you pair was on the stage at Pompey Hippodrome, two flaming nancy-boys done up like A-rabs doing a sand dance!

'OK, get up and sit on the edge of the man-hole, legs inside the drum,' he ordered, putting a stop to the frivolity. 'Left arm by your side, now work your way in.'

Sewell squirmed and wriggled, and gradually inched his way through the opening. His back resting on the rags, his head just inside the man-hole, he eased his right arm inside and lay supine, breathing heavily. . . .

Yet still to adventure and battle I ride, the voices continued in the distance.

It was incredible. He couldn't sit up; the tube ends were only about ten inches from his face. It must be something like this when the man is fired from the cannon at the circus, he thought. The Death Defying Act Of The Century. . . . Then he remembered the story of the nun who, because of some misdeed, was bricked up alive in a wall embrasure. Slowly, brick by brick, in the name of Christianity, she was cut off from life. She watched as one brick was placed upon another, her screams to no avail, anguish and terror in her eyes, and as the last brick was put in position, her madness ... scratching on the wall ... then silence.

Sewell felt himself slipping into an abyss, then the quiet but authoritative voice of Nobby Clarke penetrated his panic.

'You can get out the same way as you got in. Try it. Right arm first, now the shoulder, lever yourself up. Now your head and left shoulder, keep your left arm down until your shoulders are clear...OK?

He was sitting, dazed, on the lip of the man-hole. He felt S.P.O. Clarke watching him closely. 'Listen, lad,' Clarke said, 'if you can get out quickly, like you've just done, well then − that's half the battle, OK? Right, let's get started. There's a light inside, here's a piece of chalk.' Sewell looked at it blankly. 'To mark each row of tubes as you finish 'em,' Clarke explained patiently. 'We don't want to be doing our work twice over, do we?'

Worming his way back through the man-hole, Sewell wondered what would happen if someone put the door on the entrance. He could almost see the nun's terror-stricken face. ...

'For Christ's sake, pull the bastard down!' It certainly wasn't her voice that brought him back to reality, but Tug Wilson's, his opposite number in the top drum. Just a few inches away from his face, poking out of a tube end, was a half-inch steel wire rope about eight inches long, the end bound with twine to stop it fraying. He pulled on the wire; it wasn't easy.

'As you pull it down, push the end up into the next tube,' a voice said from behind his head; the ever watchful Clarke keeping control of the situation.

He pulled harder on the rope and suddenly a round wire brush, which was a tight fit inside the tube, appeared and quickly disappeared up into the next tube, as Tug Wilson in the top drum hauled it up. As the brush left the tube a shower of fine scale and dust fell directly on to Sewell's face. He shook most of it off and wriggled about until he was clear of the anticipated downpour from the next tube.

'Now we're learning,' said the voice from outside the drum. 'Getting on like a house on fire.'

So it went on : pull down, push up, watch not to get fingers caught in the bight of the wire rope as it was yanked away.

Though back into storyland giants have fled,
And the knights are no more and the dragons are dead.

He became quite expert at avoiding the cascade of filth from each tube. Sweat was trickling down his face and, as predicted by S.P.O. Clarke, he had discarded the goggles. Shoulders and arms were aching, but the work seemed to be getting easier.

'Tea's up! Stand easy,' shouted Clarke.

Sewell scrambled out of the boiler and joined the rest of the gang. There was a lot of light-hearted chatter as they drank their tea.

'How's it going?' Clarke asked him.

'Oh, all right. Hands are a bit sore.'

Clarke threw him a pair of leather gloves. 'I want 'em back, mind!' he warned.

Jock MacLean was impersonating Al Jolson, singing 'Mammy'. Everyone was laughing, realising that they all looked like chimney sweeps, with flashing white teeth and accentuated white eye balls.

All too quickly came the shrill whistle of the bosun's pipe over the Tannoy and the disembodied voice intoning 'Out-pipes'. Of course S.P.O. Clarke, always an individualist, had his own way of doing things, suddenly clapping his hands and shouting: 'Come on, then, lads. Don't make a meal of it. It's only a cup of tea, not the bloody Lord Mayor's Banquet.'

They drained their cups, adjusted the dust trap covering mouth and nose and climbed back into their holes, like foxes going to earth, tails first.

Pull-push, pull-push. Hell, it seemed harder than ever.

'New brush,' shouted Wilson. 'We don't want to make it too easy!'

Someone broke into the chorus of 'Maggie Maggie May', the Navy version of the Liverpool folk-song. They were really swinging along now and the leather gloves were taking the wear and tear off his hands. There was plenty of good-natured banter about the last run ashore; the merits of the new barmaid at the local pub, lewd discriptions of her physical attributes, and how this one or that one could teach her a thing or two. It seemed no time before they were told that sandwiches were ready, and speedily vacated their steel capsules.

Bully-beef sandwiches, naval pattern, washed down with hot, strong, sweet tea made a satisfying interlude. But there was no hanging about. Finished eating, a quick smoke and back on the job...the maxim being: 'The sooner you start, the sooner you finish.'

By 14.30 hours the tubes were completed to shouts of 'That's the bastard we've been looking for' as the brush was pulled through the last water tube.

This moment of elation was soon dampened by the guardian angel, S.P.O. Clarke, growling, 'Don't jump your guns, you've still got a couple of hours' work ahead of you. You can get out and stretch your legs. Go to the heads, but keep off the upper-deck or they'll think we're having a minstrels' show down here, and they'll all want to join in. I want you back in five minutes.'

When they returned, he had three wire scrubbers, one each. 'Scrub the inside of the drum and the tube plate. I want to see them shining like new pennies.' Once more through the hole. Scrub...scrub...it looked perfect to

Sewell, but as he was often reminded: 'Yours is not to wonder why, yours is but to do and die,'

Breaking through the mists of the past he was still aware of the singing.

Let faith be my shield and let joy be my steed,
'Gainst the dragons of anger, the ogres of greed.

Start from the back and work your way to the front, Clarke had told them. . . .

'OK, that'll do.' That voice again. 'Bring all the rags out.' Sewell was quite adept now at slithering in and out of the man-hole. He reached inside and removed the rags which had been pulled to the front of the drum.

'Thank God that's finished,' he muttered, stamping his feet and swinging his arms to relieve his cramped limbs.

'Don't thank Him yet,' cautioned Clarke, 'it's only quarter past three.'

'Bugger me,' grumbled Jock. 'What else?'

'One more job. . . .' Clarke was smiling, or else, as someone suggested later, he had the wind. 'Blackleading,' he explained. 'Take one of these tins, spread and rub in the blacklead using the small brush...work your way from back to front as you did before. Then polish it with the soft brush. Now make this the big effort, put some muscle behind it.' He looked at Sewell and Jock, shrugged his shoulders and went on, emphasising each word. 'When you're finished, the Engineer Officer will examine the boiler, and if it's not to the standard he requires...well, you'll have to do it again. Now, wear your goggles 'cos you'll need 'em.'

The next hour had been the worst period of the whole operation. Rubbing on the liquid blacklead was fairly easy as it dried very quickly. It was the polishing which was so dreadful. The dust and small flakes seemed to be alive, like tiny creatures; in such a confined space they were everywhere, an omnipresence, able to permeate one's very being. In spite of goggles, and covered mouth and nose, the insidious substance crept past any barrier to find an orifice or hollow where it instantly lodged. They laboured and strained in this final effort, the steel assimulating a cloak of glossy ebony.

It was eventually finished, and as they emerged from their metal wombs, filthy and exhausted, the Engineer Officer was waiting, wearing spotless white overalls.

'Even their own mothers wouldn't recognise them now,' he remarked to Clarke.

'No, sir,' dutifully replied the Petty Officer.

The Engineer looked inside the top drum, then the two bottom ones. He stretched a white-gloved hand inside and gently stroked the curve of the polished steel; an almost sensual action. He made a sound of approval and turned, smiling, to the boiler-party awaiting his verdict.

'Good, you've certainly won your spurs today. And a make and mend tomorrow, Clarke?'

'Aye, aye, sir,' answered Clarke. 'They've earned it.' And, turning, he dismissed them with: 'Off you go then.'

*And let me set free with the sword of my youth
From the castle of darkness, the power of the truth.*

It was the quiet, well-modulated voice of the Vicar, saying, 'The children sing that hymn very well, Mr. Sewell,' that brought him back from the past.

'Yes, indeed,' he replied, 'it's one of their favourites.'

'But it also takes you far away from us.'

Mr. Sewell sighed, and slowly nodded. 'But I'm back now, Vicar.' And briskly added, in a firm tone, 'Lead out, boys, back to the classroom.'

Auto-Suggestion
by Mary Andrew

Harry frowned at me. His brown leather diary lay open on the desk in front of him. It displayed the 'Family Details' section, and he had found an unacceptable gap.

'Viv,' he said, 'I accept that you have a bit of a phobia about all things medical, but I think you're getting worse. Do you realise that we have been living in Quackworthy now for more than two months, and you still haven't found yourself a GP?'

It was plain sailing for Harry. He was automatically included in the Company's medical scheme. To be fair, I could have been, too, but I tried to avoid any extra involvement with the firm. I already belonged to the Jolly Songsters, and I had always helped with the teas during the summer cricket fixtures.

Of course, Harry was right to prompt me. I must not let that 'bit of a phobia' escalate. Next morning, therefore, I found myself standing at the gateway of the nearest doctor's surgery, located on the ground floor of a shabby but gracious mid-Victorian house set a little back from the road. There were no gates; presumably they had been removed for salvage during the war and never replaced. I studied the brass plate on the crumbling stone gatepost to check the surgery hours and walked up the gravelled path. A round white porcelain bell-push set in the wall to the right of the door advised callers to 'Ring and Enter'. I did so, pushing aside the heavy black door. Thus Dr. Bentley came to be my new GP.

My first appointment with him entirely changed my whole philosophy of health, perhaps my whole philosophy of life. Patients who registered with him were automatically summoned for a check-up, which was repeated annually. I entered his surgery and was greeted by a thick-set man in his mid-forties, his hair brown but streaked with grey, and his eyes a light shade of brown. His expression was both thoughtful and enquiring.

'Good morning, Mrs. Talbot,' he exclaimed in a loud clear voice. 'How do you do? Please park yourself over there.' And he indicated a chair opposite him. Then, consulting the card I had filled in at the reception desk, he exclaimed with evident respect, 'Oh, a 1920s model, eh? Vintage, but not quite veteran. Well now, what sort of condition do you think you're in?'

Taken aback, but following his novel approach, I explained that I had had only one careful owner, and that as far as I knew, was in good condition for my age.

'Any major faults? Any serious accidents?' he enquired.

'No,' I replied, 'just the usual wear and tear on components, and a few bumps and grazes – traffic marks, really.' And I added that there were one or two accessories missing, but that they didn't affect overall performance. I allowed him to listen to my chest with his stethoscope, and then he courteously asked me to stand on the scales.

'Well, Mrs. Talbot, you're in reasonable condition for your year, but your tick-over's a bit fast and you're rather too well-upholstered; too much weight on the chassis.' He recommended that I used my gears more efficiently, got rid of some of the rear seat cushions, and tried to get more mileage out of a lower octane fuel.

I adjusted my driving mirror, signalled to move out, and chugged gleefully out into the street. I felt totally uplifted, released forever from the queasy anxiety that used to grip me whenever my — or for that matter other people's — insides, and their probable diseased condition, were being discussed. I need no longer think about those palpitating organs laid bare by the surgeon's knife, twitching and throbbing, blood everywhere. It was as though my personal health problems had become miraculously off-loaded, transferred as it were to a friendly, motorised other self, framed not of brittle bone, but of steel; clad not in feeble flesh, but layer upon layer of hardened shiny paint.

Gone was the taint of the human body about its usual daily activities; in its place was the haunting perfume of hot oil and grease, sharpened by the fragrant Sunday tang of car polish vigorously applied. But, above all, there was no blood, with its gruesome reminders of vampirism and savage ceremonial. After all, whoever would sacrifice a brand-new Mini-Metro on a dark altar at the summer solstice? Henceforth my health problems were to be borne by this friendly other self, this tough approachable structure of busy pistons, wheels and joints.

Dr. Bentley treated all his patients in the same way, as I discovered while chatting to friends and neighbours as we settled into the locality.

'Aha!' he'd say, cautiously rotating a shoulder joint, 'a bit of knock on lock, I think.' Or, 'Big end gone; have to get a replacement for that,' as he listened sympathetically to a creaking, stiffened hip-joint. A thoughtful session with the stethoscope might reveal a blocked air filter, or perhaps an engine ticking over irregularly. 'Better look into that,' he'd say, and off you'd go for an ECG. Of course, if it seemed necessary, he'd direct you over to the inspection pit for a really thorough check.

It is worth mentioning here that however he talked to his patients, he was totally orthodox in his terminology to specialists, other practitioners, or pharmacists. If he diagnosed a clogged sump, for example, he would write on the prescription list for the chemist something like 'Senna Pods, every morning' in doctor's jargon, and not, 'One pint of flushing oil, to be taken while the engine is hot.'

It is also worth mentioning that his patients benefited enormously from the peace of mind that his methods gave, the older ones especially. They felt confident that in the event of anything short of a complete systems failure, he would reach out for his spares catalogue, and get a price on a new or reconditioned part, thus postponing almost indefinitely the trip to the car-crusher, the incinerator, and that Last Great Parking Lot in the Sky.

You can't, alas, please everybody. Take Mr. Escott, for example. I saw him rush out of the surgery one day, shouting, 'I want a doctor, not a confounded car mechanic!' But then, he had access to plenty of the latter, as he owned a garage and showroom in the centre of Quackworthy.

The day came when he regretted his outburst. It was one Thursday in mid-January, freezing cold and snowing hard. Mrs. Escott was expecting her first child and she went into labour before she was due. It was impossible to get her to hospital. The only doctor who could reach her was Dr. Bentley, joined a little later by my neighbour, the midwife.

'He did a marvellous job,' she told me later, and related how, after a few initial problems, the new model rolled off the assembly line and out into the world.

'It's a boy,' cried the happy midwife to the smiling doctor, and a little later, when the baby had been through the usual finishing processes, he was deposited into the waiting arms of an exhausted but happy Mrs. Escott.

'Thank you, doctor,' said Mrs. Escott, her eyes shining, her face alight with joy, and she glanced with pride at her haggard and worn husband who had hovered near throughout her triumph-crowned ordeal. Then she looked shyly at Dr. Bentley, who was packing his tool-kit and preparing to leave.

'Doctor, you've been marvellous,' she glowed. 'May I ask you something?'

'Yes, my dear, what is it?' answered Dr. Bentley, turning to glance at her pale but radiant face, framed against the flowery blue of the freshly placed pillow.

'Doctor, I should so much like to call him after you. May I?'

'Certainly, certainly,' said the doctor, 'he's a fine little chap. Firing on all cylinders. Be pleased to have him called after me.'

'But I'm afraid I don't know your full name, Dr. Bentley,' said Mrs Escott. 'Would it be impertinent to ask what it is?'

'My full name?' answered the doctor. 'No, not at all. My full name is Austin Morris Bentley. Why not call him Austin?'

Mr. Escott groaned. 'But I'm a Ford dealer!' he wailed.

'Oh, darling, please. . . .' Pleaded his wife.

'Well, all right,' said Mr. Escott grudgingly, 'but if our next one's a girl, she'd better be called Fiesta. Well, Doctor, it was really good of you to come. Let us have your bill, won't you?' He was feeling a little embarrassed over his earlier outburst at the surgery. But the doctor had either forgiven or forgotten the incident, perhaps both.

'That's all right,' he answered, 'there are no delivery charges on this model. Treat him gently for the first five hundred miles. Good luck, Baby Austin,' he said to the child, and strode off into the blizzard.

All good things come to an end, and as far as Dr. Bentley's patients were concerned, no saying could have been more true. The years rolled on, and the doctor, by then in his early sixties, inherited his uncle's motor museum in Shropshire. We visited the museum a few months later, when our grandchildren were with us for the summer holidays, and there he was, lying under the bonnet of a 1922 Trojan.

'Bit of trouble with your waterworks here, old chap. Bladder, perhaps, or kidneys.' He clambered to his feet. 'Let's try this first. Just drink this for me, will you?' And he poured into the radiator a can of Radi-fix mixed with water.

'Well, hello, Mrs. Talbot,' he cried, suddenly realising that he had visitors. 'How are things with you?'

I replied that all his patients, especially me, missed him a lot.

'Now then, you're all going to be fine,' he said. 'The practice has been taken over by a splendid doctor. I know you'll like him.' It seemed churlish to begrudge him his obviously just and rewarding retirement, and judging by the contented smiles on the faces of his veteran charges, headlamps gleaming, bumpers set in broad grins, it had been a happy move for everyone — except his former patients.

Meanwhile, back in Quackworthy, the time rolled around all too soon for my MOT, or rather my annual check-up. By now, a twinkle in the eye of the Regional Health Authority had been translated into the splendid award-winning Quackworthy Health Centre, set high on a wind-swept hill to the north of the town. The new doctor would probably match the new order. He would probably be a brand new model, stream-lined, immaculate, straight from the showroom — I mean medical school — all quick get-away at the traffic lights, and next to no mileage on the clock. I prepared myself for the usual sickening chat about my cardio-vascular system, lungs, liver, and the rest.

I was greeted by a tall, thin man in his early forties. He was fair-haired and sunburned, with a streamlined-moustache, and eyes of far-away blue.

'Good morning. Mrs. Talbot, isn't it?' said the new doctor. He carried out the standard checks, made a few notes on my card, and said, 'Now, don't be offended, Mrs. Talbot, but I couldn't help noticing as you were coming in to land just then that you seemed to be rather heavily loaded for a pre-war aircraft. We want to keep you flying, don't we?'

I could scarcely believe my luck. Offended? Not likely! My undercarriage nearly left the ground with excitement. I already loved this new airborne other self. I would jettison any quantity of cargo to make flying this old crate any easier. I taxied out of the Health Centre, pausing on my way out to read the new brown plastic nameplate on the door so that Harry could alter his diary. The name on the plate read, 'Dr. W. Lancaster'. Good show!

Remembering that there were old pilots and bold pilots, but that there were no old, bold pilots, I lit the fires and kicked the tyres and took off down the hill. I abandoned an attempt at a Victory roll down the High Road, but completed a few circuits of the Civic Centre, and a dramatic fly-past in front of Woolworth's. Exhilarated, my mind on the King's Cup Air Race, I followed the bus route along the Avenue until I could see Harry, waving to me from the control tower.

I made a very heavy landing on the runway. Harry came out to meet me.

'Did you see that?' I cried. 'I nearly pranged! How are you feeling, dear?'

'Oh, much better, thank you, Viv. That rumble in the engine-room has gone. The doctor was right. I was using the wrong sort of oil on the prop shaft.'

He held the hangar door open for me, then steered a straight course for the greenhouse at a rate of knots to water the tomatoes.

I am so glad Harry took early retirement. He's been so much better since he registered with Dr Cunard.

Heroes
by Paul Griffin

There really were heroes once. I know, because I met some and disliked them, all except one. They were regular officers in the Gurkha regiments, and wore the medals of the North West Frontier campaigns of the thirties, plus any D.S.O.s or M.C.s they had picked up. They were dark-haired, lean, mostly unmarried, with carefully-tended toothbrush moustaches; some of them affected odd bunches of hair on their cheeks.

It must have been in my mind that these heroes represented a threat to my own safety, otherwise why should a young wartime officer have been so nervous of them? They seemed so unbending, so unoriginal, so hard; and I had read Siegfried Sassoon and Wilfred Owen. I really meant to leave our Gurkha regiment before I reached Burma and was committed against the Japanese in some hopeless cause to the last round and the last man, but somehow I clung on. And I did meet one regular officer who did not conform to pattern.

Major Felix Price was neither dark, lean, nor moustached. He was fair, clean-shaven, large even to pudginess, and carried a charge of energy that made you rise in your seat. He was not in our First Battalion, but his name was much mentioned in hushed voices. His daring on the Tochi Expedition, his brilliant and ruthless counter-attack at Dusty Col, his infallible instinct for stepping over the bounds of correctness in the most correct way, made me dislike and fear the idea of him, and expect the usual reality.

'Major Price is bringing the Band down from the Regimental Centre,' announced the C.O. one night over the Madeira, 'for our last Guest Night here.'

We in the First Battalion had finished our jungle training, and were waiting, in a tented clearing in one of the Indian States, to be launched against the Japanese. It is secondary jungle there, not the steamy Tarzan-type primary stuff; something about half as high as Epping Forest, but pretty and well provided with game. Even so, we had had enough of it. Guest Nights had been growing in eccentricity for some time, and the prospect of a band and real guests set the wilder spirits talking of rough games.

'Bloody fools!' said the C.O. affectionately. 'They'll have enough fighting soon.'

The Regimental Band beat Retreat in the centre of the clearing that was our parade ground. At the end, while the treetops loomed dark against an impossible bronze sunset, we stood to attention in the dying notes and watched the flag being hauled down. I glimpsed the large blond officer in our regimentals, but it was not till we gathered for drinks in the Mess Ante-room that I felt his impact. Half a dozen of us were sitting round the C.O., drinking pink gins, when a firm tread was heard from outside the flaps of the tent, and the stranger clicked his heels, making the conventional gesture of respect, feet together and hands stiffly at the sides, towards the C.O.

'Good evening, sir,' said a voice like a rumble of thunder. We all jerked our heads a second time in Major Price's direction.

'Evening, Felix,' said the C.O. comfortably, calling the orderly for another pink gin. He introduced us.

Unlike the other Majors, this one looked human,

amused, alert, unstuffy. His hair was on his head, not distributed in neat packets round his face. Indeed, it was unfashionably long, which in those days meant that it was not quite close-cropped. I felt a wave of respect and interest as I realised that he was getting away with murder, talking to the C.O. in a manner that would have brought a storm down on anyone else. He was joking about the camp, the Regiment, even the C.O.'s tiger shooting, and the C.O. was throwing his head back and laughing as if he were not the terror of the world. This was a man!

Apart from a nod and glance when we were introduced, Price ignored me. It was right that he should ignore a young subaltern. At the meal which followed I sat at the far end of the table from him and the C.O., but was aware that the noise and excitement at the top end sometimes rose above the music of the band outside the Mess Tent. While we disposed of the last of our stock of Madeira, a Gurkha piper marched deafeningly round the table and produced a sort of sodden quiet.

Afterwards we talked a bit, drank Drambuie, and two of us did our standard Guest Night ballet. There was a spell of 'Are you there, Moriarty?' and a chaotic rugger scrum. At eleven o'clock the C.O. stood up and said, 'I'm off. Now don't you do anything stupid. For one thing, I want to get some sleep. For another, I don't want any casualties before we get to Burma. Good night everyone.'

When he was gone, we pulled in our chairs from the edges of the tent, and sat down to talk. We spoke of Monty's new fitness regime in Britain, and decided smugly, with one dissentient, that it was irrelevant to us. The dissentient was a recently-joined officer on transfer from the British Army, a rough mature man with a career in commerce in some Midland city.

'The route marches back in England were, oh, twice as

far as any we've done here,' he declared. 'This battalion couldn't approach them.'

'Just a minute,' said the second-in-command, stroking his moustache and slurring his words. 'If you don't respect this battalion, Captain Veal, I don't know what the bloody hell. . . .'

I had heard all this before. I got up, and walked over to the tent door, noting that Felix Price was sprawled in an armchair, his eyes sparkling as the professionals fell upon the impudent amateur.

Outside, it was cool and pleasant. The band had gone to bed, and the camp lay quiet under the starbright sky. Beyond the Guard Tent was the gleam of the great river, hurrying to join Mother Ganges. A jackal howled at the edge of the camp, and a voice called out in some Gurkhali nightmare. Even now, four years from Independence, the Empire felt safe as ever. Of course, it still had to be fought for, and I reflected that many of the owners of the raised voices through the canvas behind me must be enjoying their last Guest Night on earth.

I inhaled the smells of the night, then reluctantly turned back to the bemedalled pundits in the Ante-room. The scene there had changed. Silhouetted against the lamplight were two figures. One, like a bear in an old-fashioned zoo, was Veal, halfway up the nearer of the two central tent poles. The other was Price, egging him on.

Price, it seemed, had challenged Veal to show his fitness by climbing up the pole and sliding between the two layers of canvas roof to the ground. It was mildly dangerous, and definitely banned. Small injuries had resulted from this before, and no one could walk through Burma with a sprained ankle.

Amid sporting applause, Veal reached the top of the pole, hauled himself on to the inner layer of canvas, which I noticed was ancient and inferior stuff, and slid down to the edge of the tent, the bulge of his body nearly hitting the second-in-command's head where he sat.

Price laughed, and went to disentagle Veal from the guys.

'Right,' said Veal briskly, walking over to the drinks table under the tent pole, and retrieving a glass of whisky. 'Your turn.'

Price put a foot on the table, and clutched the pole. He was much heavier than Veal, and nearly toppled the glasses as he hauled himself off. Slowly, he shinned up the pole, paused at the top to recover, then seized the canvas and dragged his bulk half on to it, out of sight. It was just as he released the pole and put his full weight on the canvas that the rotten stuff ripped and tore. For a moment, Price clutched the edge of the material; then it slid away from his grasp.

I was standing near the pole, and I saw that Price would fall straight on to the table, on which a dozen glasses and bottles stood. Quickly I stepped forward and seized the pole, arching my body over the table. A powerful blow struck me in the back and forced me down on to the glasses, my teeth hitting the edge of the table. Price slid off me, and I dragged myself up. A couple of glasses were broken, and my mouth was bleeding, but no real harm had been done.

'Quick thinking!' said Price. 'Thanks.' He patted my arm and grinned. 'I'd better not try that again. You all right?'

'We'll call it a draw,' said Veal. 'You'd have done it.'

'No, no,' Price insisted. 'You won. I need a course of slimming,'

The Mess Havildar was standing behind us with a note, which he handed to the second-in command. He read it, and raised his hand.

'Gentlemen,' he called, 'I have received a note from the Colonel. It reads: "Bloody well shut up and go to bed". I think he wants us to stop.'

We stopped.

In the morning the band set off on further travels. Felix Price shook hands with me after breakfast. It was like having your hand caught in a mangle.

'I believe I should thank you for what you did last night,' he said. 'My sincere thanks, Randall.'

My name is Brooke-Hopkins.

Major Felix Price won a bar to his M.C. with the Second Battalion at Imphal. I did not see him again during the War. Our First Battalion had a bad time, losing many dead and disabled; but I was lucky.

When it was all over I went back to Britain, and tried to make up my mind what to do. After one or two false starts, I persuaded my father to retire from the family business in favour of my brother, leaving me free to go up to Cambridge. My Fellowship came up fifteen years after the War ended, just as the terrible Sixties were beginning.

One Long Vac at that time I was down in Dorset with Father, when he reminded me of the forgotten past.

'There's a Colonel chap living in Hawfield,' he said, 'who claims to have been in your regiment. Chap called Price. Remember him?'

'Remember him!' I exclaimed. 'He was a sort of hero of mine. M.C. and bar, Second Battalion, a real bundle of energy. I'd like to see him.'

'Ask him round,' he suggested. 'You can have the study one evening and talk to your heart's content. Old times, eh?'

I rang Price, and found him flatteringly enthusiastic. 'Brooke-Hopkins?' he said. 'Of course. My goodness! We've seen a few things together, haven't we?'

It was a curious thing to say, after our one meeting. I was moved by this voice from the past, un-donnish and positive; but there was a business-like air about the way he made our appointment that reminded me of something

I could not quite place.

He was older, thinner, sparser on top, but still vibrant with energy, reducing me almost to my subalternish shyness. He accepted a whisky, and set about dictating the course of the conversation.

'Brooke-Hopkins,' he said. 'Of course. Third Battalion, wasn't it?'

'First,' I reminded him. 'Don't you remember that night you brought the band to Lalpuri, and fell off the tent pole?'

'Of course!' he said. Then, 'Of course. Lalpuri, eh?'

'You don't remember, do you? I saved you from smashing yourself up on the table.'

'Did you now? I must have been tight. Decent of you. Tell me all about what you're doing now.'

I told him, and tried to guide him back to wartime, but all the force of his strong personality seemed bent on talking about the present. I discovered he was in insurance, which he seemed to regard as a sort of crusade.

'My God!' he said, shaking his head. 'If you knew the position some people get into. Married people , dying, and leaving their families with nothing. Not a bean. It's a privilege to help. Bachelors, too. . . .'

'Don't you regret the Army?' I asked.

'Not a bit. Came out as soon as I could. Fresh fields and pastures new, eh?'

'Woods,' I murmured.

'What's that?'

'Never mind.'

'Thought you said Woods. I know a Woods — local bank manager.'

Trapped in the small untidy study with this bundle of energy, I listened to my ideal soldier talking about his new profession and putting my father's whisky back at the old Indian Army rate. I could hardly attend to him for thinking about the War; thoughts that never came to me in the vast and tidy College Combination Room.

The bottle empty, he rose to go and gave me a bear-like handshake.

'We'll meet again,' said Felix Price.

Two days after our meeting, just before I went back to face the ferment of Cambridge in the Sixties, I had a letter from him.

'Dear Richard,' he wrote, *'I am sure that after our talk you will realise how impossibly under-insured you are. I enclose details of a scheme which I feel sure will meet all your requirements.'*

Then, after three more paragraphs about insurance: *'It was so good to talk over old times. I shall never forget how helpful you were that night when the tentpole fell on me.'*

One does not like to detract from a cherished memory so I threw the letter away.

I was still keeping up with Wendy at that time, though I had already seen that marriage, even to her, was not for me. I told her about my meeting with Felix in a letter, and she wrote back: *'What is particularly funny is that under-insurance is the last mistake you're likely to make.'*

I suppose I took that as a compliment. I had been anxious to grow out of the furry charms and puppy ways of the young. Although youth was no fault of mine, and I had long ago forgiven myself my callowness, I did ask myself sometimes how far my own incompetence had contributed to the deaths of some of my fellows in the battalion and was glad of any evidence that I had grown into something better.

After twenty years as Bursar, I had reasonable grounds for hoping that the College had not suffered from my efforts. They had supported me, I had interests in the City, and my book on Macro-Economics was required reading. Sometimes I wondered whether I should not have campaigned harder for another College office; but there was always something to divert my attention, and my tenure as Bursar kept being extended.

In 1980 an Old Member offered me half a million for the College rebuilding scheme, on condition there were matching gifts. I was wise enough not to tackle the task of raising the money on my own, and we went to fund raisers.

Three years after that, we reached twice our target.

'Master,' I said one night, 'we ought to ask our Appeal Committee to a celebration.'

'Of course,' said our Master. He knew me well enough, and never argued with what I wanted. We had been Junior Fellows together.

'Don't forget the men who did the real work,' he added. 'Those fund raisers you found were excellent.'

An ex-naval Captain had done the hard work for us. I had come across him through a charity in London, and had met his Operations Manager, but not his boss, a partner who had taken over the firm and made it supreme in their field. I was only dimly conscious that his name was Price, and it had not occurred to me to connect him with Felix until I found myself sitting near him at High Table on that celebration night.

He seemed smaller, shrunken, hunched. What hair remained was sandy grey; but he still sat like a coiled spring.

I caught his eye, and nodded to him. He grinned, and leant towards his neighbour, checking who I was.

When we moved to the S.C.R. for coffee, I placed myself next to him.

'Brooke-Hopkins,' he said at once. 'Bursar, aren't you? Now...where was it we met before?'

'India,' I said.

'Of course, India. You were in the Regiment, weren't you?'

I asked him about his life, without reminding him of our meeting in the West Country. Obviously he was a very rich man. He had learnt the insurance business, then gone into fund raising at the right time. His energy had done the rest. I said as much.

He thought for a moment, and tidied up the end of his cigar.

'Don't get it wrong,' he said. 'People talk to me as if I've been given something they haven't, unfairly perhaps. But everybody has energy. The question is what they do with it. You intelligent people . . . forgive me . . . spend your energy on looking ahead, trying to anticipate events a long way off. When you're not doing that you're looking a long way back, getting things exactly right, eh? Writing theses about how some French king wore his coat. That's what this place is for, isn't it? I don't worry too much about what might never happen, and the details of what has happened don't seem to stick in my mind. I concentrate this energy you talk about on this moment, now. What's happening in the present. Lovely drop of port, this.'

'I bought it myself fifteen years ago,' I confessed.

'There you are, then, that's your function: looking ahead. We need people like you. Been Bursar a long time, haven't you?'

Someone had been telling him so.

'Yes. It seemed to be my line.' There were other, less cheerful reasons I did not want to talk about, so I changed the subject. 'I often wondered why you didn't stay in the Army.'

'Same reason. Peacetime soldiering's all about the last war and the next war. Not my line. Soldiering's a quiet sort of life, for all the moving around. Like yours, in a way. It's a life for good men. I'm not a good man.'

'That's what good men say.'

'Maybe. Did you ever know Randall, in our First Battalion?'

'No.'

'No, you wouldn't, being in the Third Battalion.'

I did not try to correct him, but let him continue.

'I hardly met Randall myself, but I heard a lot about him. He was absurdly young, but very striking. Quick thinker. Life before him. Restless energy. Always wandering around, looking at things. Had a good War. Well, do you know I met that chap only a few years ago? Where was it? Somewhere in Dorset. All the promise had drained out of him and dried him up. I tell you, he was so ordinary it wasn't true. I suppose he was what I mean by a good man. Ugh!'

He looked me earnestly in the eyes and breathed heavily. For a moment, as his eyebrows twitched, I though he had rumbled his mistake. But no.

'God save us,' he said piously, 'from good men. Remember Randall. Any chance of a rubber of Bridge? I don't feel like sleeping.'

The decanter came round.

'Let me pour you another glass of port,' I said, 'in memory of Randall. War kills the best.'

'And peace gets the rest,' said Felix Price. He grinned, and shuddered.

There really were heroes once. I think I can say they are all dead now.

Mrs. Noah's Version
by Meriel Serjeant

I just 'eard a rumour – and mind, it may only be a rumour 'cos I 'eard it from Methusaleh's girl, an' you know what she's like – that Mr. Gilgamesh is goin' to write up about the Flood. Well, I thought, the cheek, an' 'e wasn't even there, 'is family at that time bein' away on a 'Treasures of Asia' tour of the East.

'Why don't you do it yourself?' said Shem's son Tubal, 'e bein' me favourite grandson. 'I mean, people might be quite interested later on, an' Grandfather ain't goin' to, that's for sure.'

So 'ere I go.

It all began one day when Noah – that's my hubby – came to me an' said 'ad I got any gopher wood?

'Gopher wood?' I said. 'Whatever do you want that for?'

'Well,' 'e said, 'I want to build an ark.'

'An ark?' I said. 'What's that, for gawd's sake?'

An' Noah looks very serious an' says: 'It's a house, like, built on a boat,' an' not to take the Lord's name in vain.

Then I knew 'e'd been on the line again, so I didn't say nothing else. He has a direct line to God, yer know – one of them freefone things, I 'spect – an' 'e comes up with some very odd ideas from time to time. I've sort of got used to it, but I must say it gave me a funny feeling inside this time 'cos Noah don't usually ask for sensible things. Proper dreamboat 'e is, sittin' in 'is little 'ut down by the river bank. I often takes 'im 'is lunch down there so's 'e can get on wiv 'is talkin' an' thinkin' — well, really it's so's I can get on with the washing and suchlike.

Anyways, it was gopher wood 'e wanted this time. All I 'ad to tell 'im was that there was a whole forest just over the 'ill, an' before you could say 'knife' 'e was off out of the valley with Shem, Ham and Japhet, carryin' axes and saws and ropes an' so on. Next thing I knew 'e was after me measure — the one I use for the cloth.

'Mind you bring it back!' I shouted, but I don't think 'e 'eard for 'e started pacin' an' measurin' an' talkin' to hisself in the meadow near 'is 'ut, and soon 'e'd marked out with a stick a great oblong. Then 'e'd stop and think an' go back to 'is 'ut an' be on the freefone again, checkin' like, an' 'e'd come back an' alter something here or there. Well, by the time I'd gone down to get me measure back there were these little pegs all over the meadow markin' a great space.

For a week or more the boys an' 'im an' Josh, the hired hand, went back an' forth over the 'ill an' came back with logs which they dumped in the meadow, all very fast an' serious, an' they wouldn't say nothing to us women.

'Give over, Noah,' I said one night when 'e was back more exhausted than ever. 'What's all this about, anyway?'

'I told you, woman,' 'e said, 'I'm buildin' an ark — there's goin' to be a great flood soon an' we've got to save our family an' the animals.'

'What's a flood, for 'eaven's sake?' I asked. 'The river rises every year an' we don't need no ark then'

'You will this time,' 'e said, all stiff and grim like. An' then 'e looked ever so queer an' said in 'is special voice: 'An' behold, I, even I, do bring a flood of waters upon the earth, to destroy all flesh, wherein is the breath of life from under heaven; and everything that is in the earth shall die.'

That made me real uneasy, 'cos I thought: What about us, an' the harvest, an' me special pet lambs, an' Shem's wife in the family way, an' the house an' all?

Then Mr. Noah went on, still in 'is solemn voice: 'But with thee will I establish my covenant; and thou shalt come into the ark, thou and thy sons and thy wife, and thy son's wives with thee.' I couldn't help breathin' again when 'e said 'thy wife' cos I'd 'ad a sudden panic I might not be on the list. My 'ubby is ever so clever, 'e is, but sometimes I wonder if 'e knows I'm here. So I didn't say nothing more — just told Shem to keep an eye on 'im like, an' to say if 'e seemed to be getting real bad — after all, he *is* 600, 601 come 'is next birthday.

So then they all started cuttin' an' sawin' an' shapin' as if someone was after them, an' Noah was always sayin' they 'adn't much time an' the water would be risin' shortly. Our boys is good at woodwork an' did most of it, an' even Mr. N. only came to me twice for the stickin' plasters.

Then, of course, the neighbours 'ad to come an' 'ave a look.

'What's your hubby up to now?' they'd call as they passed.

'Never you mind,' I'd shout back. 'You'll see all in good time.' An' later I wished I'd never said that, for of course there aren't any of them left now, nor their farms, nor their cattle, nor their children.

'Hey, Mr. Noah,' they'd call, 'you goin' on a Swan tour?' That was when they could see the boat growin' out of the meadow. An' that made me mad because there were the boys workin' like dogs an' all the time there were bigger an' blacker clouds gatherin' in the sky each day, an' the neighbours could see them too but wouldn't take no notice.

All this went on for a few weeks, an' soon you could see the 'ouse part growin' on top of the boat with its winders an' so on. When they 'ad the roof trusses up, Shem came to me an' said 'Mother', 'e said, 'bring the girls to 'ave a look. You'll want to see your kitchen range so as to know what pots to bring.'

So we all went down to the meadow. Shem's Naomi thought everything luverly an' got quite excited, but Ham's wife, Jezebel, never said a good word but kept lookin' into shiny bits where she could see 'erself an' 'er new 'air-do. (I could go on a treat about that there Jezebel an' 'er stuck up ways — there's a nasty vicious streak in her family too.* She was me greatest burden all through those 150 days.)

Later that day that nice Ruth came to me, ever so quiet like: 'Mrs. Noah, Japhet an' me want to get married an' we don't want to wait another day.'

When she said that I saw in a flash me special weddin' 'at in the cupboard waitin' for the day and which couldn't be used now, but I saw too that when the Flood was over it was *our* family as was to be the new Adam and Eve like, an' Noah father of a new race with me boys to follow on. It made me ever so quiet for a time, but then I knew that little Ruth whom I'd known since childhood was right to want to be with Japhet at this new beginning. So I talked to Mr. Noah, an' for a surprise 'e understood an' agreed at once, an' we 'ad a quick wedding there and then, just as the rain really was startin' — so it was a good thing I 'adn't 'ad time to get me hat, after all!

For the next day an' all the followin' days it rained an' rained, an' we splashed through the puddles between the 'ouse, an' the boat, puttin' in sacks of this an' pots of

---

Author's note: It was this Jezebel's great-great-grandaughter who did such damage with a tent peg later on, so Mrs N. had something there!

that, everything we could think of, an' while the girls did the storin' an' arrangin' — of course, Ham's wife kept sayin' things was too 'eavy for 'er to carry — I managed to get the curtains up an' me brass pots 'angin' all in a row. On the seventh evenin', when it was gettin' to be quite a job to get back to the 'ouse, I came out of me new kitchen on to the gang plank, an' what did I see but pairs an' pairs of luminous eyes at the bottom waitin' for me.

'Hey, what yer doin' here?' I said, thinkin' to meself My gawd, is this what Mr. N. meant by animals? An' I knew it was. It wasn't just to be the farm flocks, we 'ad to look after all the wild beasts for posterity, too.

Then me 'ubby come up behind me an' says, ever so polite: 'Come up the plank, won't you? Ham an' Japhet will show you to your cabins' — just as if they was people! So I watched them steppin' up ever so orderly, two by two of every kind of animal around. They was that quiet and well behaved, an' all I could say was 'Mind you wipe your feet at the top!' Which they did too.

So then I went back to the 'ouse for the last time which was now quite deep in water coverin' the floor, an' got Noah's galoshes an' me umbrella an' me favourite teapot an' anything else I could carry. We'll always want a nice cup of tea I thought to meself, an' we won't be exactly short of water, *I* can see.

Well, that night it rained so 'ard I thought the new roof was goin' to collapse, an' the river rose, an' we could feel the ark creakin' an' tremblin' with the water round it. An' by the next day we were floatin', first among the tree tops an' flotsam an' jetsam, an' then driftin' on a world which was nothin' but water. When the tree tops disappeared the birds came an' joined us — Mr. N. 'ad thrown up a very snug roof space for them in the loft. They came in all eager an' good as gold, though I did 'ave to speak to them about the early mornin' chorus later.

It was then we discovered Josh 'ad stowed away in the

loft. Well, you couldn't blame 'im, not really, when 'e'd worked so 'ard alongside the boys an 'adn't any family of 'is own. (Later when we'd settled down again Ararat way, 'e turned out a real gem an' married the au pair as looked after Shem an' Naomi's brood, an' then got to be our farm manager when Noah 'ad 'is trouble with the wine. But that's another story.)

Now you'll wonder about the arrangements on this ark, 'ow we managed an' so forth. Well, we put the milking animals — that is, the ewe an' the nannygoat an' the she camel — next to the kitchen to be on tap as it were, an' at the farthest end we 'ad the wild beasts, with the 'ay and straw stored in the middle to try an' keep the smell of the big cats away from the antelopes an' domestic animals, which they found disturbing as you'll understand. An' upstairs we 'ad all the smaller animals — rabbits an' foxes an' 'edgehogs an' so forth. Mr. N. 'ad even made a place for the snakes, but I must say I never took to those creatures — after the rain stopped, when we was on deck they used to swallow the little frogs that plopped on to the timber in one mighty gulp. 'Orrible it was.

While it rained, which it did for 40 days an' 40 nights, we all 'ad to sleep in the store room next to my kitchen, an' it wasn't none too comfortable. Of course Jezebel 'ad to say she didn't like the blankets I'd brought and preferred a continental duvet. Anyhow we all made out somehow, eatin' light, feedin' the animals an' cleanin', an' sometimes after supper making up Garden of Eden stories to while away the time. An' all day an' all night it rained, an' if we looked out of the winders we saw nothin' but water an' grey skies, an' even Mr. N. wasn't able to get a proper answer through 'is direct line on account of it bein' disconnected.

Come the thirty-fifth day there seemed to be slight stirrin' among the beasts, an' the birds got more talkative, an' four days on we could see gaps in the clouds, until on the fortieth day we woke up an' there was silence all round outside 'cept for the lappin' of the water an' the creakin' of the ark. Then we went out on deck an' saw the sun risin' over the rim of water an' the woodwork of the ark beginning to steam an' the water drops sparklin' on the eaves. I'll never forget that moment, seein' the sun again after all that time – we was that excited. Mr. N. 'e just fell on 'is knees an' started talkin' to 'is god, line or no line.

'Now, girls,' I said, 'let's get all the blankets out an' give them a good airin.' An' put me tubs of tomatoes out on deck to bring them on.'

After that, an' for many days, there was silence outside an' sometimes a little gleam of sun, but still nothin' to see but water, water everywhere, an' the ark driftin' 'ither an' thither. Then it got ever so windy an' we 'ad our time cut out with the beasts bein' seasick. An' of course Jezebel, though there was some doubt about her as she was probably puttin' it on, or there again she might 'ave been in the family way. An' when the wind died down we could see far away a small bit of land stickin' up through the water. We could 'ardly believe it. So Noah, all excited like, let out a raven from the loft, an' that raven never came back so we knew it'd found dry land. Then we waited a few days more before Mr. N. again opened the winder one mornin' an' sent off a dove. But blow me if that dove didn't come straight back into the attic to 'er billin' an' cooin' with 'er mate!

Each day the sun was out more an' more, an' we'd be busy giving the animals their aerobics on deck an' 'avin' picnics. We watched the small triangle of the distant mountain gettin' bigger an' bigger all the time. Then again Noah sent out the dove an' this time we thought she wouldn't return, for the whole day passed an' the other birds was gettin' restless, wantin' to have a go themselves. But in the evenin', just as we was turnin' in, there was a tap at our winder an' there she was with a sprig of olive leaves in 'er beak. Well, you can imagine 'ow excited we got then, wonderin' whose orchard it was — for of course we didn't know if the ark 'ad drifted far or if we'd be able to get back to our own place — an' thinkin' of all the things we was goin' to do when we was on dry land again.

I often used to wonder to meself, during all them days when we was cooped up in that ark with the rain an' the water all round: Why did *He* do it? For we 'umans are all just the same as before, no better nor no worse. An' I come to the conclusion that 'E 'ad something to 'ide which 'E was ashamed of an' the flood was some great cover-up — 'E'd made a mistake somewhere an' the only way 'E could get out of it was to start all over again. But if 'E was savin' all them that was perfect, an' the animals, why did 'E save Jezebel along of us? Well, I still don't know the answer, an' Jezebel went off a long time ago with some feller from over Caspian way, an' Ham 'as a right blue stockin' of a wife now — mind you, I'm not criticisin' but she can't look after Ham an' the family any better than Jezebel. Foreign, you see.

Anyhow to get back to the ark. ... After the dove returned, each day we watched the water gettin' lower an' lower, an' more an' more mountain appearin', an' one day we felt a bump an' knew that the ark 'ad touched ground at last. High ground it was, but ground, above the water in the valley where the river should be.

'We'll call the ark Lake View,' I said when I saw where we were, an' I 'ad very mixed feelings about gettin' back to normal, I can tell you. All in all I'd enjoyed me bit of travel — made a nice change anyway.

Well, first thing, after we'd let all the beasts out — and mind you, they all said thank you ever so nice when they left — we gave the whole ark a good scrub out, an' tidied up the storerooms an' gathered the lime from the loft to put on the land when we started cultivatin' again. An' it all looked so nice an' smelt so sweet again, but my, 'ow it echoed with no one but our family on board. I fair missed the animals, I did. We stayed in the ark waitin' it seemed forever, until the waters 'ad gone down in the valley. An' each day the sun got stronger, an' small green things started pushin' up through the mud, an' gradually the earth dried out in front of our very eyes.

After a time I said to Noah: 'Find out what we 'ave to do now,' but 'e just sat there, starin' out into space that was water once, sayin' nothin' an' doin' nothin' — it was as if 'e was fair played out after the flood.

But one day some time after we was once again buildin' — this time a place for the boys, with a granny flat alongside — we looked out an' saw there was a great bow of many colours in the sky. Then Mr. Noah stirred an' got real excited as 'e used to in the old days, an' said it was God who 'adn't forgot 'im after all. So I realised, poor lamb, 'e'd been worrying that the line would never be put back and that all 'is efforts were for nothin' an' that the end of the world was comin'. But the arc in the sky — ha! ha! — was a sign that 'E was still there an' 'E wouldn't send another flood an' we could settle down an' plan our farm.

Now Mr. Noah he jus' sits there with 'is flagon beside 'im on the bench outside Lake View — only no lake now, of course — an' gets real talkative when the rainbow shows, an' tells stories to the people of the wanderin' tribes who come down from the north an' pass the time of day. An' they'll listen with unbelievin' faces an' say: 'Reelly!; an' 'Fancy that now!' an' think it's the wine an' 'is great age.

But I remember it all, an' sometimes I wish we was back again, all cosy an' tucked up in the ark an' sittin' quiet like of an evening — me an' Shem's Naomi workin' on the layette, an' Japhet an' Ruth teachin' the monkeys to play dominoes, an' Mr. Noah tellin' us stories of the first days. It was real nice then, an' 'cept for the creakin' of the timbers an' the milk bar animals munchin' in the next room, an' sometimes a heavy foot movin' when a big beast was dreamin', it was ever so peaceful an' 'omely. Yes, it was real nice in those days. . . .

The Man Who Was Scared
by Patricia Nielsen

A thick, pallid fog shrouded the station. Heavy, cold and insinuating, it crawled over the smoke-grimed buildings, dimmed the yellow lights and clung round Margaret's small figure as she stood waiting at the edge of the deserted platform. She shuddered. What a night! What a horrible, depressing, dreary night!

In a passion of longing she thought of the warm, brightly-lit room at home and Charles, in slippered ease, deep in one of his favourite books. Hurry up, train, hurry up! she pleaded, and wished again that her parents did not live so far away. Every Friday she came to visit them, and every Friday night she took this long journey back home. A whole hour in the train lay between her and the warmth and security of her house. Hurry, Hurry!

As if in response to her silent pleading a distant rumble was heard, and a few seconds later the little local train loomed through the fog and fussed and grumbled its way to a halt. She opened the nearest door and climbed thankfully in.

The compartment showed no appreciable difference in temperature from outside. She turned up her coat collar and huddled into a corner seat. The fog pressed white against the window, blotting out everything else. Mirrored in the glass was her own dim reflection and that of a man in the opposite corner. He was the only other occupant.

A muffled whistle, a sharp jerk, and they were on their way.

The man in the corner had glanced up as she came in. She had been conscious of a rather yellow face and unnaturally large dark eyes. But now he just sat hunched up, his head bent and his eyes on the floor. Occasionally he twisted and untwisted his fingers, but otherwise scarcely moved.

What a peculiar man! thought Margaret, studying his reflection in the window. Believing himself unobserved, the man behaved more oddly than ever. At the slightest sound his head jerked up and he would gaze apprehensively at the empty corridor. He seemed incapable of keeping his hands still; they kept writhing and twisting on his lap. Reluctantly fascinated now, Margaret watched him more closely. Once his face turned fully in her direction. She met his eyes for a moment and then looked quickly away. What she had seen was fear — fear in all its pitiable nakedness. His eyes were those of an animal at bay.

Margaret felt her spine prickle; a strange electric thrill ran through her body and her heart began to beat painfully.

Don't be such a fool, she told herself angrily, what have you got to fear? But the tension in the atmosphere increased and she felt as though she were suffocating. She longed to go out, to step into the corridor, but she knew she could never bring herself to pass the man in the corner seat. Or perhaps, worse still, to meet whatever it was he feared in the corridor.

She felt a slow tide of hysteria rising in her mind, and she knew she must take immediate action. She spoke.

'Beastly night, isn't it?' she said.

Her voice sounded unnaturally high-pitched above the roar of the train. The words seemed to hang in the air — she could almost see them floating up to the ceiling like so many bubbles. He *must* reply, she thought wildly, and at that instant he did.

'It was a night like this when it happened, you know, Miss. A night just like this.'

Margaret felt icily cold.

'I'm sorry,' she replied helplessly, 'I don't quite understand.'

'No, no, of course not,' he said. 'No one really ever understands.'

He turned suddenly towards her and she was again aware of the huge dark eyes, looking strangely unfocused in the dim light.

'Of course, *you* don't believe in ghosts.'

Margaret smiled nervously.

'Well, I prefer to have evidence first,' she said.

'Ah, evidence!' Again his head jerked in the direction of the corridor. 'Who knows but you may have plenty of it tonight. . . .'

Margaret felt pity overcoming her fear. She spoke to him as one might coax a child frightened of the dark.

'Won't you tell me what's wrong?' she asked gently. 'What is worrying you. Perhaps I could help.'

The man stared hard at her. The face was thin and yellow — in the dim light it shone like wax. A small muscle twitched just above the left eyelid.

'It's my brother Jim,' he said. 'He's dead now, is Jim. Died three years ago on this very train. You may not believe it, but actually in this carriage!'

Margaret gasped.

'But how?'

'Oh, no, it wasn't murder, and not suicide either. Not Jim! Heart failure, that's what the doctor said.'

'I'm so sorry,' said Margaret.

'No need, no need. I'll tell you something, Miss. . . we hated each other, Jim and me. Like poison. Jim was the worst, always had his dagger into me, and now — even now, it's not done with. He comes back, I tell you...he comes back to this carriage where he died, and I've just got to sit here waiting — waiting for him!'

The voice took on a high, hysterical note.

'But why do you travel on the train? Why torment yourself?'

The man gazed despairingly into space.

'It's got to be,' he said with an air of finality.

I don't believe one word of it! thought Margaret crossly, and decided to question him more closely.

'What was he like, your brother?' she said aloud.

'Jim? Oh, he was a great brute of a man. Bigger'n me, much bigger. Strong, too — not the sort to kick the bucket so easily. His face was one you wouldn't forget in a hurry. He had a great scar all down one cheek, and now that I come to think of it, it's still there. That's most horrible of all — that the scar should be still there!'

'What caused it?' asked Margaret.

The man looked up. His eyes narrowed to slits. Margaret had a sickening premonition of evil.

'I did,' he said abruptly, and disappeared into the corridor.

The train thundered on. Its persistent rhythm beat in Margaret's brain. She felt sick and frightened and prayed for the friendly lights of her home town. The compartment suddenly seemed misted and unreal. It's like a nightmare, she thought, but how soon can I wake up? She closed her eyes for a second. When she opened them she saw a large figure blocking the doorway. The face turned slowly to the light and she saw across it a searing scar, running the length of the cheek-bone. In one moment Margaret lived through an eternity of terror, and then darkness closed in. ...

'Oh dear, I'm dreadfully sorry! Are you feeling ill?'

The banal words roused her as nothing else would

have done. Gradually the noise of the train, the sway and rattle of the carriage, was borne in on her and she remembered where she was. When she opened her eyes she saw the young man bending over her. This was no phantom. The eyes were clear and steady, the mouth firm and human, and the scar a real thing and no ghostly deformation.

'I'm sorry,' said the man again, 'I was getting worried about my brother and came to look for him – it annoys him, you know, if he feels he's being watched too much. That's why we travel in separate compartments. I saw you looking pretty ill and came to see if I could help. Are you all right now?'

'Yes, thank you,' said Margaret shakily. 'But please tell me what this is all about. Who is your brother?'

'Poor Larry, I'm afraid he's not quite right in the head. Been like it for years now. We kept him at home as long as we could, but then – ' he touched the scar – 'three years ago this happened, so we had to send him away. He's not really dangerous though, not now, and sometimes I fetch him home for weekends. I'm really terribly sorry if he frightened you. Usually he doesn't even speak to strangers.

Margaret smiled. The sense of relief was almost unbearable.

'I'm afraid I encouraged him,' she admitted. 'Anyway, he left here just before you came along.'

'Oh, I expect he'll be sitting in an empty compartment further along. I'd better go to him. Sure you're OK now?'

'Perfectly,' she replied. 'In fact, we'll soon be coming to my station.

'Good night, then,' said the man.

'Good night.'

When the train stopped at her station, she jumped out and ran like a mad thing across the platform.

'In a hurry, are you?' smiled the ticket collector.

'I'm going *home!*' cried Margaret over her shoulder, and vanished into the mist.

First Day
by Peggie Cannam

He had imagined that it would be a continuation of play school but he soon found that there were subtle differences.

This school was bigger, there were children here whom he had never seen before, and the teacher was a stranger too. When she drifted over and told him that he could play with the bricks which were set out on a low table in front of him, he had smashed them away with his fist in a defiant gesture of indifference.

She said nothing but studied the small scowling figure as she brushed away a wisp of blond hair from her forehead.

He waited for an admonishment, for some pernicious attention which might ease the situation, but she only said quietly, 'Pick them up, please.'

He knew he wasn't going to do any such thing and watched her covertly under lowered eyelids, still sitting stiffly in the chair, hoping that she would use his name.

All the noise in the room had stopped; the air charged with tension as though an electrical fuse was about to blow. He knew the others were watching him and the slight but satisfying moment of power strengthened his resolve.

'Pick them up.'

He pursed his lips, shuffled in his seat, cringing as the

teacher came around to his side. He knew she was looking for the Mickey Mouse badge which he had ripped off not long after she had pinned it on him.

'I said — pick-it-up.' She was near enough now to be disconcerting, and the silence of the others started to bother him.

'I'm waiting,' the teacher said, smoothing the soft velvety fabric of her skirt as she sat down on a corner of the table. She had the look of someone who was going to stay there indefinitely. He knew that this time he was beaten, but there would be plenty more.

Slowly and noisily he picked up each brick in his grubby hand, and dropped it into the box, every deliberate movement a challenge to her authority. Yet when she moved away to talk to a pair of children who were working on a jig-saw together, he felt abandoned.

When at last the box of bricks was full, he got up, slithering along the floor on his heels, finishing alongside her and looking up into her face, waiting for her denunciation.

This time it came quickly. Holding his arm in a strong grip, she took him up to her desk at the top of the room.

Again he was in a strange twilight of longing and despair, the desire for notoriety vying with a desperate longing to be wanted.

The teacher, sitting down in her chair, gripped him between her thighs and held him firmly; their eyes met, charged with a question that was unanswerable just then. 'Where's your name badge?' she asked.

He made her wait for the answer, then unwillingly muttered: 'I don't know.'

'If you won't wear your name badge, then I don't know your name,' she explained, 'and I have twenty other little girls and boys who are new, and I have to know all their names.'

He was aware of her puzzled stare, but could think of no reason to give her that much. Giving was a commodity that had accompanied trust and his had been severed a long time back, almost as far as he could remember.

A boy across the room suddenly cried out, 'It's Stephen, his name's Stephen. He lives in our road.'

The teacher was looking at him with a kindly expression. 'Stephen – that's a nice name. Now, Stephen, we do have to try to get along together at school. When we're asked to do something, then we do it. That makes it easier for everyone. Do you understand?' Her face was close to his. She was looking at him with eyes bluer than his own; eyes that seemed to penetrate his thoughts.

He felt uncomfortable again, vulnerable. Frowning and biting his lower lip in frustration he tried to wriggle away from her, but when she stood up, releasing him, he didn't move away.

'Would you like to paint, Stephen? If I get you a nice big sheet of paper you can do a picture, a nice big one.'

He pursed his lips, grunted and followed her, wondering if there might be a catch in it somewhere. He liked painting, he always had. It was a therapy that released the tensions that he could not control; as if some rottenness inside him were spilling out, distancing him from the scars.

He allowed the teacher to help him into the plastic overall and tie the strings properly at each hip, as he looked with longing and pent-up excitement at the upright easel with a large piece of brown drawing paper pegged to it. Play school had never been like this. There had been no easel, the painting had always been done on the floor. He noticed with an almost unwilling excitement that there were small jars of ready mixed paints ranged along the front of the easel in a deep groove so that they would not spill. There was a big jam-jar of water too, and the teacher explained that he must dip his brush into the water jar after he had used one colour and wanted to change to another. It was very important to change this *every* time the colour was changed.

That was different to play school, too. There they had a brush, one for each colour, so you didn't need a jar of water on its own.

The teacher smiled down at him, and at first he thought that she was going to stand there beside him and watch. He was relieved to see her move over to another child who was painting nearby, and then go to her desk and sit down.

For a moment he waited, unsure how to begin, then decided that he would have a look at the other child's efforts before starting his own. Half sliding, one shoe scuffing the floor, he approached her from behind and stood watching.

The child looked around with no surprise, which annoyed him.

'What you painting then?' he said.

'That's a house,' she replied. 'Look – there's the chimney, see?' She squashed a finger against it. 'Look – there it is with the smoke coming out.'

'It's a soppy old house,' he said, frowning.

'It's not then!' Her lip trembled and he thought she might cry, so pretending indifference he scuffed his way back to his own easel.

Slowly, he dipped the brush into the thick vermilion mass which moved reluctantly in the jar, like mud at the bottom of a pond. Then, lifting up the brush dripping red, he transferred it to the immense space of paper in front of him, dabbing it so hard that the bristles of the brush flattened, making huge red whorls on the brown paper. Fascinated by the thick coagulation of the paint, he bent over, watching intently as tiny bubbles of red appeared and vanished as they dried.

After that, he became quickly confident, splashing on all the colours, scrubbing them in together with the flat of the brush, almost making a hole in the middle of the paper. But his experimentation didn't stop there; with a dollop of yellow ochre on the end of the brush he dipped it into the jar of red paint, watching with delight threads of yellow, like thin veins, disappear then emerge, a new colour.

'Orange, that's orange,' he muttered, and for a moment he had a sudden urge to tell the teacher the magic of it. But doubts, fears, crept up and he knew he wouldn't but would just go on until he finished.

When the other child appeared at his shoulder, staring at the great mass of paint on the brown paper, he said, 'I made orange then, did you see?'

The child pouted. 'I can too. I can make orange.' She was still there, staring at the conglomeration of colour. 'What is it – your picture?'

'Nothing,' he said.

'It can't be nothing.'

He didn't answer but moved in closer to the easel, concentrating on the middle of the paper, twisting in yellow and red and blue, dabbing on more and more colours to form a darker, heavier mass of impenetrable density. And as the painting darkened on the already smudgy background, like smoke billowing in heavy clouds, he remembered the pain, the beatings, black like that – the bruises and the hate alongside the fear, the shock that remained in him, nagging, waiting to be released.

He was back with it all now, trying to break through, forcing it along in a surge of energy, obliterating the whiteness, the purity of daytime, bursting to get through cleanly.

The child was watching again. 'That's not a picture. That's nasty – not a picture.'

Without looking at her, he said, 'It's not meant to be a picture.'

'It's nasty,' she repeated, and went away.

He stood back from the easel to study it, hardly

noticing that the teacher had returned.

'Well, Stephen, is it finished?'

He was surprised at her tone. People didn't usually like his paintings.

'Is it finished?' she asked again.

He nodded, not looking at her but towards the floor in sudden embarrassment, his cheeks flushed.

Saying nothing about the mixture of paint in the jamjar, she showed him how to rinse the brush and where to put the dirty water, then she said, 'We'll take it down and find a place for it on the wall.'

Surprised and puzzled, he gazed at her as she unpegged the heavy wet paper and took it carefully on the flat of her hands to the pin board at the other end of the room.

'I think it's dry enough,' she told him, and looking around, 'Now where did I put my staple gun?'

'I know — I know, Miss,' he sang out in a loud grating voice. He ran over to her desk and although he knew that running wasn't allowed, nothing was said. As he came back to her with the staple gun and handed it to her, a feeling of warmth closed in on him. His skin tingled with it.

When the teacher started to pin the picture on to the pin-board, he stretched up on his toes and held the corners of the paper for her.

Once, she glanced around at him, watching the eyes alight with concentration. That was when she knew that from then on he was going to be all right.

'Tomorrow,' he asked, his face tilted towards her, 'can I do another one?'

'Of course you can, Stephen,' she said, smiling. 'Of course you can.'

Spider's Web
by Peggie R. Kerr

There was something about the girl that attracted Joe straight away. At first he couldn't quite pin it down but as she glanced up at the brasses she was positioning in the window of the antique shop, he knew it was her eyes. Deep brown they were, like the brown velvet dress that had been his mother's and which she had worn on Sundays, when he was a child.

He pushed the memory away. He didn't want to think of the past now but of this girl with delicate features like fine china. Kneeling there, she fitted so well into the world of beautiful things, like those she handled with such loving care.

Brown velvet and fine china! He felt a warm glow spread through his body. She was just what he needed. The perfect girl for his next bride, and one who would understand about his collection.

He moved away. He couldn't let her see him watching, not yet. First he must prepare the setting, then get to know her gradually. The old routine. Turn on the charm, something that had always come easily to him, and a little subtle make-up did wonders with the years.

It took three keys to open the complicated locking device on the front door of his detached Victorian villa, but he was well pleased with his discovery as he turned the ordinary key that finally let him into the house.

He walked through the door to the back room he used as part sitting room, part study, swinging the key chain jauntily. A further key was needed to open the middle drawer of the large oak desk. He seated himself in the leather chair and drew out a notebook and a fountain pen, before reaching for his calculator. He leaned back in the chair, alternately studying the book and glancing round the room. Much as he hated parting with any of the treasures he had acquired, some of them would have to go. A painting, a vase, or perhaps jewellery. It would be an almost physical wrench, hurting him deeply, but he knew there was no other way of maintaining his life style.

Once he had tried. He remembered with a shudder the sheer boredom of sitting in an office all day, helping others to make a fortune. And at the end of it all, a mere pittance ... until he learned the art of helping himself while helping others. He smiled grimly. *That* way was too risky, even for him. Unseen, that was the way. He knew now the satisfaction of building his own fortune over the years. A little here, a little there. Change frequently. Different names, different homes, different jobs – work from one, then another.

Excitement, that was what he needed. His eyes gleamed as he remembered the thrill of the casino, the stimulation of the urge to possess, the danger and satisfaction of a job well done. And he'd paid – the thought brought a frown. Once or twice – three times, perhaps – he had paid with his freedom, but it had all been worth while in the end.

One day, he thought, he might retire with the right woman. But not yet. Brief interludes with the women he met in fashionable resorts or on world cruises were frequent and pleasant. They liked his charisma and the money he spent gave him the pick of the best, but they were not for real. Not for the collection. Only those specially selected would ever know about that.

He got up at last and walked across the thick carpet to

the oil painting on the opposite wall. That one might have to go, he decided ruefully. It had been here in what he liked to think of as his headquarters for quite a few years now. It was one of his father's acquisitions from a well-known French gallery, so it wouldn't be so bad as losing one of his own. A smaller picture on the right revealed a wall safe when he moved it upwards. He whispered the figures aloud as he dialled the combination, and finally opened the inner door.

Lovingly, he handled the labelled packages, one by one. Sapphires would be saleable, he decided, and the pearls for the girl. Just right. Not easily identified, pearls. Joe ran three strands through his fingers and nodded with satisfaction, then selected a few more items. He hesitated over an opal and diamond tie pin. Opals were unlucky, so he'd heard, and pearls were for tears — or perhaps the other way round. But he was not superstitious and beautiful things should be seen sometimes. He fastened the pin into his tie, making a mental note to remember to remove it before leaving the house. He would wear it for the wedding, he decided. He selected rings for the girl and closed the safe.

He left the house early in the morning and drove more than thirty miles before parking in a back street and walking to a lock-up garage, where he kept his plain van, ready for removals. There was only a small child in sight when he removed the pictures and other items from the car boot and transferred them to the van, but Joe made sure she was well occupied with her scooter before he made the transfer.

Removals, he thought, were hard work but he was used to it and it provided his bread and butter. He hummed to himself as he drove deep into the country. Several hours later, he pulled up outside a disused warehouse that he had found by accident ten years before. From outside it appeared derelict, war-time camouflage still visible amongst the rust. He unlocked the door and then an inner one and drove the van inside, relocking them both. Joe felt a glow of satisfaction as he regarded his neatly stacked shelves, all labelled and covered for protection. He knew they were safe here in this isolated spot, and even if a wanderer sought shelter, they would never be able to penetrate the inner sanctum, it was too well fortified.

In the comfortable apartment he had set aside for himself, he poured a whisky, then set about selecting a meal from the well-stocked freezer. Leaving it to defrost, he began his usual tour of his possessions. He had already assessed the relative risks of the items he planned to dispose of, but Joe took great pleasure in handling his treasures from time to time, making sure they were dust free and in good condition. This, he knew, was the best of his various safe houses, but contained only a portion of the whole.

He knew now that his father had been right to advise this kind of life, and regretted that it was years too late to tell him. Father would have been proud, Joe thought, if he could see the accumulation here, just as his mother would be proud of the girls. Joe frowned. It was the one thing he had never understood, his father's harsh treatment of his mother. But he was making it up to her now, giving her the companionship she needed. Ultimately, the whole collection was for her. His mood lightened again. They had never found the house, or the warehouses, and the collection went on growing. Even when he had to go away, they only found the flat he was using at the time.

When he finished his selection and had them packed on the van, Joe switched on the television and settled down with his meal. By the time he returned to the villa, he had successfully completed several sales. He knew it was a weakness, entering everything in the books, but it gave him a certain excitement to know its possession could reveal every transaction he had ever made, as well as every name and address he had ever used. He knew, too, that it was quite safe in his headquarters, where he was known locally as a very quiet man who lived with his invalid mother and travelled a lot. He never allowed anyone inside the house, except those who were invited to the weddings or to see the collection.

It was almost dark when he stationed himself outside the shop, later that same day. He could feel the old anticipation bubbling inside him as he waited.

Finally, she emerged and his pleasure swelled. She was everything he had expected. Small, dark-haired, with an unconscious grace; a fresh, living creature who might have belonged to a more gracious age.

'Excuse me, Miss,' he began, stepping forward as he spoke.

The girl paused under a street lamp, her face a suitable mixture of surprise and wariness. Joe felt himself drawn once again to the deep brown of her eyes. He could almost feel the soft texture of velvet.

He swallowed.

'Excuse me,' he repeated, 'am I too late? Has the shop closed for the evening?'

She smiled then, her lips parting to reveal small white teeth.

'I'm sorry, but it has,' she said.

He rubbed his chin with his forefinger.

'That's a shame,' he said. 'I was interested in those vases — Victorian, aren't they?'

She nodded. 'We open at nine in the morning,' she said, moving on.

Joe fell into step beside her, aware of her apprehensive glance towards him. It wouldn't do to frighten her off, right at the beginning.

'You see,' he said, 'I've got this Victorian villa and I'd like to furnish it with all the right items — right period, you know.'

'Oh, yes?' She looked interested, as the brown eyes turned towards him.

'My name's Joe Thorn, by the way,' he said. 'I work all day, you see, so it is difficult to get here when you're open. Do you think it could be arranged for me to view some pieces in the evenings?'

'We're open all day on Saturday,' she offered.

He smiled ruefully.

'I'm afraid that's no help!'

She gave a small answering smile.

'Mr. Green might arrange to see you after hours,' she suggested. 'If you're looking for several items, it might be possible for him to come along to your house, make suggestions, if you need them.'

'Who's Mr. Green?'

'The owner,' she said simply, and began to walk more quickly.

Joe hesitated, annoyed with himself for overlooking the obvious fact that it might not be her own shop.

'Do you ever do that — visit people's homes?'

'Occasionally,' she said.

'You see,' he said softly, 'I need advice on soft furnishing, the right fabrics, er . . . the feminine touch.'

She laughed, the lights from passing cars illuminating her face. Then she stopped abruptly, staring at him.

'I know what you mean,' she said stiffly. 'I must go, I'll miss my bus. But ring me sometime.'

'I'll do that,' he said, and waved to her slim figure, darting across the road to join a bus queue on the opposite side.

He walked away, humming to himself. He wouldn't rush anything. Build up a telephone acquaintanceship first, buy a few items and gain her confidence. Never an impatient man, he had already decided that the old world charm approach would be best. He could see she was intrigued. It was a good start.

Joe waited a few days, then made the first call.

Her voice was charmingly deepened by the telephone and he warmed to her in a way he would not have believed possible.

Keeping up the pretence of being unable to call in at the shop during the day, he discussed prices and ordered the vases he had seen in the window, as well as a pair of lamps. Then he discussed delivery. He had already rented a garage nearby specially for the purpose.

'I'll be there and pay cash on delivery,' he said finally.

'We could have kept them until you have the house ready,' she said.

'No, this will suit better. I want to get things laid out in my mind before moving them — the garage is big enough to try out the effect.'

'All right,' she agreed, 'if that's what you want.'

A few months later, he felt he had gained her confidence. Their brief telephone conversations had now developed into friendly chats. Her name, he discovered, was Dorothy. She lived alone and had no regular boyfriend. He almost purred with satisfaction. Everything was going smoothly.

Gradually he transformed the sitting room and bedroom with Victoriana. The perfect setting for his gem. His mother would be pleased, he thought, and it was some time now since he had taken a girl downstairs to see her.

'You've bought some lovely things,' Dorothy said, as they settled the price for a pair of chairs. 'Your house will be a picture.'

'I've almost everything I need now,' he said. 'It does lack something though, those feminine touches we talked about. Would you care to see it — give me a bit of professional advice along those lines?'

Her deep-throated laugh reached his ears.

'Well, I suppose I could. Mr. Green's away, though, on his honeymoon.'

'Well,' he said carefully, 'how about popping along this evening? I can get off a bit earlier today. Meet you outside the shop, after closing. What do you think?'

He held his breath, his hands trembling a little. Nothing could go wrong now. It would be too cruel.

After a brief pause, she said, 'All right, I will. Just after five-thirty, then?'

'Fine — I'll pick up a bottle of wine, just to celebrate.' His lips stretched in an evil grin as he replaced the receiver.

Joe was there early and crossed the street when he saw the door sign being changed to 'Closed'. He watched as a young man left, followed by a blonde girl in a short black dress who walked slowly past, tottering on high-heeled strappy shoes. He saw her pause and look up and down the street.

No one else appeared in the doorway. Thoughts chased themselves through Joe's mind. Perhaps Dorothy was ill, or had developed cold feet.

He was just considering knocking on the shop door, when the blonde girl came back, walking towards him.

'Mr. Thorn — Joe?'

He gulped and stared at her questioning eyes. He could not discern their colour in the street light but they were not brown. He nodded miserably.

'I'm sorry, I expected an older man,' she said. 'I mean, I didn't realise it was you. I'm Dorothy!'

His heart sank. He would have known the voice anywhere. He had made a mistake! It was the wrong girl!

He nodded to gain time and hide his disappointment.

'Have you been waiting long?'

He shook his head. 'No,' he said, 'not long.'

His mind was whirling. If he took her to the house, she'd see the flowers, the ring and the prayerbook. He thought of the bridal gown and the brown velvet dress laid out on the bed upstairs. They were not for her. She would not fit into the specially prepared rooms.

'Geraldine told me what you looked like,' she said. 'But you're younger than I expected, and better looking. She didn't say anything about that.'

She was smiling. Joe frowned. She shouldn't be talking like that, flirting with him! It was wrong!

'Who's Geraldine?' he asked, convinced he already knew.

'The girl you met the first time you came to the shop,' she said, confirming his suspicions. 'She's just got married.'

'Yes,' Joe said through clenched teeth, 'I remember.'

She was looking at him expectantly. 'Married the boss. Aren't we going to see the house, then?'

She was asking for trouble, Joe decided, watching her smooth the right skirt over her thighs. She leaned close to him and took his arm. He caught a glimpse of rounded breasts and a whiff of heady perfume.

'Of course,' he answered, switching on the charm to match her mood. 'Come along, then. Don't let the wine get cold!'

They laughed together and walked towards the place where Joe had left his car.

One more wouldn't make much difference, he thought, and he was in the mood now to enjoy her company. He knew he wouldn't be able to let her leave, once she had seen the house. Perhaps a wedding after all, he thought, as he ushered her into a chair and poured the wine.

'What a lot of flowers,' she said.

'For a beautiful lady,' he replied gallantly, handing her the glass with a flourish.

Once she had sipped the wine, everything would slip into place. The drug was a strong one.

'Cheers,' she said, raising her glass, and, as if on cue, the doorbell rang.

Joe sighed with annoyance. No one ever came to the house uninvited, but he knew how to get rid of casual callers. He'd have to answer it or she would become suspicious too soon. She was already hesitating over her drink.

He put his glass down.

'Drink your wine,' he said, smiling at her, 'while I see who it is.'

He couldn't quite fathom the look in her eyes, as she raised the glass to her lips.

Joe was completely unprepared for the police. He had been so sure he had covered all his tracks. He stared stupidly at them, only half-hearing the words.

'Ah, an old friend! We've a few questions about some stolen property, sir. An opal tie-pin.'

Joe gaped. As his head began to clear he realised Dorothy had followed him to the door.

'You want to see this lot through here, Inspector,' she was saying.

It was useless trying to make a run for it. There were too many of them. Nowhere to go either. Once they found the notebooks, they'd have all the addresses.

'How did you know?' he stammered.

'Opal tie-pin. The other young lady recognised it from lists of stolen property in the shop,' the Inspector said. 'Looks like we've hit the jack-pot. Been looking for this place for a long time.'

So opals really were unlucky. Joe cursed his own stupidity, forgetting to remove it that night. Caught in his own web, like a careless spider.

He smiled grimly to himself as he stood back and let the police into the house. There was nothing else he could do, but they were in for a bit of a surprise when they went down to the cellar, where his collection was hidden under the floorboards. All his brides, and his mother still in her brown velvet dress, where his father had put her all those years ago, when Joe was six years old.

Hot Cockles For Tea
by the Very Reverend Fenton Morley

Even on the darkest night I could find the house of my Great Uncle Morgan Morgan by my nose. A distinctive smell oozed out under the front door. Part of it came from the kitchen oven where chopped-up bits of pit-prop were drying for firewood. But most of it came from the bamboo medicine cupboard, packed with herbal remedies and patent back-rubs, by the side of the bed in the front parlour where the old man had been dying for the past two years. At least, that was what he claimed and the family had come to accept it philosophically.

If you ever asked him how he felt, he always gave the same reply: 'Middling, only middling. I don't expect to see the year out.'

As a child, I took his prognosis seriously. When each year drew to its close, I waited with some excitement for Morgan's grand exit. One New Year's Day, I asked him why, after all, he had not departed this life.

He did not resent the question but replied solemnly, 'I suppose the Good Lord wasn't ready for me. So I've got to be patient and struggle on as best I can.'

Not that it was much of a struggle, as far as I could see. The old chap spent his time in the front room downstairs which had been taken over for his sick room. His main occupations were studying the racing pages of the *South Wales Echo* in preparation for his weekly sixpenny bet, and reading the Bible. In a voice like that of a street-corner evangelist, he would declaim at me long chunks of the Old Testament. He did not care much for the New.

'Weak stuff, most of it is,' he would insist, 'No poetry. No blood. None of that beautiful wailing and gnashing of teeth. Now listen to this, boyo ...' and he would turn joyfully to one of the more bloodthirsty denunciations by the prophets. He was particularly fond of the curses pronounced upon two rather dubious ladies rejoicing in the names of Aholah and Aholibah.

'If we'd had them two in the Chapel, we'd have exposed them good and proper. Shameful, that's what they were, shameful,' he pronounced wrathfully.

But old Morgan could afford to indulge himself. He was reputed to have quite a decent stocking of money put by somewhere. This was what remained of the compensation received from the local colliery after the accident which caused the amputation of one of his legs many years before. I heard the saga of that disaster so often that I could have recited it by heart. I knew every detail, from the wild dash of the pit pony which had hurled him to the ground and dragged the coal tram over him, to the moment when he awoke after the operation and thought he was in heaven — until he asked for a Woodbine and was denied it by a hard-hearted nurse.

Now, at last, it looked as though Heaven was going to be his destination pretty soon, for the old man was sinking. At least, that was what his daughter, my Auntie Joyce, had told my mother. She reported that Morgan was off his food — unusually and ominously. He also had a persistent cough which had resisted every remedy. Even having his chest rubbed with hot goose-grease had not made any difference.

So my mother sent me down to pay a visit, taking with me half a dozen eggs reluctantly contributed by our temperamental Rhode Island Reds.

I found Morgan lying there in the darkened room. His gaunt face was topped by his white night cap. His stringy neck emerged from a wreath of red flannel. The long bony hands were motionless on the quilted cover. His eyelids were closed. They looked like cream walnuts in the deep shadowed sockets.

My aunt motioned me to be quiet. As she smoothed the bed cover, she gently pushed the old man's good leg more into the middle of the bed from the side.

A quavering voice came from the invalid. 'Put my leg back where you found it, gel.' It was like a voice from the grave. It went on 'Who's that with you by there?'

I admitted my presence.

For a moment there was silence, then the old man asked: 'Joyce *fach*, have you sent Thomas the Bookie my usual?'

My aunt shook her head disapprovingly. 'For shame, our Dad,' she said, 'to think of that old gambling at a time like this.'

The old man sighed. 'Go on, gel, do it. Like Sunday, the better the day, better the deed, as the Good Book do say. If my horse do come in first, then you can give a bob here to the boy for going, and keep the rest for my funeral tea. I want to be buried proper, with ham, mind you.'

Reluctantly my aunt gave way, to humour a dying man. She pushed at me the envelope containing a sixpence and a bit of paper. Then she went off to the kitchen to prepare the evening meal for her husband when he returned from the colliery.

My Great Uncle was now wide awake.

'Come and sit down by here on the edge of the bed, boy *bach*,' he invited. 'That's right. Sit you down a minute. You're young. You've got all your life before you. I wish I had my time all over again. Then I wouldn't be here now.'

A long pause, while his mind roamed over endless

possibilities. 'America, that's where I should have gone,' he decided, at last. 'But instead I went down the pit, poor dab. And I got married. Big mistake that, boyo. Ties you down. Ball and chain. I'd have made my fortune in America. Chicago, that's the place I've always fancied. Like Sodom and Gomorrah rolled into one ... beautiful.'

I had a sudden vision of Great Uncle Morgan Morgan in splendid affluence, like the big shots of the silent films I saw every Saturday morning in the local flea pit. Morgan Morgan in a Rolls-Royce, smoking huge cigars, instead of the customary Woodbines stuck damply beneath his yellowing moustache.

I sighed in sympathy for What Might Have Been.

He opened his eyes again. 'Did I ever tell you about my accident?' he demanded. Without waiting for my reply he went through the whole drama right up to the heavenly awakening.

'Heaven, that's where I'm bound for now,' he asserted confidently. 'Beautiful palaces and crowns of glory and magnificent choirs. I used to have a lovely voice. Always in the front row of the tenors at the Eisteddfod ... And I'll have my leg back, too, I shouldn't be surprised.'

But that idea certainly surprised me. I had never thought of Heaven as having a spare parts department. It seemed sensible, though, come to think of it.

The old man frowned. 'The only trouble is, according to Richards the Minister, Heaven is strictly T.T. No booze allowed. Ah, well, you can't have everything. But I'd have thought that even the angels would sing better for a bit of a gargle.'

At that pious thought, the door opened. The old man immediately closed his eyes and lay inert. Two faces appeared round the door. One was that of my aunt. The other was that of Pugh the Insurance, looking as ever like a friendly ferret. He gazed with professional interest at one of his 'Names' soon to depart this life and so bring The Policy to a belated harvest. For years and years, my aunt had been paying Pugh's Company sixpence a week so as to cover her father's funeral expenses, and every week Pugh had marked off this payment on one of the cluster of insurance booklets stuck behind the marble clock on the kitchen mantelpiece.

'Very sorry, very sorry, to be sure,' he hissed. 'Well, fair play, it comes to all of us. You know where to find me when The End comes,' he could be heard whispering to my aunt as she ushered him out to the street.

Old Morgan opened his eyes and gave me a wink. 'Like the Bible says ... where the corpse is, there will the vultures gather. It'll be Shinkin the Undertaker next to give me a quick look-over on spec, mark my words, boyo. But they tell me that old Shinkin is failing a bit. I hope he'll see me out, anyway. He's got a posher hearse than the Co-op. Though it would be funny for our Joyce to get a dividend from them on my funeral!'

Weakly, he began to laugh, which turned to a bout of coughing. He subsided on to his pillows. 'Ah, well, I suppose it's high time,' he murmured.

For a while there was silence. I gazed around the room with its pot-plant and antimacassers, and the terrifying picture on the wall of a huge unblinking eye with the legend 'Thou God Seeest Me'.

Then the old man's nostrils twitched. 'Can you smell something?' he demanded.

Amid the mingled reek of liniment and hot firewood, a new odour was evident.

'Hot cockles!' Morgan decided. 'They're having hot cockles and bacon for their tea! Ring that bell, boy *bach*.'

Obediently I rang the small brass bell marked 'A Present from Barry Island' which lay on the bedside table. My aunt scurried into the room, thinking that her father had taken a turn for the worse.

'I can smell cockles and bacon,' he announced in a surprisingly strong voice. 'I fancy a bit of that.'

My aunt argued that the doctor would not allow anything except invalid foods. What about a nice bit of calves' foot jelly? Her father said something in Welsh about calves' foot jelly which was terse and vulgar — as I found out later when I relayed it to my mother. She threatened to wash out my mouth with soap if ever I used such language again. My aunt flounced out of the room. But when she came back it was with a plateful of hot cockles and fried bacon for old Morgan, and one for me too.

'Now, boyo, pass my teeth,' he demanded, motioning to a tumbler of water where his yellowed dentures reposed like miniature tombstones. Gingerly, I passed them over.

When we had finished the meal, Morgan said, 'Well, if that meal was my very last, it was worth it.' And he settled back with a comfortable burp.

But of course it was not his last meal. Great Uncle Morgan Morgan lived to see the year out, and in fact he did not die until December 31st of the following year. So his theory had been right all along. The only trouble was that he'd got the year wrong.

And he had a beautiful funeral, with two ministers and four hymns at the graveside, and my mother and Auntie Joyce weeping buckets. And afterwards, at the funeral tea, we had ham and mixed pickles and jelly and trifle and Welsh cakes and lots of pop for the youngsters. Then we kids went and smashed the pop bottles in the back lane to get the glass marbles out of the bottlenecks.

By the way, as for that bet ... his horse came in first even though it was called Last Chance. It paid twenty to one and I got the shilling as promised. But my mother would not let me keep it. She was dead nuts against gambling. So I had to put it in the missionary box. Grown-ups have no sense of justice, I decided, but perhaps when they get as old as Great Uncle Morgan Morgan, they think differently.

Neighbourhood Watch
by Susan Ashmore

Grace completed the satisfying task of hanging the new curtains, adjusted the tapes, smoothed the folds and opened the top of the sash window to its fullest extent. With her elbows on the window frame and her chin in her hands she surveyed the prospect before her. Huge dark cloud shadows moved swiftly across the distant fells, now purple and pink in the summer sunshine; curlews bubbled overhead, and shrilly squeaking swifts whistled past her face.

Directly below lay what had once been an extensive, well-designed garden. It was a wilderness now. Long grass obscured the paths, weeds choked the flower beds, brambles and nettles rioted along the outer fence. From this second-floor window Grace could see, as in an aerial photograph, the underlying plan: the central lawn, more like a hayfield now, the rose beds around it, and here and there glimpses of paving stones which marked the lines of the original paths. To the left of the so called lawn, in what had probably been the vegetable patch, she could see her two children crouched in the undergrowth, intently observing some small object on the ground between them.

A feeling of immense contentment flooded warmly over Grace. She seemed invaded body and soul by happiness, it drenched her whole being. Adorable children, a permanent home where she had always wanted to live, and tomorrow the return of her beloved husband. Life on earth, it appeared to Grace, must be very close to heaven.

The children were upright now and making their way slowly towards the house. It was a toilsome business traversing the rough ground and there were broken steps to be surmounted. Rachel, the elder by two years, appeared to be in a maternal mood and was endeavouring to assist the plump Jonathan over the difficult terrain. Their wordless voices rose up like the squeaking of the swifts. Grace jumped down from the window sill and hastened to meet them; she did not want them to attempt the stairs alone. As she passed Mrs. Martin, hugely and fiercely scrubbing the hall floor, she said over her shoulder, 'I'm going to put the kettle on. It's time you had a break.'

'Not yet, Mummy,' said Rachel from the kitchen. 'Come and see what we've found.'

'Little donkey,' said Jonathan gravely, 'found a little donkey.' He twisted a small, pink and exceedingly grubby hand into the folds of his mother's skirt and pulled her towards the back door. Rachel took one of Grace's hands in both of her skinny little claws and exerted pressure. They moved as a group out into the sun-dazzled wilderness, the children twittering with excitement all the way.

'He thinks it's a donkey because he's only a baby,' announced Rachel with devastating condescension. 'Donkeys are furry and have great big ears, he should know that.'

'Got big ears,' mumbled Jonathan. He looked up at his mother. 'You'll see,' he added with confidence.

'A snail,' Rachel continued, ignoring the interruption. 'Told him. A snail. Crawling under a snail shell. Look, Mummy, there it is!'

And there it was − a large grey snail promenading

slowly along a dock leaf.

'Dear little donkey,' said Jonathan tenderly.

There certainly were similarities, particularly to someone devoted to donkeys who enjoyed building stick houses for Eeyore at every oportunity. Grace was about to say as much when Mrs. Martin appeared at the door and announced that coffee and orange juice were ready and waiting. They left the donkey snail to pursue his untroubled way and repaired to the kitchen for elevenses.

Although large quantities of crockery and utensils were still in packing cases, Mrs. Martin had succeeded in finding all that was needed and had set out mugs and a plate of biscuits, tastefully arranged on a sheet of clean newspaper. It looked and smelt inviting.

'How are you getting on with the floors?' asked Grace. 'It's hard work I'm afraid. They must be filthy.'

'The better for a good bottoming,' said Mrs. Martin darkly. 'They'll want more than one going over, I don't doubt,' she added. 'You nobbut lay t'dust with once.'

Jonathan approached her and laid a crumb-speckled paw on her sacking apron. His pink mole's hand had dimples in place of knuckles. 'Daddy come 'morrow,' he said, gazing earnestly into her face. With a lightening swoop Mrs. Martin gathered him up and set him on her lap, pressing her cheek to the back of his silken head. He sat enthroned, placidly munching his biscuit. Rachel moved in closer, her hand on Mrs. Martin's elbow.

'I'm nice too,' she said. 'And I'm cleaner than he is.'

'Aye, tha's a reet bonnie lass,' Mrs. Martin agreed, and enfolded her in a warm embrace. When she had a free hand she reached over to the newspaper on the table and indicated a certain paragraph. 'They've no caught yon chap yet,' she said to Grace over the top of Jonathan's head.

Grace leaned forward and took the paper. 'Which chap do you mean?' she asked. Sensing that a tedious adult conversation was about to begin the children slipped away, bent on some ploy of their own.

'Him as killed the little lass over Yorkshire way,' Mrs. Martin stated grimly. Grace no longer needed to read the paper. The horrible details flooded uncalled for into her mind, and suddenly the beautiful morning seemed to fade and the glorious summer's day appeared dark and overcast. The little girl, abused and then strangled, had been just a year older than Rachel.

'Police are watching all the schools round here,' Mrs. Martin continued, 'and all the mothers meet their bairns at night and tak them to school in't morning. T'isnt safe to let them walk by theirselves.'

'But it happened a long way from here,' said Grace weakly. She did not want to think of such terrifying obscenities or pursue the conversation any further, but Mrs. Martin was not to be deflected.

'They reckon he came this way,' she continued, '"answering to the description" it says in't paper. There's only one answer for the likes of him — and I don't mean hanging neither! You'll have told your two not to speak to strangers or tak sweeties and such.'

Grace blushed guiltily. 'Well, no, I haven't,' she faltered, 'I want them to grow up trusting people and being friendly. I wouldn't want them to be suspicious and afraid. In fact, I encourage them to offer their sweets to other children and talk to anyone who talks to them. Perhaps I've been rather stupid. I know it's different in cities, but surely in the country . . .' She paused, feeling foolish and embarrassed.

'Not stupid, love,' said Mrs. Martin, 'but things are different now. I mind when folk knew everybody else and you could spot a stranger for miles. It's not like that now. Folk come and go so fast. You must be careful and tell the little ones to mind what folk they gang with. But Rachel and Jonny are safe enough in't garden,' she added encouragingly, 'and till they start school they'll not go out without you. It's when they're in the road alone there could be trouble.'

The earlier mood of joy and optimism had deserted Grace entirely. Moving house alone and working hard to make it habitable before Mark returned no longer seemed a great adventure: she felt lonely and afraid. Until this morning it had all been such fun. To find an old house being sold cheaply due to neglect and disrepair had seemed like a dream come true. Packing up and moving, helped and advised by her mother and her mother-in-law, had been a stimulating and happy experience. But now all she wanted was Mark, and another twenty-fours without him seemed to stretch ahead like an eternity. A nameless unease nagged her. She did not as yet know any of her neighbours and Mrs. Martin would soon be going home. The thought of being alone was chilling.

'You are an idiot,' she told herself firmly. 'Stop standing around moping, and do something useful. Goodness knows there's plenty to be done. Prepare some lunch for a start.'

After lunch they sat on the newly covered sofa in the freshly cleaned drawingroom and Grace read a story aloud. It was going to be a long hot afternoon so a rest seemed indicated before the children returned to the garden. They had already announced their plan of building a stick house for the little donkey. Rachel had agreed that it should be known as a donkey until its house was completed, after which it was to resume its identity as a snail. Jonathan agreed to this compromise, though with reservations. The story completed, they hurried outside to commence operations and Grace went upstairs to make a start on the big bedroom, intending to have it bright and welcoming when her husband returned the next day.

She had not been working for more than half an hour

when the noise began. Noise is a totally inadequate word to describe the hideous cacophany that suddenly burst upon the air. Pandemonium broke loose in the garden. The children were screaming and crying, a man was shouting, shouts which seemed to change suddenly to yells of terror, and above it all a dog was baying. It was no barking of a small dog or yapping of a terrier but the full-throated sound of a hound who has picked up the scent. Grace rushed to the window. Across the field at the bottom of the garden a man was running as though for his life, his hair on end, his coat flying out behind him, his hands thrashing the air. Staggering through long grass, stumbling over mole hills, he rushed headlong down the slope to the main road in the valley at the bottom. The baying of hounds reverberated behind him.

She pelted down the stairs and out into the garden. The children met her at the bottom of the kitchen steps. Rachel buried her face in her mother's thighs, Jonathan clasped her round the knees. They were panting and sobbing so much that it was a few moments before they could speak.

'A great 'normous dog,' gasped Rachel. 'It was huge, Mummy, huge!'

''Normous,' puffed Jonathan.

'It rushed out of the bushes and chased the man away,' Rachel resumed.

'What man?' demanded Grace. 'I saw a man running across the field, but where did he come from? What was he doing?' Fear gripped her heart. 'He wasn't in the garden, was he?'

'Oh, no,' said Rachel. 'He was in the field, talking to us through the hedge. He wanted us to come through and he would show us something, but we couldn't — it was too prickly and thick.'

'He had sweeties for us,' Jonathan interjected. 'Couldn't reach them,' he added sadly.

'We couldn't get through the hedge,' Rachel repeated, 'but the dog did. He just jumped straight through, roaring. Poor man, he was frightened.'

'Ran away,' said Jonathan.

'I think,' said Grace firmly, 'that I must make a telephone call. Come on, my poppets, we'll go indoors.'

She took their hands and led them in, through the kitchen to the hall. There they stopped abruptly. The front door stood open, and on a table flanked by suitcases lay a Naval cap and a pair of gloves. Grace stood stock still, trembling with delight. Her joy was such that she seemed momentarily to have lost the use of her legs. Not so Rachel. With one joyous shout of 'Daddy!' she bounded across the floor and out through the door. Jonathan stood close to his mother, gripping her hand in both of his. He raised a pink and radiant face, his eyes huge and shining with excitement.

'Mummy,' he breathed, 'Is it tomorrow now, today?'

Mark came in from the porch carrying Rachel in his arms. He put her down and embraced his family, then he embraced them all again, and then once more just for good measure.

'Couldn't find you when I first arrived,' he said, 'so I went out again to pay the taxi. Were you in the garden?'

'Yes, we were,' said Grace unsteadily. 'But I came in to phone the police.'

'The police!' Mark exclaimed. 'Whatever for?'

As quickly and briefly as possible Grace explained, the children making excited additions the while. Instantly Mark took charge.

'I shall ring the police,' he said, 'while you put the kettle on. I've been travelling for hours. The exercise finished at dawn this morning and there was no need for me to stay on so I caught the first train I could. I'd been away from you all quite long enough.'

* * *

The telephone rang the next morning while they were having breakfast. Mark went to answer it. Returning shortly, he said quietly to Grace, over the heads of the children, 'It seems they may have got him.'

Her hands flew to her throat. 'And is it the same man? The one in the news recently?'

'Who knows?' he replied. 'It may be weeks, months even, before they get it all sorted out. Anyhow,' he continued, drawing the children into the conversation. 'the police are most impressed with our dog – a grand protector, they called it. You said it was a big one, I think.'

''Normously huge,' Rachel pronounced. 'Biggest you ever saw. Big as ... as ...' She paused, at a loss for words.

Jonathan did not hesitate. 'Big as a donkey,' he said with great emphasis, and gave his sister a long hard look.

For once she did not correct him but nodded her head in agreement. 'That's right,' she said. 'Grey and furry and big as a donkey.'

'Sounds like a wolf hound,' said her father with interest. 'What did you think, my darling?'

Grace was silent for a moment. 'Strangely enough,' she said, 'I didn't actually see it – but I certainly heard it. What a din, it was terrific! And of course I saw the man running away. He looked scared out of his wits.'

'Probably belongs to one of our neighbours,' Mark observed. 'When we meet it we can say thank you and make friends. We certainly owe a big debt of gratitude there.' But seeing the fear in his wife's eyes he forebore to continue the subject. He started to carry the plates out to the kitchen then turned in the doorway.

'If you don't need me in the house this morning, I think I'll make a beginning in the garden. Nothing technical, of course, I wouldn't do anything to the flower beds till you are there to advise, but I thought I could start clearing the paths and discovering the lay-out of the place. The fences need attention, too. Is the billhook unpacked yet?'

'I put all the tools in the shed behind the garage,' Grace replied. 'But do you really want to start at once? You must be so tired. You could take it easy for one day at least.'

'I'm longing to get on with it. Besides, I need fresh air and exercise. Most of the past few weeks have been spent underground and in artificial light. Not exactly a life on the ocean wave.'

Grace raised her eyebrows at him. 'Really?' she said. 'Not at all as I imagined it. However, I know better than to ask any questions.'

'That's my girl!' he said, and kissed the back of her neck. 'Shout if you need me, I shan't be far away.' He went out by the back door and Grace started preparations for lunch. She was still standing at the sink, peeling potatoes, when Mark appeared at the window and leaned in.

'Come and see what I've found,' he invited. 'A milestone at the bottom of the garden. It's covered in moss and mud, and there seems to be an inscription on it that I can't quite read. Probably the distance in miles. Anyhow, I think it's a number – looks like nineteen and then something else. If you've got an old knife, a strong one, we might be able to clean it enough to read the rest.'

Grace found a suitable knife and joined him outside.

'Odd place for a milestone,' she observed. 'It's not on the road to anywhere. Perhaps it's something boring like a hydrant.' While Mark held back the undergrowth, she stooped over the stone and scraped at the moss with the knife.

'It's not a milestone,' she said. 'Look, a date, 1910. Do you think it might be a tombstone?'

'Well, hardly, my sweet. People weren't buried at the bottom of gardens in 1910. In fact that date ruins all my theories. When I first uncovered it I hoped it was Roman, and started to scrape off the moss looking for a dedication to the gods of the shades, or perhaps I.O.M., but no such luck.'

'Wait a minute!' Grace exclaimed, continuing to scrape and scratch. 'There's a line further down and it's got an I in it, but I don't think it stands for Jove or Jupiter, it's not at the beginning of the word. And as you say, it's quite a modern stone anyway.'

She worked with great vigour and a large slab of earth and moss fell away, revealing one short word below the date. Slowly and shakily, Grace rose to her feet. Hot tears streaming down her cheeks, she stretched out her hands, groping blindly for her husband, and clutched his arm tightly.

'Tiny,' she whispered. 'Tiny. It must have been the most prodigious hound to have a name like that. Oh, how I wish I could have seen it, too.'

'You had no need,' Mark told her gently. 'At no time was there any personal threat to you. Only the babies were in any real danger, and Tiny certainly protected them.'

From a nearby bush he picked a bright red rose and laid it gratefully on the forgotten grave.

Grey Dolphin
by Doris M. Hodges

Dora Ken bustled to the bottom of the stairs, and tilted her small, round face, framed in its helmet of grey hair, towards the spare bedroom. The acrid smell of paint drifted down. Dora sniffed. She did hope Ernie had the windows of the small room open, so that he wasn't inhaling too much of the paint. She heard him, hand-planing away on the wooden hull of his model boat, *Black Witch*.

Model-making was his hobby, as cooking was hers. One of hers, she amended, with a curious feeling of mixed mischief and guilt as she opened her full, rather pouting lips, and yelled, putting an edge to her voice: 'Do come on, Ernie! Coffee's spoiling, love!'

Back in the somewhat cluttered kitchen of the small, semi-detached house — Dora was a loving wife, a first-class cook, an indifferent housewife — she placed freshly baked rock cakes on a plate, then nodded with relief at the sound of Ernie's light footsteps coming down the stairs.

'Catching the 11.30 bus then, are we, Dor?'

The diminutive didn't irritate her, as it might have a more sophisticated woman. Instead, she warmed inside to the special note it held still, after thirty years of marriage. These days, there weren't all that many couples who could claim they were still as much in love as in their courting days, but she and Ernie could.

She sighed. If only the poor man didn't worry so much about money. Of course, now they were both retired – he from engineering, Dora from a cashier's post – things weren't quite so easy. Their combined Pensions were just enough to keep them in decent comfort, but there was certainly nothing left over for extras. Dora glanced quickly at the battery clock above the sink, which was another example of Ernie's patient and individual handiwork.

'Got a lot of shopping to do in Westcombe,' she nodded. 'And I want to take a look at that new supermarket that's just been opened next to the Orion Cinema.'

'Back about six, then?'

Ernie dunked rock cakes into his coffee. The homely habit had long since ceased to irritate her, though she still felt it wasted good cakes. Ernie smiled over at her. Both were small, somewhat stocky in stature, with greying hair and indeterminate features. Ernie's eyes, though, were hazel, deep-set and inclined to be brooding. Dora's were big and blue, usually bright and alert. They gave her the look, at times, of an amiable, giant-sized doll. But there was a shrewdness in them which matched, in its own way, Ernie's introspection. It was a speculative focussing, as if both their minds, at times, split off from the everyday world and entered another dimension. The land of dreams, perhaps, and unfulfilled ambition ...

'You go off to the Library, Ernie? It's a wonder they don't give you a special chair in that place.'

Each and every Wednesday, Dora went into Westcombe shopping, and her husband to the County Library to study the books on the history and craft of model-making.

'I've a chicken casserole and apple pie for supper. If you're in first, Ernie love, just put it in the oven.'

'If we'd got one of those microwaves you fancy, I could hot it up in no time.'

'There's a difference,' said Dora quietly, 'between what we need and what we think we want!'

'Birthdays, too, tomorrow,' Ernie reminded her, seeming not to notice or mind, her sermonising. 'And we both know what we'd like, eh? 'Course you never know, we could be lucky.'

Dora would be sixty-seven and Ernie sixty-nine next day, because they shared birthday dates as to the day and month, but not the year. They parted outside the trim front garden, Dora kissing Ernie's lean cheeks, he giving her a hug around the waist. Fondly she watched his straight, sturdy figure marching down the suburban tree-lined road towards the County Library. Such a clever chap, her Ernie! He ought to have been made charge hand, at least, in that car factory where he'd spent most of his working life. Instead, they'd kept him in a routine job on a machine, never giving him a chance to show his real potential. There was hardly anything he couldn't do with his hands in the way of turning and shaping and accurately measuring things, especially small, delicate objects. Good thing he'd always had his model-making to console him. Just as Dora had her cooking, and could shut herself in her kitchen and work on her favourite recipes when the world turned sour on her.

Up glided the multi-coloured double-decker bus. Dora frowned at sight of the painted elephants, giraffes, monkeys, lions and tigers cavorting all over it. Then, suddenly, her face broke into a smile of pure delight. Over the wheel nearest to her was a tumbling grey dolphin, so realistic Dora half expected the creature to give one of those fascinating dolphin chuckles.

'Do I pay in monkey nuts, then, to get on?' she asked the driver-conductor, as she plonked forty pence and her pensioner's pass on his tin tray.

'That's real art, that is, love – don't knock it!'

But the man, middled aged and genial, winked at

Dora's spry little figure, her orange mackintosh and windblown grey hair, as she began to climb the stairs. 'Best watch it up there — them creatures might just try and get in at you through the windows!'

Dora cut herself off in a giggle — mature ladies weren't supposed to giggle — at this fantasy, then further indulged it with the thought that the poor dolphin would soon perish, thus deprived of water. Giraffes and monkeys, now, Dora could take or leave — mostly leave. And lions and tigers were carnivorous, and liable to devour you when hungry or provoked. But dolphins, now, who could help being fascinated by those tumbling grey forms, the faces set in a perpetually amiable smile, the quaint, whistling calls which could sound so like chuckles? Ernie was just as fascinated by them as Dora. Once, when there was a serial on the television with a super-intelligent male dolphin as star, her husband actually neglected his model-making to follow the tumbling grey mammal's adventures. He would sit, hand to cheek, staring in fascinated delight, almost as if expecting the dolphin to come leaping right out of the screen into their lounge.

She remembered Ernie's shy comment about their birthdays. She could expect a card with nice, appropriate words, her breakfast in bed, and either a few of her favourite Malmaison pink carnations, or a small box of chocolates — hard centres. Funds just wouldn't run to anything else, certainly not to the microwave oven. She sighed, thinking of the money she would save on fuel bills, and the jacket potatoes Ernie loved which you could cook in just a few minutes in a microwave.

Ernie hated breakfast in bed, but he always appreciated the cards she got, with sailing ships or perhaps birds or some other wild creatures on them. He was a great one for watching everything in the natural world, from waterboatmen on ponds or hovering hawks over motorways.

to the horses competing at point-to-point races. His birthday card, this year, had a horse on it, a big brown Shire pulling a plough. There was also a copy of his favourite model-maker's magazine. What he really wanted — what Dora hungered, in fact, to get him — was a brand new Micrometer, (called, by him, a 'mike'), with decimal markings. His old one, used since his apprentice days, was in feet and inches. But she just didn't have the money. 'Unless,' pondered Dora, and that odd, dreamy look far back in her blue eyes suddenly grew in intensity, I tried *that* again! Only I oughtn't to, not really. Because whatever would Ernie say? Or think? And not only him, of course . . .

Dora considered this thought and its implications, her face intent, lower lip caught between small, even white teeth. She looked then as she did when, as a child, she had contemplated something forbidden. But she also looked faintly mutinous, as if a war was being waged in her mind between the dictates of respectability, even orthodox morality, and her own instincts and desires. 'I don't see that it's so wicked,' she murmured to the top of the now empty bus, 'just as long as I don't go too far. Now that would never do.'

'Mind them monkeys as you get off!' said the driver-conductor, poker-faced but eyes dancing. 'Play havoc in the supermarket, they would.'

Dora shot him a conspiratorial smile, saluting a kindred spirit, as she disappeared into the giant, shining maw of the new supermarket. To her, this had all the fascination of some Aladdin's Cave, with its long counters with their arrays of all manner of food, drink, fruit, sweets, and clothing. She viewed it all, especially the exotic foods and fruit, with something of a child's delight and wonderment.

There was also a handicrafts and hobbies counter, with the exact mircometer Dora yearned to give Ernie displayed in a polished wooden box with an imitation velvet interior. Almost like a jewel, or perhaps a magic key or talisman, she brooded, plaintively aware that to her husband the delicate instrument would certainly have near-magical qualities. She sighed for she noticed that the micrometer had gone up yet again in price, since the last time she'd studied one in the older supermarket. It was really as much beyond her reach as the Koh-I-Noor Diamond she and Ernie had gazed at in awed admiration last time they went to the Tower of London to see the Crown Jewels.

Crossly Dora pitched margarine, tea, coffee and other basic necessities into her basket. At the bottom lay the newspaper she'd bought at the book counter. Thoughtfully, she made her way to the cafeteria area, got a cup of coffee and a cake, and found a quiet corner. She bit into the cake with professional interest and grimaced in disappointment. It tasted of sawdust! But soon her interest became wholly focused upon the newspaper – primarily, indeed totally, on certain pages. Her teeth again gnawed her lower lip, and her gaze became hard and focused. Stacked by the Exit was a splendid display of microwave ovens, with even the free gift of a turkey or chicken if you bought one now! Ernie would have got her a microwave in a flash, for her birthday, if only there'd been the money to spare.

'Evening, Mrs. Kent.' It was a neighbour from their road, on his way out of the cafeteria. He lingered briefly. 'I ran into your husband over in Paulton, earlier – he's looking well, like you! Lovely, this new supermarket, isn't it? Spend all your money under one roof, eh?'

If you've got the money to spend in the first place, Dora thought, as he passed on. And fancy making that stupid mistake about Ernie. He'd be in the Library, as he always was on Wednesdays! Planning the super new models he'd build, especially if he had the help of that micrometer for his delicate measurings.

Abruptly, Dora left the supermarket, dived down a narrow street, and halted. There, she took an old felt hat from her bag, and a pair of dark glasses, and put them on before entering with a certain nervousness a particular doorway.

Her return bus had no bright cavorting creatures on it, but was painted in circus stripes and brilliant flowers. This joyous note didn't match the driver-conductor, however, for he was stern and unsmiling, eyeing Dora impatiently as she struggled with bulging plastic bags to the only downstairs seat. But Dora's cheeks were flushed pink with triumph, her blue eyes sparkled, and she even smiled at him. As a bus glided by in the opposite direction, she suddenly spotted the grey dolphin on it . . . Her smile and the look in her eyes deepened.

At a quarter to six she opened her front door to the delicious aroma of chicken and apple pie. Leaving her carriers on the hall table, she took from the top of the nearest one a long narrow parcel wrapped around with one of the glistening plastic supermarket carriers.

Ernie had the table laid. He looked unwontedly flushed, but, at the same time, both triumphant and uncertain. There was something different, too, about her kitchen! As she neared the table, something fluttered from the turn-up of her coat sleeve. Ernie stopped and picked up the slip.

Dora nearly cried out, standing there with the long oblong of the parcel in her hand, gazing at her husband. The slip was small and yellow. It had on it, in Dora's neat, square handwriting: *4.00 p.m. Heydock. Grey Dolphin. £5 win and place.*

'Dor, this – this is a betting slip!' cried Ernie, in a very strange voice indeed. At the same split second, Dora spotted behind him the microwave oven, glittering with newness.

'The — the microwave?' she cried, torn between delight and uncertainty. Could her gentle, mild-mannered, clever husband have robbed a bank? Or something even worse? Then the memory of her own activities returned, and a flood of crimson rushed to her cheeks. She held out the parcel, watched as Ernie unwrapped the new micrometer . . .

'Snap,' said Ernie, in the same odd voice, and took from his pocket a small yellow slip. On it was written, in his larger, backward-slanting script, with the address of a Paulton Betting Agency at the top: *4.00 p.m. Heydock. Grey Dolphin. £10 to win.*

'He — he was twenty to one,' breathed Ernie almost reverently. 'I didn't exactly lie to you, Dor. I do go to the Library, every Wednesday, for an hour. But then — well, I get the 'bus to Paulton, and — and . . .'

'And have a little flutter on the horses?' said Dora. 'Like me, Ernie! Every now and then, when money's extra tight, I do the same. I never bet too much, you know.'

'Nor me,' said Ernie. 'Only you did want that microwave oven, and it was your birthday. And on the way to Paulton, I saw the old grey dolphin painted on the side of a bus.'

'Snap!' said Dora this time. 'Only we mustn't ever do it again, must we, Ernie dear? 'Cos it's really too — '

'Too habit-forming?' suggested Ernie gravely. And Dora nodded, as solemnly. But that look was still there, at the back of both pairs of eyes: speculative, dreaming, and bright with the promise of the sporting chance.

Poor Betsy
by Helena Bovett

I was only six when I met poor Betsy. It was in November 1914 when Mum and I were visiting Gran. I'd had croup and the doctor said I must be taken out of the London fog. Every detail of that visit comes back to me so clearly, from the minute the train rattled across the points into Newton Abbot station.

'There's Uncle Harry,' I called excitedly, my head hanging out of the window.

'Don't put your head out or you'll get a smut in your eye.' Mum was getting our things from the rack.

I pulled my head in but waved to the big man I could see through clouds of steam, standing by the ticket collector. The train drew slowly to a halt with much hissing and there was my Uncle Harry, opening the carriage door, catching me up in his arms and giving me the usual swing in the air before putting me on the platform.

'Run under cover, Dolly, it's pouring with rain.' Uncle Harry turned his attention to Mum and the luggage. 'How are you, Alice? Whatever made you come to this benighted spot in such weather? It's been raining for days.'

'Better than our fog, I can assure you,' said Mum as we hurried to cover under the station roof. Uncle turned to me.

'Now let's have a look at you. Why, you do look a

peaky little maid! You've had that nasty cough again?'

I nodded and demonstrated my particular croupy cough which always set everyone on edge and gained me a lot of sympathy and attention.

'The doctor said that she should get out of the fog or she wouldn't lose it all the winter.' Mum was tucking my scarf in and buttoning up my coat until I nearly choked.

'Well, Mother will feed her up all right but I doubt if she'll be able to get out much. It looks as if this weather has set in. I'll dump these in the trap and come back with the umbrella.'

Uncle dashed out into the rain and came back with the largest umbrella I had ever seen. I was hoisted into the trap and Mum and I cowered under it but Uncle didn't seem to bother a bit about the lashing rain.

We set off at a fine pace along the country lanes. It was very dark; the only light cast on the road was made by the flickering lamp at the side of the trap. And it was very quiet, just the sound of the horse's hooves and the rain. I snuggled closer to Mum and listened to what they were saying.

'You know Mother's got poor Betsy with her now?'

'Yes, she wrote and told me. How is it going? Mother's been alone so long now that I shouldn't have thought she would want anyone else to live with her.'

'Well, her rheumatism is so bad now that she can't scrub those stone floors anymore or wash the sheets. Poor Betsy's very strong, although she looks such a little thing, and she's been a real godsend to Mother. Steady there, Brownie.' Uncle gave the horse an encouraging cluck as one of the wheels of the trap went into a rut and had to be pulled out.

'I've never seen her, you know,' said Mum thoughtfully. 'She's Mother's second cousin, isn't she?'

'You wouldn't have seen her. She was away, you know what I mean, while we were growing up, and anyway she lived in Somerset and visiting wasn't easy.'

'What's she like? Is she strange in any way?' Mum sounded curious.

'She looks a bit peculiar sometimes. And talks to herself. But what can you expect? Twelve years shut up in that place, and then to come home to an empty cottage. Her husband died while she was in there. The villagers didn't mix with her much, the gossip lingered on, but she's devoted to Mother and that's all that matters.'

I wanted to ask questions but I had already found out that you heard more if you didn't ask, especially if the grown-ups were talking in the way they did when they hoped you weren't listening. But I didn't much like the sound of poor Betsy.

A few lights were beginning to appear and I knew that we must be nearly there. I recognised the village street by the brook running along its side. There was no one about and no street lights, not even a light in the village shop. Uncle pulled up outside Gran's cottage, quickly sprang down from the trap, then picked me up and carried me to the open door where Gran was waiting.

'Here they are, Mother, safe and sound, if a little wet. You run in, Alice. I'll bring the bags, then I must dash. It's choir practice tonight – I'll look in later.'

I followed Gran into the kitchen, blinking for the light from the oil lamp seemed very bright after that long, dark ride.

'How's my little maid?' Gran was busily taking off my scarf and coat. 'Come over to the fire and get warm. You've had a nasty cough then? Never mind, we'll soon make it better. Take your things off, Alice, I expect you're dying for a cup of tea. Betsy, the kettle's boiling.'

I was rubbing my hands in front of the fire when Betsy shuffled across the floor with the teapot in her hand. As she bent over the fire to fill the teapot, I thought she looked exactly like the witch in my picture book, bending over her cauldron. Her black hair fell over her face and she wore a shabby black dress with a shawl around her shoulders. Now that I had seen her I didn't much like the look of poor Betsy.

'Betsy, this is my daughter, Alice, and my granddaughter, Dorothy, whom we call Dolly.' Gran proudly introduced us and Mum shook hands and gave Betsy a pleasant smile. I hung back. 'Shake hands nicely,' commanded Gran, and slowly I obeyed. Betsy stared at me, muttered something and gave me a sort of twisted smile.

'Now come to the table and start, we've had ours long ago.' Gran was already pouring the tea. 'When you've eaten a piece of bread and butter, Dolly, there's splits and strawberry jam, and junket and cream. But bread and butter first.'

I enjoyed my tea but I was getting sleepy by the time I'd finished and made no complaint when I was taken up to the little bedroom and tucked into sheets that smelt of lavender. I squealed with delight when my feet touched the warm brick wrapped in flannelette and fell asleep at once.

It was still raining the next day. I couldn't go out and I soon got tired of my books and toys. I would have followed Gran and Mum about, watching what they were doing, but Betsy was nearly always there too and she kept looking at me. Later, Gran sent her out on an errand and I heard them talking about her as they prepared the vegetables in the scullery. I sat quietly in the kitchen, turning the pages of my book but listening intently.

'But what really happened?' asked Mum.

'She wanted a boy so badly but had three girls, one after another. They only lived a few days. Then the gossip started and, what with that and the disappointment, she went out of her mind. Twelve years they kept her in there, and when they let her out she lived alone in that cottage.

No wonder she talks to herself and acts a bit strange.'

'Do you believe that she ..?'

'Of course not.' Gran sounded very sharp. 'These things happen. Mind you, Betsy is partly responsible for the gossip because she kept on about only wanting a boy and that she didn't like girls.'

There, I knew it! I felt Betsy didn't like me. She was always watching me and I couldn't get away from her, the cottage was too small. It rained all day long, and the next day. There was nothing for me to do and I began to wish I was back in London.

The evenings were the worst time. Gran and Mum would sit on either side of the fire and I sat on a stool beside Gran. Everything was so cosy. The lamp stood in the middle of the table and threw a lovely circle of light on the brown chenille tablecloth. I could smell the apples in the blue bowl on the dresser. Occasionally Gran would use the bellows to rouse the wood fire into sparkling life again. But it was all spoilt for me, for in a dark corner sat Betsy. Now and again she broke into a few words that sounded like gibberish, then there would be a dry cackle of laughter. Whenever I looked in her direction, Betsy would be looking at me.

The next day the rain had stopped and Mum said, if I put on my hat and coat, I could go out in the garden for a while but I must keep to the path. I was out in a flash. It was lovely to be standing in the sunshine after being cooped up in that small, dark cottage. I walked slowly down the path, enjoying my freedom. The garden, looking very different now from when I had seen it in the summer, was a long narrow one. First a bit of grass, then a flower bed, next the vegetable patch, and right at the bottom the chicken run and henhouse. Then I saw Betsy. I stood and watched her. She came out of the henhouse, scattering corn from her apron, walking amongst them, peering down as though she was looking for a particular one. She was, for suddenly she pounced and had the squawking chicken in her hands. Then, with one quick twist of her wrist, she wrung its neck. She gave her little dry cackle, looked up and saw me, and laughed again.

I ran, screaming and sobbing, up the garden path, burst into the kitchen and hurled myself against Gran.

'Betsy's killed a chicken,' I sobbed. 'Betsy's killed a chicken.'

'Don't take on so, Dolly,' Gran tried to soothe me. 'I told her to. That's for our Sunday dinner.'

Gradually they calmed me down. I knew that animals had to be killed so that we could eat them. But Betsy killing that chicken had looked horrible, as though she had enjoyed doing it. That night I lay awake in that dark cottage bedroom, thinking. Had those babies really died or had she killed them?

One night, after I had been in bed a while, Mum came up.

'Not asleep yet? We're just going next door to Uncle Harry's for a while, shan't be long.'

She bent over me and straightened the sheets. I grabbed her hand. 'Don't go,' I begged.

'Why ever not?' Mum was surprised. 'You never make a fuss about being left a little while at home. Now behave like a big girl. We're only going next door and you're not alone. Betsy's downstairs.'

Reluctantly, I let go of her hand. 'Don't stay long.'

I heard her footsteps go down the stairs, then the front door banged and I was alone with Betsy. The house was quiet but outside the wind moaned and the rain pattered against the window. I lay very still, straining my ears for the sound of movement below.

Time passed very slowly and I had begun to hope that they would soon be back. Then, there it was, the sound I dreaded, the scrape of a chair on the stone floor and a slow shuffling sound as she crossed the kitchen. I heard the stairs creak, one after another, and I knew she was coming up. I fixed my eyes on the door and watched it slowly open. There she stood with a lighted candle in her hand. I tried to speak but no words would come. I could only lie there, unable to move as she slowly crossed the room. Carefully she put the candle on the table and then came over to the bed and peered down at me. I saw her hands coming towards me. They clutched at the bedclothes and raised them ... she was going to smother me! Slowly, and with the utmost difficulty, I opened my mouth and screamed and screamed.

It could only have been minutes after that Mum was in the room, holding me in her arms and trying to pacify me.

'Whatever did you do to frighten her so, Betsy?' she asked angrily.

Betsy looked startled. 'Nothing,' she said sullenly. 'I was only going to cover the little maid up.'

Mum and Gran were quite satisfied with Betsy's explanation but I was still terrified and from then on wouldn't leave my mother's side. She could see that I wasn't going to settle so we went back to London soon after. Back at home I gradually forgot all about it.

I wasn't to see poor Betsy again, for the terrible epidemic of influenza of 1918 reached the village and she, amongst many others, died. The cottage remained in the family and now it has, at last, come to me. I love it and, as old people do, spend hours reliving memories of the happy times I had spent there during the holidays, playing with my cousins in the sunshine.

But sometimes, as I lie in bed on a wild November night, when the wind is moaning and the rain in pattering on the window, I find my eyes drawn towards the door and, for a moment, poor Betsy appears. I see her clearly, standing there with the candle aloft − and I see the look in her eyes.

Then the vision fades. In spite of the warmth of my bed, I shiver and doubts return. Did she really only intend to cover me up?

Mr. York
by Dorothy Gibson

Aunt Lucy, with whom Laura had lived for three years, since she was seven, had a few stock phrases, one of which was: 'I never go out to tea and I never invite anyone back. I don't hold with afternoon tea and gossip.'

Laura wasn't in agreement about afternoon tea. She thought thin fish paste sandwiches and biscuits from a biscuit barrel the height of sophistication, like pink satin blouses and patent leather shoes — all of which her friend Muriel's mother went in for. But she too did not hold with gossip. She found it boring. And she knew about gossip since Aunt Lucy and Grandmother, who lived with them, gossiped about neighbours and the family quite a lot.

They often forgot Laura was there.

'A quiet child,' Aunt Lucy used to tell people.

It hadn't taken Laura long to discover that she was not expected to join in their conversation unless she was specifically addressed. At first she had done so, but that had only led to misunderstanding. Now she listened and thought her own thoughts.

Aunt Lucy belonged to the local Ladies' Conservative Club. Not that, from the things she said, she held rigid political views but she enjoyed whist and music and company and, it must be said, gossip, and she found all these at the weekly afternoon meetings. These meetings also gave her an excuse to wear the classy hats which were some of the perks of Uncle Fred's occupation. He was a buyer for a large Singapore Department Store and he patronised the top firms since the customers were mostly rich rubber planters of the European colony and a few wealthy Chinese or Malayans. Besides hats, he placed orders for cut glass, silver, shoes, whisky, cigars and Christmas cakes, and parcels containing gifts of these and other luxuries frequently arrived at home, with compliment slips.

The tradespeople served Aunt Lucy well and were eager to deliver since she plied them generously with handfuls of the best cigars, tots of whisky, or Sherry, cigarettes, or whatever was most plentiful. It also staved off the monthly settlement of accounts on the frequent occasions when Aunt Lucy was 'short'. Laura often heard her say how dearly she would have loved a fur coat, but they did not seem to export fur coats to Singapore. Perhaps this was a blessing in disguise, Laura and Grandmother agreed privately – Aunt Lucy did not really have the build for fur coats.

But despite the fur coats and floral hats of the other Conservative ladies, Aunt's Henry Heath hats and Bally shoes marked her out as one of the most expensively dressed to anyone of taste. And the Major, the local Tory M.P. who was also a lord, and whose name was spoken in almost reverent whispers, on his rare appearances made much of Aunt Lucy.

She came home from one of the weekly meetings, obviously very excited.

'You'll never guess what I found out this afternoon,' she said.

Grandmother was willing to concede this.

'May Moore is living at the other end of our road – next door to Janey Scott!'

Grandmother looked puzzled for a moment and then her face cleared. 'You mean May Pavey that was? You were her bridesmaid?'

'Of course! May Pavey that was! Maisie, the young lady who comes along to sing and play the piano – I think you've met her –'

'Yes, of course. Gingery hair.'

'Blonde,' Aunt Lucy corrected firmly. 'She's May's daughter. I was chatting with her and she told me they used to live in Highgate – Delaware Road. Then it dawned on me, Maisie Moore! I said, Was your Mother's name Pavey before she married – May Pavey? And your Dad Cyril Moor? When she said yes I told her that her mother and I went to school together ... then we'd lost touch after she married.'

Grandmother said, 'Didn't they move up North somewhere?'

'Yes, but Maisie said Cyril had abandoned May and her when she was a little girl. So they moved down here to May's brother Jack. And Jack goes to the local pub where Janey Scott serves behind the bar. And Janey said the flat next-door to her was to be let. May got a job as a waitress, and the flat –'

'I never took to that Cyril Moore. I reckon she's well rid of him,' Grandmother stated.

'But's she's not!' Aunt Lucy played her trump card. 'Cyril turned up again, after all those years. Out of work and flat broke. May wasn't going to have him back, and you can't blame her, but they didn't like to see him so down on his luck so Janey let him have her box room till he gets back on his feet.'

'She's a good sort, that Janey Scott,' Grandmother said under her breath, qualifying her statement with 'Underneath', and as an afterthought, 'Mutton dressed as lamb!'

Laura knew what she meant. She had met Janey Scott, and she had seen her with an insipid-looking woman who might be May-Pavey-that-was. Janey had a white face, very dark red lips, huge brown eyes circled with black mascara, and straight black hair with one or two kiss curls on her forehead. She wore rows and rows of beads, and was always saying she had Spanish blood. Laura found her fascinating. She was curious to see this Cyril Moore who was down on his luck, too.

'Cyril manages to do the odd job apparently,' Aunt Lucy went on. 'One thing about him, he can turn his hand to anything.'

Mr. Moore, soon after, at Aunt Lucy's invitation did turn his hand to several things over the next few months. He repaired the wireless set and put connections in other rooms so they could take the speaker round and plug it in. He put up shelves and put down new lino in the kitchen. He painted doors and window frames and re-upholstered chairs. He shared meals and Uncle Fred's whisky and cigars and Aunt Lucy paid him more than she could really afford.

Whether Uncle Fred knew how many meals Mr. Moore consumed at his expense, Laura never knew. Uncle's hours of work were erratic and he was often not home till ten o'clock. Laura knew where he spent most of his evenings. She had seen him get off the tram and go into Joe Pryor's when she had been coming home from Brownies. No women frequented Joe Pryor's – it was only licensed to sell beer. It looked more like a cottage than a pub, and it had no sign outside like the Red Lion. Uncle was not a spirits drinker and he did not want much dinner at night. He ate well in the City, on other men's expense accounts – or perhaps his entertainment was classed as advertising, as Aunt Lucy explained. The arrangement suited them all and what he might be engaged in during the evening was never mentioned.

Neither Grandmother nor Laura liked Mr. Moore. Grandmother admitted that he was 'gentlemanly' looking. His navy blue suit, although slightly shiny in places, was clean and well-pressed. His shoes were highly polished, his shirts starched.

He had distinguished-looking wavy silver hair and his pink face had a sort of matt finish as if he powdered after shaving. But his eyes were light brown and rather narrow and Laura did not like his mouth. She thought he seemed to watch her, waiting to catch her out in some misdemeanour like answering back or telling fibs. When he succeeded he would shake his head and click his tongue quietly, glancing at Aunt Lucy to encourage her to reprimand Laura. Strangely, she rarely did when he was there.

Even less did Laura like an undertone which she thought she detected in his manner: that he and she were really in the same boat, partakers of Aunt Lucy's benevolence, and so, like him, Laura should adopt a more grateful manner. If she had known the word 'creep', she would have nick-named him that. Instead, she and Grandmother, and later Aunt Lucy herself, called him by the nick-name 'York'.

For York seemed to be his Mecca. He never missed an opportunity to compare London unfavourably with York. And every month he would go off for four or five days to York where, apparently, he had numerous friends.

Then there were the evenings of whist. He and Aunt Lucy enjoyed whist, and Grandmother and Laura were dragged in to make up a foursome. Uncle Fred was a lifelong abstainer from card games.

York taught Laura whist. He was a good teacher but he could never resist the post-mortem. After every game he would tell her what she had done wrong. If she attempted to answer, he would say crisply, 'Children must not argue with their elders and betters.' If she lost her temper and flounced away, flinging her cards on the table, he would shake his head in quiet exasperation while glancing at Aunt Lucy, who always looked slightly embarrassed.

As the months went by even Aunt Lucy eventually admitted that he was beginning to wear out his welcome.

But if he noticed a cooling off, he did not take the hint.

It was on one of his trips to York that, guiltily, it was decided that when he returned there would be only bread and cheese produced for his evening meal.

They waited, when he was due to return, rather fearfully. But there was defiance in Aunt Lucy's face too. She was generous to a fault, but she was beginning to be persuaded by Grandmother that she was being 'taken for a ride'.

The knock on the door did not come. They waited anxiously for several nights and it still did not come. Gradually, with relief mingled with curiosity, they began to stop listening.

'Perhaps he got a job and stayed up there,' Aunt Lucy suggested.

'Perhaps he got the message,' Grandmother hazarded.

Laura was able to read or paint instead of playing whist. Aunt Lucy listened to the wireless and knitted.

It must have been two or three months later when one day Laura arrived home from school to find Auntie May Pavey in the kitchen, sipping tea. It was the first time Laura had seen her for ages. She had been vaguely aware that there was 'coolness' between her and Aunt Lucy over Mr. York. It seemed Aunt May thought that Aunt Lucy had 'encouraged' him.

Laura slipped out of the room to get her slippers and a book, and when she returned Aunt Lucy was saying, 'Funny about Cyril. Did you hear from him?'

Aunt May shook her head.

'You'd have thought he'd have dropped you a line.'

'He meant to come back,' May said. 'All his personal documents are at Janey's, even his post office book — not that there's much in that — but his clothes, insurance card, references . . . everything.'

'So you don't think he got a job up there?' Aunt Lucy continued, puzzled.

'At his age — not a hope. And he would have sent for his papers, his insurance card, if —'

'It's a mystery,' Aunt Lucy went on.

'Maisie and I think we know what happened to him,' May whispered.

They waited, not liking to press her.

'We think he was murdered.'

Two shocked gasps from Aunt and Grandmother dropped into the ensuing silence.

'Murdered?' Aunt Lucy was incredulous.

May went on. 'We made enquiries — well, Jack did. Cyril used to get lifts up and back, along the Great North Road. He arranged his trips to coincide with his regulars ... commercial travellers and that ... he couldn't afford to go up there any other way.'

'I suppose not,' Aunt Lucy murmured. 'I used to wonder'.

Aunt May's voice trembled slightly as she went on. 'The night he was coming back ... that last time ... was the night when that burnt out car was found, with a body in it ... on the Great North Road ...'

Grandmother, an avid reader of newspaper reports of murders, said: 'You mean the insurance swindle case ... the man who faked his own death?'

May nodded. 'His wife was to collect the insurance money and follow him out to Australia. Only they caught him at the docks.'

'And charged him with the murder of an unidentified man,' Grandmother finished.

There was a long silence.

'What makes you think that Cyril ...?' Aunt Lucy asked.

'Apparently the man he picked up was a loner. He often picked him up ... they had a sort of arrangement. He probably planned it all and picked Cyril. He killed him with a blow on the head then set the car alight. The body was too charred for identification. But when Jack made enquiries about Cyril, the police seemed pretty sure ...'

'How terrible if it was,' Aunt Lucy whispered.

Grandmother glanced at Laura but her head was down. She pretended she was deep in her book — she was not supposed to listen to grown-up talk. But all she could see on the page was a tall, silver-haired man with a pink face and a shiny blue suit ... the loner they had called York, and had been going to reject when next he knocked at the door.

A Rather Elderly Buttons
by Heather Johnson

At seventeen, our Fanny was a little beauty. People would say 'Eh, your Fanny's a sight for sore eyes', and I, several years younger, would look at my sister curiously and see the cascade of bright honey-coloured curls, the deep blue-grey flecked eyes and peachy skin, and even I could appreciate her. Now that I look back I recognise that she had a good neat figure, too, and carried herself well.

I knew also that the manager of the weaving shed 'fancied her' (all three sisters worked in the local mill); but it wasn't until years later that I connected him with Fanny getting stouter, stopping work, and baby Maggie's arrival.

I remember being astonished at this latter event and asking where she'd come from and why we needed a baby, and being slapped down as usual.

My questions were never answered. I would sit and listen to the stream of female chatter issuing from my elders and then make some perfectly straightforward observation of my own on a different and – to my mind – much more interesting subject, and get withering looks from them all, all except Fanny, as they paused for a second, their flow interrupted.

'Don't teach yer food to talk!' my Grandmother would say sourly.

'If it needed any teachin',' I'd mutter to myself

rebelliously, 'it'd be shoutin' by now, after listenin' to you lot!'

My mother had died when I was born. They said she lived just long enough to be pleased to have a son at last, which gives me some satisfaction though I don't remember her at all, and if my father was pleased too, he went into the army when I was only four years old so I have only a very hazy recollection of him too. He was killed in 1916, so Grandma Cash, already widowed, had looked after our household as far back as I could recall. She was a stern, humourless old woman – not without cause as I can see now – but she had the strength that was needed to survive in those bleak days in a frequently depressed Northern town between the two world wars. Living in a cramped and crowded terraced house, with not much money coming in, must have been trial enough for the women, without me – and then the baby – to contend with as well. Being the only lad meant I was shielded somewhat, but I missed male company sorely.

I remember that only Fanny looked after the baby, and after its arrival she stayed at home, got up first every morning, cleaned the grate and laid the fire, and started making the porridge, waiting on everyone – often with the baby on her hip. When company came, the baby was taken upstairs and Fanny either stayed there with it or sat at the back of the room sewing and never joining in the conversation.

She even stopped talking much to me; I didn't know what to make of it. The others just seemed to ignore her and the baby, even more than they did me ... I noticed it particularly whenever there was a special treat, a church or works outing. While baby Maggie was small I could understand someone having to stay at home, but when she started walking and could have come with us, I asked about it.

'Why isn't our Fanny coming with us?'

'Because she's not fit, that's why,' declared my Grandmother, shortly.

I looked at Fanny. She looked well enough to me and a darn sight better than the other two who were dressed up to the nines; overdressed, in my opinion. I said as much and got the usual cuff around the ear from Annie, the eldest.

She was a real bossy-boots, our Annie. Why, she had even chosen Maggie's name, Marguerite. Fanny had wanted Isobel, Bella for short, which she said meant beautiful. I supported her, glad of the chance to feel close to her as in former days. They never even listened to us and Marguerite it was, though she was never baptised.

When Grandma Cash died, Annie took over and ruled us all with her haughty looks and sharp tongue. I kept out of her way, spending most of my time after school kicking a ball about on the nearby croft. I suppose they were glad to be rid of me, but I thought they were rotten to our Fanny who, it seemed to me, lived like a prisoner. I said so frequently, but nothing changed.

When I started work, one of my mates told me what had happened (with a few crude embellishments, of course). Fanny had 'given in' to the boss at the mill; she said because he'd threatened her with the sack and she couldn't have faced our grandmother without a job. When she became pregnant he didn't want to know, and in the way of families in those days, with all their jobs at stake, the Cash family closed ranks and supported her and the baby between them. At least they didn't force an abortion on her, but from then on Fanny and her baby were regarded as a mark of shame on the family name, hidden from outside view and never spoken of.

Far worse, it seemed to me, was that as Maggie grew older and really pretty like her mother, my other two sisters started treating her as if she belonged to them. Fanny made all her clothes, but as she still stayed at home to look after the house and do all the cooking and washing, she didn't earn anything, so it was Annie and Liz who bought the material for Maggie's dresses and it was they who had the pleasure and satisfaction of showing off the little girl in public. They took her to church and on outings and when she won a scholarship to the grammar school, they basked in her success as if it were all due to them.

Liz had got married by then, but in the fashion of those days she still spent a lot of time at our house. It meant that Annie ruled the roost more than ever. Fanny never complained and she seemed well and happy enough – probably because she was always busy – but I got really sick of it. If I'd had enough money to get wed, I'd have been off out of it years before the Second World War.

As it was I spent a good deal of the inter-war years unemployed or on strike, and so without much say in family affairs. As a method of getting away from petticoat government I joined the Territorial Army. That at least gave me a little money, some masculine company and annual training camps to look forward to, but it also meant I was one of the first called up in 1938, a sergeant by then, and among those who 'bought it' at Dunkirk. Really, I was lucky because I got away, even though I left a leg behind. At least I got a bit of a pension, had time to get used to my artificial one and was taken on by the local council in a reasonably paid job before the rest of the lads came home.

For the first time that gave me a bit of status in the family, and I saw to it that Fanny got more out of life than in the past. We used to go on bus rides together, and to the pictures. Marguerite (we were all trying to call her that by then) had been to teachers' training college and when she started teaching we were suddenly quite well off. Annie was no longer at the mill, of course, but she had quite a good job and with our three wages, and by pooling what

Annie and I had saved, we were able to buy a semi-detached house in a better neighbourhood. The day we moved in there was a red-letter one, I can tell you. It's much easier to live with people like Annie when there's some space around you — and her — and best of all, for me, a garden to escape into. And though Fanny and Marguerite had to share the biggest bedroom they didn't seem to mind.

When Marguerite married one of the other teachers in her school and went to live on the pleasant outskirts of the town, we really felt we'd 'arrived'. Not that if you'd seen a photo of the wedding group you wouldn't have thought it was our Annie who was the bride's mother; *she* organised everything ... but *I* gave the bride away and had the satisfaction of pointing out that she owed her good looks to her mother, making the guests give Fanny a special round of applause. That made her blush of course but she was so happy I don't think she minded. By then Maggie's — sorry, Marguerite's — illegitimacy was long forgotten; I suppose they must have told her husband-to-be but he's a good chap and wouldn't have given it a second thought.

Anyway, when I told you that Fanny made all Maggie's dresses, and did all the family sewing and mending for that matter, I didn't tell you she'd done a deal of fancy sewing — crochet and embroidery and that sort of thing, too. I expect it was the years of sitting in the background and always staying at home — her Cinderella years, I call them now — that started her off. If she did any outside sewing for someone she'd spend the money they paid her on linen and silks, and she made some beautiful things.

Marguerite was always lively and a good mixer, and as her own kids got older she got quite involved in the Women's Institute. They do other things besides making jam and running jumble sales, of course, and every now and again they display all the work they've done at local fêtes and agricultural shows. Marguerite persuaded Fanny to join and occasionally she'd go to one of the meetings, though she was too shy really to mix in. Until the day when Marguerite said they were a bit short of needlework to put on display and went off with a kind of tapestry picture her mother had made; apparently she got it properly framed and Liz, who saw it, said we'd never believe how beautiful it looked. We never saw it again because someone asked if they could have it on permanent display in a room at the local community centre which the W.I. was decorating, and of course Fanny agreed.

Two years after that it was a special celebration year of the W.I. and all the areas had to do a project representing their own county. A sort of deputation led by Marguerite came to Fanny to ask her to design something special. At first she was very doubtful, but all the nice things they said about her work boosted her confidence and she said she'd have a go. What she produced, helped by other members doing the stitching – a sort of map illustrating the history of local industries and famous people and places, surrounded by the moorland countryside people forget we have up here, looked a real treat, and everyone was tickled pink about it.

When the finished masterpiece had to go to London to be put on show with work from other counties, Fanny and Marguerite went with it. They showed me the specially printed notice that would be placed beside their effort: 'Designed by Frances Cash', it said. Just think of that! I was so pleased I took our Fanny out and treated her to a complete new outfit; suit and shoes, hat, gloves and handbag, the lot. She'd put on a bit of weight, but she was still shapely and her hair still waved, and with it up on top and that nice straw hat ... she looked every inch a Frances Cash. I could see Marguerite was feeling really proud of her.

But that wasn't the end of it. Came the Silver Jubilee and Fanny was chosen to design an altar cloth for the new chapel in the Cathedral. She was ever so frightened at first but soon got interested when the committee started telling her the sort of thing they wanted.

I got Annie to help us clear our front room — we still hadn't got into the way of making much use of it. Then I fixed a huge curtain pole, the old-fashioned sort with big rings on it, along the longest wall, and a big trestle table from the church hall beneath it. When the beautiful big piece of linen was delivered, we attached it carefully to the pole and Fanny looked at it for ages before she plucked up the courage to start on her design. It took her weeks and several trips to the library and she got very tired, but by the time they came and took it away for other ladies to continue and complete each motif that Fanny had started, indicating what sort of threads and colours and stitches she wanted to be used — all the pale reds and greens and greys which would merge into a gold sort of woven background — you could see it was turning into a real work of art.

Fanny was so tired at the end of it all that we were quite worried about her for a while, but she's all right now, I'm glad to say. By now Annie and Liz treat her as an equal; in fact, they're quite glad to be known as her sisters, and Annie isn't half as dominating these days.

We were disappointed that the Queen wasn't able to come to the Cathedral during Jubilee year, but only last week, Fanny got a letter through the post — in a large stiff envelope, with a crest on the back — to say that Her Majesty would be visiting the city next month for the bi-centenary and Fanny would be presented to her as the designer of the chapel altar cloth.

Just imagine, Fanny Cash going to meet the Queen! (Cinderella going to the Ball, at last, I thought.) She was allowed to take one guest with her.

'Who'll you take, Fanny?' asked Liz, looking rather pointedly at Annie. 'Marguerite, I suppose?'

'No,' said our Fanny, without even considering. 'Marguerite's had plenty of special occasions. No, I think I'd like to take Bertie, if he'll come.'

'If he'll come!' I couldn't believe my ears. So Fanny carefully wrote, 'And Mr. Herbert Maurice Cash' on the invitation next to her name, and I'm collecting my new suit tomorrow.'

I reckon we'll look all right, Fanny and me? Cinderella and a rather elderly Buttons, going to the Ball at last ...

Safety First
by E.P. Fisher

They were classified Home Service troops, but some 'brass hat' decided that the twenty-one miles between Dover and Calais was near enough to be included in that description. D-day plus six found them deposited on a beach which looked like the world's junk yard. Less than A1, but between that and outright rejection, they had been used for a variety of jobs, releasing fitter men for combat.

C company was detailed to follow the tide out and recover useful stores from sunken barges, weapons, and also to mark any unexploded charges they discovered. That these charges might explode at any time created in them a more sober attitude than their work might normally warrant, but apart from that and Sergeant Watson most of the men enjoyed their tasks especially the 'perks' that went with them.

Private Joe Unwin was one of the exceptions. Manual work of any kind was anathema to him, as was the Lee Enfield rifle whose mechanism defied all his efforts to master it. It had already got him into trouble, having slightly wounded an officer, who had staggered about the beach clutching his rear and shouting: 'I've been hit!'

Corporal Bates saved Unwin from the wrath of officialdom by shouting louder still, 'Snipers! Take cover!'

Unwin appreciated the gesture but resented Bates'

constant gibes about the state of his rifle.

On their third day at this work the loads got heavier and the loose sand a trial, and all of them began to voice their opinion of it. On one of their meal breaks some were too tired to eat and sat with eyes closed, backs to a groyne, ignoring the sand which trickled into their mess tins. Lance Corporal Charlie Weeks opened his in time to see Sub Lieutenant Dean and Corporal Bates approaching.

'Officer!' he warned the men, and the most anxious of them rose wearily, raising their hands in salute.

'As you were, men,' he said. 'We can dispense with those formalities. You may be pleased to hear that your services on the beach are no longer required as we have been entrusted with an important job in support of the R.A.F. After you have eaten, stow all your loose gear in your kit-bag, retaining rifle, ammunition, gas mask and cape, water bottle and First Aid kit.

'You will depart from exit H, stowing your kit-bag on the truck as you leave.' He let that sink in and added, 'Smarten yourselves up and be ready to march off at 1400 hours. That is all for the moment.'

As he went Corporal Bates hushed the inevitable questions. 'No, I don't know where we are going. What I do know is that the infantry captured an airfield and handed it over to the R.A.F. What *they* didn't know was that some Jerry snipers crept back and lay doggo, while the ground staff were busy trying to get the airfield serviceable. By all accounts the R.A.F. boys copped it good and proper. Don't ask me what we are going to do, all I know is we're walking it . . . so wash feet, empty sand from boots and change socks!'

Two hours later the weary column wondered if the march would ever end. Charlie Weeks' feet were the cause of his downgrading. He found the going very hard, and the constant diversions a trial that left him speechless and without a smile. When the sullen murmur of battle came to them on a shift of the wind, he cocked his head at Joe Unwin as though he might know something. Joe shrugged his shoulders; he, too, was beyond speech.

'Fall out – take ten!' Corporal Bates called out. 'Check your safety catches before you perforate somebody,' he added, looking at Joe. He ran his hand up the barrel although he had checked it five minutes before.

'Where's Sergeant Watson, Corporal?' asked William Willie.

'In the truck, where I'd like to be. My feet ache, too, you know.' As they voiced a protest he added, 'When you get to be Sergeant you pick your own jobs – well, almost.'

'Well, 'ere comes old Deansy,' said Charlie. 'I wonder what 'e's got for us this time.'

'Hope it's a taxi,' said one wag. 'I'd give double fare for two hundred yards, the way I feel.'

The officer squatted on an upturned bucket. 'I'm afraid I can't let you brew up yet, lads, we've come to the tricky bit. We don't have too far to go but between us and the airfield are some snipers. Sergeant Watson has taken the truck along the road to create a diversion. A detachment of infantry will use that diversion to pinpoint their position and hopefully clear them out. I am going with them as observer and one of their runners will relay my instructions as to changes in the operation.

'I can't rule out any danger to you but must emphasise that speed is vital. I know you're not infantry in the accepted term, but from now on – at least the next half an hour – you must think like soldiers and act like soldiers. Your lives will depend on it. Do what Corporal Bates tells you – he's been shot at before and knows the drill. Keep your heads down, and save me some tea.'

Bates mustered them. 'Right! Move off in groups of four, ten yards between groups. I will take point with the first four. Keep each other in sight. When I raise my hand you'll stop and go to ground. Don't bunch up. Cradle your rifle muzzle down. Don't turn round, don't talk. You won't stop for anyone who gets hit or falls out.'

'Lance Corporal Weeks, you will take over if I get hit. Now, safety catches off! Did you hear that, Unwin?'

'Yes, Corporal,' Unwin winced as all eyes turned to him.

Bates went on, 'Caress the trigger guard in front of the trigger, you may have to use it.'

They moved off with mixed feelings, some wishing they were back on the beach. Every ruined house or barn held fresh terrors for them as the minutes dragged by. At one point they crawled on hands and knees as a furious fire fight developed around them, but one hour later they limped onto the airfield to be greeted by Sergeant Watson.

'Well, it's nice to see you again, boys.' He showed them the perforated truck. 'Your kit bags came in useful, or I'd be full of holes instead and I know you wouldn't like that.'

He pointed to a long, low building. 'There's tea over there for you, but first I want to post guards. Any volunteers?' No one moved. 'Well, you can't all do it so I'll take you-and-you-and you.'

Private William Willie sipped his tea and grimaced as the soreness of his feet rose up his calves and caused his knees to ache. 'Don't know what we're doing here,' he grumbled. 'We don't know nothing about aeroplanes.'

Joe Unwin, who'd just been over for a re-fill, said, 'Don't need to, Willy boy. There are none.'

'What d'ye mean.'

'What I said. Their planes are still in England. There's plenty of jobs to do besides mucking about with kites. I've just been talking to that bloke over there dishing out the tea. He's ground crew. Lost one of his mates in that attack . . . nine in hospital and two officers killed. That's why we're here — to replace 'em.'

'That's right,' said Corporal Bates. 'Lieutenant Dean's just come out of the Station Commander's office. The only planes here are what Jerry left behind. Some are booby trapped and others junk. We'll have plenty to do sorting that little lot out and we've got airfield defence as well. After tea, I'm going to show you how a Lewis gun works.'

'We've already done that, Corp, in our basic training,' said Willy.

'Not like these you haven't — these are twins on high angle mounting. I'll put you, Unwin — you can show him where the safety catch is — and Lance Corporal Weeks on one big boy, and two pints each to the team that knocks down a Jerry.' He added with a grin, 'The Germans have already dug the gun pits so you're saved that job.'

Charlie Weeks exclaimed: 'That's nice! They know the address, too, don't they?'

Bates laughed. 'I shouldn't worry too much, Weeks, I think they're rather busy at the moment.'

Three days passed during which the selected men were kept busy practising loading, training, stripping and reassembling the guns until each became confident that they could give a good account of themselves if ever an ME 109 or Junkers 88 got in their sights.

The cool winds of early June gave way to hot and humid weather. Lacking sufficient numbers, they had to spend more time in the gun pits before being relieved. Nothing ever came their way except the high flyers coming out from England leaving contrails in the blue vault above. On the ground the RAF 'erks', assisted by the 'brown jobs', gradually brought the field into service. Daydreams of cold baths and long drinks replaced all thoughts of valiantly repelling enemies.

The sandbagged gun pit of Charlie Weeks' crew was

half way down the field. Sixty feet away was a tempting cluster of shady trees beneath which flowed a small stream of clear, cold water. Charlie had had a quick shufti whilst the guns were being positioned and noted it for future use. Being stuck out in the open in a sweltering pit was becoming an ordeal for him. He had never been able to take too much sun, and his feet had never quite recovered from the pounding on the beaches and the long march to the airfield. If only something would happen to take his mind off of this torment!

But apart from visits from Lieutenant Dean on his daily round, and the random sudden appearances of Sergeant Watson, nothing of interest came their way. He had dwelt for hours on end on the fobidden prospect of trotting over to the stream and dangling his feet in the water, but had never voiced it to his companions. They wouldn't have it anyway; too scared of retribution.

And still Charlie pondered. Lieutenant Dean was no problem, you could hear that old bike start up a mile off, but Sergeant Watson was something else. You could be on the alert all day and then relax for one minute and he would pop up like a mole with his sarcastic remarks, beady eyes roving over each man, the weapons and the pit; nothing escaped him. What the penalty would be for absenting himself, Charlie shuddered to think about, and tried to put it out of his mind with furious bursts of useless activity.

Charlie considered paying a visit to the stream when their relief crew came, but was afraid that it might invite curiosity and lead to his being moved to sites further away from temptation.

After the customary cup of char he stood with his mates under the showers which the Germans had left intact. It was nice to get the dirt and sweat off of his body. Even his feet lost some of their sting. It wasn't like the stream, though. In his mind the elusive trickle under the trees attained the sparkling beauty of a stream in the Sussex countryside with a vista of cows in a meadow and a water mill on the bend, instead of what it was — a tiny tributary of some larger river.

On the fourth day opportunity knocked not once but twice. Sergeant Watson was stricken with peritonitis and whisked away to an encounter with the surgeon's knife, all thoughts of his charges erased under anaesthesia. His place was taken by a Sergeant from the R.A.F. An armoury technician, his main concern was the continued efficiency and preservation of the weapons. He found it irksome to have to pay the periodic visits to the untried soldiery. He hoped that no harm would result from the guns being fired whilst in their hands, but being a peacetime servant of the R.A.F. he had learned to be philosophical. His war had come when he was about to retire.

He arrived at their gun pit on a ladies' bicycle. After consulting a slip of paper he introduced himself. 'I'm Sergeant Pedlar — you won't forget my name,' he said, nodding towards the bike.

'And you're Lance Corporal Weeks?'

Charlie drew himself up. 'Yes, Sergeant.'

'And Private Joseph Unwin?'

'That's me,' said Joe, and added 'Sir' quickly.

'You don't "sir" me, son — Warrant Officers upwards.' He looked at Willy. 'You must be Private William Willie.'

'Yes, Sergeant,' said Willy, emulating Charlie.

'Well, don't tell anyone you don't have to — some people can be unkind.' Before Willy could digest this statement, he added: 'How's my babies?' and climbed into the pit to examine the twin Lewis guns. After a couple of minutes he climbed out and picked up his bicycle.

'They are nice and clean, lads,' he said in his soft lilting Welsh voice, 'Keep them well oiled, and they'll never let you down.'

His subsequent visits were as predictable as his first words: 'How's my babies?' Charlie made sure that he never had cause for complaint on that score, and was rewarded by the most perfunctory glance and wave of his hand as Sergeant Pedlar wobbled off to the next position.

Hot and high the sun rose. Waves of heat caused the distant buildings to dance, shimmering, across the scorched grass. Charlie's dream of cool water became even more insistent. He glanced at Joe who was sitting on the sandbagged wall rubbing his ankles.

'Feet 'urt, Joe?' he asked.

'Too right!' exclaimed Joe. 'What wouldn't I give for a bowl of good cold water.'

Well, thought Charlie, it's now or never.

'Joe, boy, I can do better than that.'

'What do you mean?'

'See just behind them trees? There's a lovely stream just waiting for us.'

Joe looked askance. 'You're crazy! Do you want to get us shot?'

'We won't get shot, we won't even be missed. Willy can work the guns — he loves 'em — and he can keep his eye out for us.' He added quickly: 'Then he can have a go', looking at Willy. 'Right mate?'

Reluctant as he was, Willy's vision of being in sole charge of the guns was too strong for him to raise any objections.

'All right — don't be too long, though.'

'Twenny minutes and we'll be back,' agreed Charlie. 'Deansy never comes near us now and Pedlar's just gorn, but if you see anyone come near start singing "The Campbells are coming".'

They were gone before Willy could ask how it went.

Slithering down the bank they whipped boots and smelly socks off, giving blissful sighs of contentment as the running stream caressed their tired feet. All too soon the twenty minutes passed, wrapped in the delicious easement of their aching limbs.

At the gun pit, Willy began to worry. He imagined that he heard the Lieutenant's motor bike start up, and convinced himself that Sergeant Watson would somehow find a way to catch him out. Ten minutes later he could contain himself no longer. Leaving the weapon, he ran towards the trees.

'How much longer you gonna be?' he whispered.

Charlie turned in disbelief as he saw Willy's pale face through the branches.

'Get back to the guns, you stupid idiot! You wanna get us all hung?'

'You've had over half an hour,' objected Willy.

'We're coming now,' said Joe, frantically drying his toes with his handkerchief. As Willy withdrew, Charlie said, 'What a dope, fancy leaving – ' His words were cut short by the ominous snarl of aero engines at low level. They looked at each other, appalled.

'Oh no!' shouted Joe.

'Oh yes!' grated Charlie as the mournful wail of the siren started up, followed by the stutter of a distant pair of Lewis's. Galvanised into action, Joe started to pull his socks on to wet feet. Three shadows swept across the glade and more guns joined in.

'Leave yer socks, stoopid!' Charlie snarled furiously, pulling his boots on.

They scrambled up the bank, Joe puffing and sobbing for breath as he tripped over his laces. Charlie hobbled through the trees desperately trying to roll down his trouser legs. Willy was standing still, as though mesmerised, by the sight of two aeroplanes receding into the distance. By then all the guns except one pair, their pair, were spraying the sky with tracer as the third aircraft, streaming smoke, belly flopped on to the grass and slithered through the boundary fence, shedding a wing en route. Finally it ground looped to a standstill amid a cloud of dust and smoke. A figure emerged from the cockpit and ran in crouching fashion away from the wreck.

The guns stopped firing, and hoarse shouts and running figures all over the field seemed to bring Willy round, from a dream. He ran towards their guns.

'You dimwit! You should've been in there shooting. What's the matter wiv yer?'

'I dunno,' said Willy, 'I couldn't move – all that noise – ' his voice petered out.

'Well, it's too late now,' Charlie said as the aeroplane erupted into flame.

'Too late for us as well,' said Joe.

'They'll want to know why we didn't fire.'

Charlie looked at him. 'If you don't tuck your laces in they won't have to ask, will they?'

Joe said desperately, 'We've got to think of something – quick!'

Willy offered a suggestion. 'Tell 'em the safetycatch got stuck.'

Joe glared at him. 'Any one else 'oo mentions safety catches will get me hung for murder.'

Amid the commotion at the scene of the crash they heard the familiar putt putt of Lieutenant Dean's motor bike.

'He's got Pedlar on the back,' said Charlie 'Well, that's our lot.'

'The motor bike stopped at each gun pit and when it arrived at theirs the trio could see that Lieutenant Dean's face was suffused with anger. Sergeant Pedlar's face reflected a mixture of sadness and resignation. Charlie opened his mouth to speak but was cut short.

'Before you say anything foolish, Weeks, we will examine your weapons.' Lieutenant Dean worked swiftly, lifting off the ammunition drum and sniffing for spent cordite, but all he got from the guns was the sweet smell of machine oil. The ready to use ammunition was neatly stacked, no shell cases were visible. His anger seemed to soften.

Turning to Charlie, he said: 'Congratulations, Weeks. Thank goodness I have one team on the ball.' He climbed back on to his machine. 'You coming, Sergeant?' he asked.

'I'll walk back if you don't mind, sir, there's just a little item I'd like to have a look at.' He stared the trio up and down.

'Your mates will be on extra drill for today's display,' he said softly, 'while you'll most likely get mentioned in despatches.' Charlie didn't miss the glint in his eye but was mystified by the obvious sarcasm. Pedlar patted his babies lovingly. 'These guns are in beautiful condition,' he said.

Charlie looked at Joe. Joe looked at Willy. Willy was puzzled too. 'But *they* got the Jerry didn't they, Sergeant?'

'Oh, didn't I say? It wasn't a Jerry, it was one of ours – a Tomahawk. But you knew that, didn't you?'

'Er ... his aircraft recognition ain't too good, Sergeant,' said Charlie as light dawned.

'No, but yours is perfect, isn't it, Lance Corporal Weeks?'

'Pilot all right, sir?' asked Joe.

'Yes, but a bit bruised. The Americans will be very annoyed with your officer,' said Sergeant Pedlar. He patted his babies once more and as he turned away, said: 'Why don't you put your socks back on, boys? It's much more comfortable for your feet – and safer, too. Wouldn't want Lieutenant Dean to find out the truth about his crack team, would we now?'

About the Authors

Robert Wood was born in 1917, the son of a master butcher whom he reluctantly followed into the trade. He spent six years in the Army during the Second World War, in Infantry, Ordnance and R.E.M.E. After the war he worked in airline catering until his present semi-retirement. Thirty years ago one of his stories was broadcast by the B.B.C. in their morning story slot, and he had various short articles published in film magazines in the U.K. and America. *The Exorcising of Ruby* is his first short story to be published.

Arthur Thrippleton is a retired language teacher who took early retirement in order to write. A keen member of a writers' group in Leeds, he has written several short stories and a novel, so far unpublished, and is currently working on his second and third. He served in the Western Desert during the Second World War, where he first felt the urge to write, and afterwards lived for a time in Durban, Natal, where his first short story was published. He currently lives in the Aire Valley with his wife, the head of a girls' preparatory school, and his other interests include painting in oils and water colour, crossword solving and compiling – and enjoying a quiet drink with friends.

Pamela Margaret Pennock was born in Redcar by sea, North Yorkshire, and now lives in Leeds. She is married with two daughters and one grandchild. After studying as a mature student, she became a teacher and was finally Head of Drama at a Leeds school before her retirement. Her interests include theatre, amateur dramatics and hiking, particularly in the Yorkshire Dales, and she is a member of a writing class. She is currently engaged in writing a historical novel set in Leeds.

Ted Hayball was born in Bristol in 1911, and now lives in Hinckley, Leicestershire. During the Second World War, he saw active service in the Army, was commissioned in 1942 and took part in the D-Day landings. After the war he worked as a teacher until his retirement in 1976. His hobbies include drawing, painting, woodcarving and writing, and his short stories have been broadcast on Radios Bristol and Leicester.

Monica Goddard was born in Macclesfield in 1925 and grew up in Stoke-on-Trent. She trained at the Royal College of Art as a book illustrator, and her chief claim to fame is that she designed a recruiting poster for the Women's Land Army in the Second World War — with the result that there were so many Land Girls the authorities didn't know what to do with them! She retired from teaching in 1980 and now lives on the edge of the Peak District in Marple, Cheshire. Since her retirement she has written plays for an amateur dramatic company, and started to write short stories two years ago.

Heather Johnson describes herself as a 'compulsive scribbler', and is the only entrant to have two stories included on the competition shortlist. She was born in India, but spent most of her childhood in the Manchester area, where she later met and married her husband, Bill.

A primary school teacher by the end of the war, she eventually left the profession to care for her three sons and two daughters. As her children left home, she began to travel widely with her husband, a successful academic, in Canada, Iran, Japan, China and Singapore. They are currently enjoying their second two-year stint in Purdue University, Indiana, U.S.A.

Kate Greenwood retired in 1977, after a varied career in banking, the Civil Service, and fifteen years in hospital administration. She took an O level in English for mental exercise, and joined a creative writing class. She has written and submitted several previous short stories, but none have been published so far. As Assistant Editor of her local parish magazine, she contributes items of local interest and traveller's tales of holidays in Germany, France and Switzerland. Other interests include the study of comparative religions, and voluntary work in First Aid and beauty care in hospitals.

Barbara Roberts is an ex-teacher of drama and art, now an energetic grandmother with fingers in many pies, both artistic and literary. *Like Mother, Like Daughter* is her second prize-winning short story, and she is currently engaged in writing an historical novel.

Pat Earl is a retired RAF officer, and an ex-golf club secretary. He was born in Chalford, Gloucestershire, but educated in London. Widely travelled, and a lover of sea and country, he now lives quietly in Devon, where he devotes his time to writing, gardening and playing golf. He is currently working on two books – one a collection of Charlie Puddington stories, the other based upon amusing everyday incidents in the life of a golf club secretary.

Katherine Parry was born in Wales but has spent most of her life in London. After the War, she won a scholarship to the London Academy of Music and Dramatic Art, but left the theatre when she married, later training as a teacher and ending her career as deputy director of a London teaching centre. She and her husband now live in Staffordshire, near their son and three grandchildren. *Relative Strangers* is her first ever attempt at story writing.

Ivor Middleton was born in the mining village of Tonyrefail, South Wales, in 1907. He left school at the age of 14 to work in the local coal mine. During the 1929 Depression, he left his native land and arrived in London where he settled in Cricklewood. After his marriage in 1947, he moved to South Buckinghamshire, where he and his wife live today. The Middletons have one daughter, who lives in Canada with her husband and two children.

Eva Lomas was born in 1920, and worked in insurance in Manchester before wartime service in R.A.D.A.R. She and her husband, a mechanical engineer, have three daughters and four grandchildren. They now live in Melton Mowbray where they are pursuing an active retirement, swimming, dancing and walking, and particularly enjoying word games on television.

Iris Taylor lives in Harrogate, North Yorkshire. A war widow, she has one son, one grandson and two great grandchildren. Besides writing, she enjoys knitting and embroidery.

Glynne Jones is a retired London schoolmaster, and a translator from Thai, Spanish and French. Born in Wales, he has travelled widely, and at one time was interned in Bangkok for three and a half years.

Nell Arch was born in London but now lives in the heart of Kent. She worked as an Executive Officer in the N.H.S for over twenty-five years before her retirement. She has three children and five grandchildren, and enjoys writing and painting, badminton, dancing and music.

Bruce Cameron Firth took early retirement from his headship of a comprehensive school, and has since been kept overwhelmingly busy writing short stories, learning to play golf, decorating the house and a holiday cottage, and doing the housework necessary to support a working wife. He has two grown-up daughters and two grandchildren, and plans to devote more time to his writing in future.

Mallie Aarstad was born in the North East, where he has lived all his life, the son of a Norwegian father. During the war he was an ambulance driver with the C.D. and afterwards worked in various jobs, but particularly enjoyed his years in an advertising agency. Since retirement he enjoys attending adult education classes, in Literature, Local History and Philosophy, and the company of his many friends.

Robert Sharpe has written an autobiographical story in *The Boiler Party*. During the Second World War he served in the Royal Navy, and his experiences aboard *H.M.S. Belfast* provided the background for this story. After the war he became a school teacher, retiring in 1979 from his post as headmaster of a village school in East Devon.

Mary Andrew was born in London in 1926. She began a career in teaching in 1948, and this remained her chief occupation until her recent retirement. She married a Cornishman, and in 1959 moved to Cornwall, where she has been lucky enough to live and work ever since. She now assists her husband in his retirement hobby of Aviation History, and has been a member of Newquay Writers' Circle for one year. She also enjoys babysitting for young friends, attending touring theatre or opera productions, and entertaining family and friends from all over the world.

Paul Griffin was born in 1922, and graduated as an M.A. of St Catherine's College, Cambridge. During the Second World War he was a Major in the Gurkhas. He later worked as a schoolmaster and was given the M.B.E. for his work running the English School in Cyprus during the Emergency of 1956–60. He was Headmaster of Aldenham from 1962–74, and in his retirement enjoys writing comic verse and prose for magazines and anthologies.

Meriel Serjeant lived her early years in India before returning to England. She spent a brief period in the WRNS then worked in publishing for a while, before, in the fifties, setting out to live in Europe, equipped only with £30 and determination to succeed. Three glorious years in Rome followed, before she returned to England to work on the *Oxford Mail*. She later married an architect and had three children. She and her husband currently divide their time between their London home and a house in the country.

Patricia Nielsen was born in 1927 in the South of Ireland. From 1944-7 she served in the W.A.A.F. In 1950, she graduated from Trinity College, Dublin in English and French literature, later teaching English in France, Italy and Sweden. She married in 1970 and made her home in Denmark. She has done a little freelance writing and given travel talks for Radio Eireann.

Peggie Cannam spent many years teaching in Africa before her retirement. She now lives in Norwich where she enjoys pursuing her hobbies of swimming, reading, travel and membership of the Norwich Writers' Circle, of which she is currently Secretary.

Peggie R. Kerr first became interested in writing during a spell at home, looking after her two children some thirty years ago. Return to work as a medical secretarial supervisor intervened. It is only now that she and her husband, an ex-engineer, have retired that she has been able to return to writing and finds it a satisfying retirement occupation.

The Very Reverend Fenton Morley was born in 1912 in South Wales, the setting for his story *Hot Cockles for Tea*. He was ordained to the ministry in 1935 and served in six dioceses before retiring as Dean of Salisbury in 1977. An honours graduate of Wales, Oxford and London, he has lectured in the U.S.A., Canada and Africa and many European countries, and given more than 150 radio and television broadcasts. Formerly a Chaplain to H.M. The Queen, Dean Morley was awarded the C.B.E. in 1980 for his work as Chairman of the Church of England Pensions Board. In 1987 he and his wife celebrated their Golden Wedding. They have one son, one daughter, and six grandchildren. Dean Morley's hobbies include music, writing and after-dinner speaking.

Susan Ashmore was born in 1925, and educated at Clifton High School, Bristol, and St Hugh's College, Oxford. She married in 1949 and has two daughters, one son, and two grandsons. Before her retirement, she worked as a Residential Socialworker.

Doris M. Hodges was born and educated in North Somerset. She is unmarried, and like many ladies prefers to keep her date of birth to herself. Her hobbies include travelling, reading, writing and Siamese Cats. She is also interested in West Country legends, and would like to make an anthology of these. She has completed a novel about the Monmouth Rebellion of 1685, which took place not far from her home, and is currently seeking a publisher for it.

Helena Bovett is a retired civil servant, now living in Devon where her roots are. Her hobbies include entertaining friends, reading and writing — she belongs to a local writers' group in Brixham — and especially travel, a lifelong interest which has taken her from her first escorted tour to Lucerne in 1936 to a solo trip to the Great Barrier Reef in 1987. There is still a lot of the world she would like to see.

Dorothy Gibson is a retired civil servant. Widowed after 45 years of happy married life, she has one son, one daughter and two grandchildren. Writing has always been important in her life. She has written several plays for amateur dramatic groups, a number of short stories which she has not yet submitted for publication, and, most notably, a sizeable body of poetry. She has won or been placed in several poetry competitions, and currently holds the cup for the 1987 John Clare poetry competition for Essex. She also acts as a tutor for the London District W.E.A. for Creative Writing classes in Southend and Basildon. She is at present collecting a volume of poems for publication, and is halfway through a novel. Other interests include art, music, philosophy, natural history, gardening and people.

E.P. Fisher received an elementary education in the

thirties, which laid great stress on the 'three R's'. He mastered the first two but failed lamentably in the third, until rallying somewhat in later years to get a job as turner/fitter (Instruments) during the war. He enjoys writing chiefly for his own amusement and entertainment, but has collected a few kind words of praise along with the rejection slips. His chief hobby is aeroplane spotting, and he thinks he must be among the oldest 'plane spotters, as he started at the age of five.

The World of Saga

Saga Holidays
Over the past 35 years Saga has become widely acknowledged as the international leader in providing holidays for people aged over 60. In that time Saga has grown into a worldwide organisation with international offices in the USA and Australia.

Saga Financial Services
Our experience has enabled us to provide a wide range of other Saga Services such as Home and Car Insurance, the Saga Retirement Health Plan and Saga Accident Insurance.

Saga Publishing
Saga has its own Club and award-winning Magazine specially designed for mature people. Topics covered include consumer affairs, pension rights, motoring and gardening. There are many benefits available to Club Members and Saga Magazine also keeps you up-to-date with the very latest in holiday offers.

Useful Telephone Numbers
Here is a list of telephone numbers which we are sure you will find useful. All calls to Saga's special 0800 telephone numbers are FREE.

Saga Holiday Reservations — 0800 300 500

Customer Services (for holiday advice and brochure requests) — 0800 300 600

Saga Services — Folkestone (0303) 47021

Saga Magazine Club Membership — Folkestone (0303) 47062

Saga Holidays PLC, The Saga Building, Middleburg Square, Folkestone, Kent CT20 1AZ.